More Critical Praise for Pete Hamill

for *Forever*

"His remarkably imaginative new novel is an exciting mix of realism and fantasy ... Hamill writes with great detail, which adds texture and spice to, rather than impeding, the narrative's swift movement. As always, he is perfectly enjoyable to read for his great felicity of style (obviously derived from his years as a journalist) as well as his originality of plot. This absolutely embracing novel is certain to hit the best-seller lists."
—Booklist

"If September 11 was a terrible warning of New York's mortality, Hamill's entertaining panhistorical fantasy is a paean to its immortality ... The book's central conceit could almost have come from the pages of Twain or Bellamy, but Hamill pulls his story fiercely into the present by centering the final phase of Cormac's narrative on the World Trade Center attacks themselves."
—New Yorker

"[*Forever* is] a superior tale told by Hamill in the cadence of the master storyteller ... This rousing, ambitious work is beautifully woven around historical events and characters, but it is Hamill's passionate pursuit of justice and compassion—Celtic in foundation—that distinguishes this tale of New York City and its myriad peoples.   *—Publishers Weekly*

for *North River*

"Hamill has crafted a beautiful novel, rich in New York City detail and ambiance, that showcases the power of human goodness and how love, in its many forms, can prevail in an unfair world."
—Publishers Weekly (starred review)

"Famous New York City writer Hamill is as closely identified with his native city as the Empire State Building or the Bowery. As usual, his new novel draws closely and intensely from the streets of New York (details are plentiful, and all of them are just right) ... Hamill is not ordinarily thought of as a historical novelist, but if, as the saying goes, the shoe fits, wear it. It is an extremely good fit here."
—Booklist (starred review)

"Hamill's quietly engrossing novel skillfully conjures the gritty world of lower Manhattan during the Depression, weaving elements of suspense, comedy and romance . . ."
—*Publishers Weekly* (review of audio book edition)

"Lovely, richly textured . . . Is there another living writer with as firm a grasp on the city's sidewalks, its buildings, its history?"
—*Cleveland Plain Dealer*

"Hamill's love story casts an engaging spell, and Manhattan-lovers will delight in the gritty particulars." —*Entertainment Weekly*

"*North River* . . . seduces us with the author's sweetly convinced nostalgia for his city . . . Hamill's a smart guy and a fluent writer, and few people have written quite so beautifully about New York as he has . . ."
—*Los Angeles Times*

for *Snow in August*

"[M]agic . . . this page-turner of a fable . . . [has] universal appeal."
—*New York Times Book Review*

"Strongly evoking time and place, Hamill . . . serves up a coming-of-age tale with a hearty dose of magical realism mixed in."
—*Library Journal*

"An intelligent, heartfelt, and ironically charming novel that will certainly enhance the reputation of this popular writer." —*Booklist*

for *Tabloid City*

"*Tabloid City*'s subplots really shine—this is where Hamill's attention to detail and talent for writing memorable characters are most apparent . . . *Tabloid City* is, at its core, exciting to read. The story is engaging and the characters distinct and fascinating." —NPR

"Hamill's exhilarating thriller explores a world where newspapers are as soaked in adrenaline as they are in ink." —NPR, "New in Paperback"

"[E]ngrossing . . . a gritty tone-poem in prose on New York City life— and death." —Alan Cheuse, *San Francisco Chronicle*

A
KILLING
FOR
CHRIST

A
KILLING
FOR
CHRIST

PETE HAMILL

BROOKLYN, NEW YORK, USA
BALLYDEHOB, CO. CORK, IRELAND

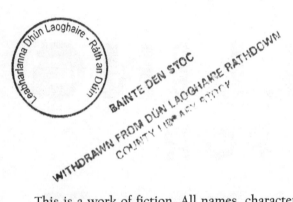

This is a work of fiction. All names, characters, places, and in-
cidents are the product of the author's imagination or are used
fictitiously. Any resemblance to real events or persons, living or
dead, is entirely coincidental.

©1968, 2018 Pete Hamill
Originally published in 1968 by The New American Library

Hardcover ISBN: 978-1-61775-590-3
Paperback ISBN: 978-1-61775-578-1
Library of Congress Control Number: 2017936107

Akashic Books
Brooklyn, New York, USA
Ballydehob, Co. Cork, Ireland
Twitter: @AkashicBooks
Facebook: AkashicBooks
E-mail: info@akashicbooks.com
Website: www.akashicbooks.com

TABLE OF CONTENTS

To my wonderful wife Fukiko

And in memory of Tim Lee, Jimmy Vlasto, and Paul Sann

Donde están los amigos queridos de entonces?

INTRODUCTION

One morning in 1967, in my office in Dublin, I took a deep breath, gazed a moment at the gray Irish sky, and began to write this novel. I had by then written many thousands of words for newspapers and magazines, several movie scripts, and a dozen short stories, but this was my first novel.

It was to be a thriller, the story of a man driven by negation and anger who sets his sights on assassinating the reigning pope. It would take place largely in Rome. I had lived there for a while with my first wife and two very young daughters in the Parioli neighborhood. But I was in many ways a stranger. So I needed help to have the sort of details that persuade readers to suspend disbelief. That is, to believe a work of fiction. The details you know only from friends.

One such friend was a publicist named Harvey Matofsky. He had prospered during the postwar golden age of Italian cinema. He was also a friend of the producer Joseph Levine, with whom I once sat at a café table on Via Veneto along with Marcello Mastroianni, Federico Fellini, and—be still my heart—thirty-year-old Claudia Cardinale. I kept my mouth shut and listened, thinking, *Hey, I'm actually getting paid to do this.*

I was also shown around Rome by Mickey Knox, a marvelous New York guy who was initially an actor after

World War II, before being driven into European exile after being blacklisted as a "leftie" by a cowardly Hollywood. Mickey moved first to Paris, and then to Rome, where he helped translate dialogue for Italian films. He helped coach actors in English too, for dubbed versions. And he certainly helped me. In Rome, I didn't know what I was looking for (beyond the guidebook banalities). Mickey and Harvey did, and told me.

I loved Rome, its sensuality, the sense it exuded of knowing every variety of sin—and forgiveness too. In Rome, time itself was visible, not an abstraction. This suited my own beloved profession. As a reporter in my native New York, I had seen many varieties of horror and violence, treachery and delusion. But I also learned the limits of the craft. My first great editor, Paul Sann of the *New York Post*, said to me once, "Remember: if you want it to be true, it usually isn't." Yes. In journalism. In life. Romans could have embraced that line, preferably in Latin.

I had been reading as a writer for a long time when I entered my thirties. Hemingway, of course, Fitzgerald, John Dos Passos, Sherwood Anderson, James T. Farrell, and Irish writers too. (My Catholic parents were immigrants from Belfast, driven to exile in Brooklyn by Ulster bigotry.) But many kinds of writing had helped shape me: *The Story of Babar*, the *Bomba the Jungle Boy* books, *Treasure Island*, Sherlock Holmes, Howard Pyle's *Book of Pirates*, *The Count of Monte Cristo*. They fed my curiosity about the world beyond Brooklyn, and helped to drive my emerging wanderlust. I was a familiar figure at the local public library, which had been put there by my favorite rich guy, a Scottish immigrant named Andrew Carnegie. He was a man who didn't want to be the richest person in the cemetery and used his money to open more than 1,600 public libraries in the United States.

I was also a student for two years at Regis High School in Manhattan. It was run by the Jesuits, whose standards were rigorous. They gave me great gifts: exactitude, wonder, pity, irony, and, many years later, my most prized possession: an honorary diploma. They also gave me doubt. Its enduring challenges are all over this novel.

Another huge influence in my boyhood was comic books, then in their first golden age. I was a fan of Will Eisner *(The Spirit)*, Milton Caniff *(Terry and the Pirates)*, and Bob Kane and Jerry Robinson (DC Comics's *Batman*). All could have become movie directors or novelists.

For this book, I helped lay out the big plot moves as if planning a comic book—in panels (then on index cards and eventually on storyboard pads). This visual plan showed me if I had too many static scenes in a row, and needed to dissolve (or cut) into a street scene or an action scene. All I had to do at my typewriter then was fill in the blanks. Or so I thought.

From the beginning, I was giddy with a sense of freedom. In journalism, the writer must adhere to the knowable facts. Fiction was a work of the imagination. And unlike a movie script, in a novel the writer (with guidance from an editor) would have the final cut.

Until *A Killing for Christ*, I had never tried a story of such length (my first book was a paperback biography of Ernest Hemingway, written in collaboration with Alfred G. Aronowitz after Papa killed himself in 1961). I had learned how to write magazine pieces by writing them.

But the experience of this novel more closely resembled setting down a fiddle and picking up a cello.

At the same time, I was still writing journalism and that caused me to discover the great creative value of the nap. I had taken the hint from Hemingway to finish a day's work when you know what comes next. But to make the transition from one form to another on the same day, I'd lie down, thinking of choices, and wake up an hour later, almost always knowing what to write. No pills. No whiskey. Just a nap.

Reading *A Killing for Christ* again for the first time in a half century, I now believe that it is overwhelmingly about the loss of faith. Religious faith, eroded by doubt and disillusion and history. Where the hell was the all-knowing, forgiving God during the Shoah? And why didn't He intervene in Vietnam? Faith was mortally wounded by the political and moral disillusion that came with the long Vietnam War. My Father Malloy has already lost the internal struggle. Harwell, the self-hating Jew, has embraced a form of fascism. Mary Wilson, the aging actress, uses whiskey and laughter to ward off critics. Other characters are unhappy with Italy and Italians, deeply cynical, seeing nothing but sour corruption everywhere (not true of me). To many, ideology is not thinking now—it's a substitute for thinking. Like E.M. Forster, many could say: "I do not believe in belief." It's a lot easier to make love in the moist shadows.

My various times in Mexico, where I was first a student on the GI Bill in the 1950s, and later as a part-time resident, had opened new ways of writing to me (and others). I embraced the new writers such as Gabriel García Márquez, Mario Vargas Llosa, and, above all,

Carlos Fuentes. The last was a master, a superb essayist, an extaordinarily splendid writer of fiction. His *The Death of Artemio Cruz* was a revelation and a spur. Don't rehash Hemingway, it said. Get deeper. And make the prose resemble music.

A Killing for Christ was first published fifty years ago, in early 1968. None of us then knew what awaited us in the sardonically labeled "real" world. Up ahead, true believers waited to kill Martin Luther King Jr. And Malcolm X. And Robert Kennedy. And John Lennon. And on May 13, 1981, a young Turk named Ağca waited in crowded St. Peter's Square under the Roman sky and shot at Pope John Paul II four times, hitting him twice. In spite of severe loss of blood, the pope survived. So did the guns and the fanatics.

Pete Hamill
Brooklyn, New York
November 2017

A
KILLING
FOR
CHRIST

HOLY
THURSDAY

Q. How should Christians look upon the priests of the Church?
A. Christians should look upon the priests of the Church as the
messengers of God and the dispensers of His mysteries.

—ADVANCED CATECHISM OF CATHOLIC FAITH AND PRACTICE

*The spirit that dwelt in the church has glided away to animate other
activities, and they who come to the old shrines find apes and players
rustling the old garments.*

—Ralph Waldo Emerson

CHAPTER 1

〰〰〰〰〰〰〰〰〰〰〰〰〰

He dreamed a storm, with seas gone wild and brutal, and the crippled bark adrift across its face, rudderless; and the old commander propped upon the deck, his face yellowed and waxen, the mouth a darkening bruise. The crew knelt around him, mates and seamen and cabin boys, begging his indulgence, howling softly for salvation. And beyond the bark, spread out across the roiled waters, he could see the dead and the dying: a sailor bloated with salt and sin, an old man clinging to a rotting spar, a girl become a chancre floating like a wood chip in the tide. And children, always children, going down and under, sucked away to hell and gone, while the old commander's slackened jaw tried to move, tried to speak, tried to save.

Suddenly Malloy was awake. He could hear the gulls screeing and the long slow steady roar of the sea, and he knew it was still night. There were no other sounds: no screech of autos, no garbled murmuring of children, no young men shouting after girls. It was still night. The drunks and the lovers and the homeless and the wild were gone; it was that empty moment before day's first true light, and the beach at Fragene slept. It was almost like peace.

He reached for the pack of Camels. If nothing else does it, he thought, you surely will. He felt something move in his chest, some long-impacted wad of phlegm or bone or waste or filth; some timid trophy of decay, lodged there like a reminder of long passage. His hand trembled in the darkness.

The struck match broke the darkness, and in the orange glow he could see that picture of the Virgin and Child, with sweet face, empty smile, golden curls on the Son of God, gone all soft and corrupt, like a bad copy of Raphael. It was a Neapolitan vision of heaven.

"What time is it?" the girl said.

"Half past five."

She slept again, and he could hear her sated breathing, heavy and regular, and in the light of the second match, he could see the bulk of form: the small line of waist and back, the heavy roll of hips, the slick black hair spilled out across the violet pillow. She had bought the pillowcase for his birthday in some shop on Via Margutta, for three thousand lire, and she had sulked for three days when he told her it was the color of Lent.

"You and your God," she had said.

"That's close to blasphemy," he said, laughing.

"What can he do, this God?" she said. "Can he take you to bed? Can he do to you what I can do to you? What is this big God of yours?"

"God is God," he said that wintry afternoon, thinking piously that only the pious explained.

The match guttered and went out. He pulled a long hard drag on the cigarette, stepped into his bathing suit, walked across the splintered floor, and slipped out to the beach. It was Holy Thursday.

The sand was cold and damp and he walked carefully, afraid of broken glass. Ahead was the sea. He had had that dream again, but this was another sea. The dream sea was a gnashing piece of private history, a personal mystery. He had dreamed that sea for years. But here the sea lay still and black, its surface glossy, scribbled on by dead stars. There were no clouds. Above him, the stars exploded away, in wild combat with the black, fierce roof of sky. Away off, he could see the lights of the fishing boats, and hear the quiet, almost polite ding ding ding ding of the buoys. Ahead, coming from the bungalows, he saw a red pinhole, bobbing, jittery, moving toward him.

"*Buon giorno,*" the man said, offering a drag on the cigarette. He had a small, moustached face on a large head. On the collar of the dyed black Army greatcoat, he wore the red-white-and-green pin of the night watchman.

"Well, they've gone," he said, looking at the ground. His voice was a question.

"Yes," Malloy said.

"They were children, only children."

"Oh?"

"I told them to leave when they first came. They were too young and it is cold here. They insisted. They said they wanted to look at the sea. They never know what could happen to them here. Killers, rapists, the world is full of them these days."

"Yes, I suppose it is," Malloy said. "Perhaps we should pray for them."

"Nobody prays anymore," the watchman said. He kicked sand over the contraceptive.

"Some people do," Malloy said.

"Women pray," the watchman said. He said goodbye, and disappeared among the bungalows, checking the doors and shutters that now lay sealed, waiting for the season. Malloy was waiting too. He needed warmth. The last chill of winter remained, and in their room these past two weeks, he and Franca had bundled against the cold, or lit the small gas heater left behind by some other transient the year before. He remembered the terrible feeling of intrusion the morning they first rented the house at the sea. A crumpled piece of loose-leaf paper lay dusty under a bed, the name *Susan* written in tall spidery child's letters upon it. American matches were in the kitchen drawer, an old copy of *Time* on a table, a scurf-clogged comb in the second drawer of the bureau, a moldering jar of French's mustard on guard in the tiny icebox. It was like walking into another's life; those sheets were stained by the defeats and small wins of strangers. He wondered about those people, with their child just learning to write, and where they came from and where they had gone, and who would take this house when he too had gone and what souvenir he would leave. Perhaps it should be the rosary beads. He longed now for the brutal heat of summer and the stunned mile of oiled bodies on the beach, when sin was more general than it was now. He stood for a moment, staring at the sea, and then ran, legs pumping, the muscles bunching in his calves, and dived.

He could not feel his body. He felt the swirl, the red Ferris wheels of shock, the cold blue dimensions of suspended time. The floor of the sea moved away from him and he heard a high fine singing in his ears. For a moment, he thought he would freeze and drown. And then he was out again, sloshing through the surf, watching the sky come up sullen and gray, and the first banks of cloud moving in from the Mediterranean. The fishing boats were gone, but a mile out a cruise ship moved against the horizon, like a white tin cutout in a shooting gallery. He wondered if it had come from New York.

Franca slept. Malloy shaved himself in the small cracked mirror over the kitchen sink, watching the coffeepot bubbling on the stove. At last, he thought, I am growing old. He thought once the malaria would do it. He had heard stories of men lost in malarial fevers, whose hair had whitened, whose bodies had gone suddenly old. He remembered lying in the cot in the highlands, and awakening from the fever, with the mosquito net over him, and the smell of the jungle everywhere, asking what color his hair was. They thought he was still in fever. Now, staring in the mirror, he saw the beginnings. Pouches under the eyes, something soft and ugly happening around the mouth. His gums were sore from too many cigarettes, but perhaps it was more than that.

A spider jumped from his shoe as he dressed. It was small and yellow and skittered away under the bed. He tapped the heel to empty the rest. There was nothing. He hoped the spider had not just arrived. He preferred to salute him as a brave survivor, the spider who had made it through winter. The coffee was ready.

He had been awake every morning at five thirty for the past twenty-five years, he thought. He could not break that habit. It was like the cigarettes. You start as an altar boy, then you are a seminarian, and then a priest, and then the Army, and when you finally are allowed to change, you can't. Altar boy. He thought of crisp white surplices, and the long walk through the snow to the great red church on the hill, the smell of wax and piety in the mornings.

"Oh my God, I am heartily sorry for having offended Thee, and I detest all my sins . . . all my sins . . . because . . ." He couldn't remember the words. Once, in the confessional, he smelled whiskey on a kind priest's breath, the first chip into belief, and later, when the sliding panel of absolution had shut, and he had passed through those rustling wine-colored drapes, he had gone to the altar and prayed. He had prayed for everyone that day, for his mother and father and the men away at war, for the British and the Russians, and his Uncle Tom, and his cousins and for the priest with the whiskey breath. It was what they called then a state of grace. Now he no longer remembered the words.

He remembered the names of countries, and the ranks of soldiers, and the way some of them walked. He only remembered names of people if they were old enough. The girls were named Rosemary and Catherine and Lorraine and Jean. He remembered their first names, not their last. He poured a cup of coffee. And Kathleen. She was different: he had never forgotten her name, or her address, or even her telephone number; but he could no longer remember her face. She was lean, thin-boned, angular, and wore a green sweater from St. Joseph's that fall, and always wore a blouse to the beach because she thought her breasts were too small. Malloy chuckled. They had a private park bench, respected by everyone. And on Sunday afternoons at the beach they would eat hero sandwiches at Mary's on Surf Avenue. He frisked his memory for a glimpse of her face, but it was like going through an old steamer trunk for a cracked photograph you saw there once years before. It wasn't there anymore.

There were spots of grease on the surface of the coffee, and Malloy tore a lid from the flour box and skimmed it clear. The kitchen was domesticated and he wondered if sin, like grace, could become domesticated too. He had heard that men in the wilds of the north had taught wolves to love children. In his list of sins, nostalgia was the most forgivable.

Poor Kathleen: she must have thought him a curiosity, the rough boy from the seminary, home for summer. That was eighteen years ago, and the place was Ocean Tide on the boardwalk at Bay 22, away out on the end of Coney Island. It was the summer of Korea too, but no one they knew was yet dying, and they all were certain they would live forever. She had not survived.

"Roberto," Franca said. Day streamed grayly through the open shutter and he could see her in the slate light, sitting up, watching him, her skin dark against the sheets, the legs pulled tight against her buttocks. She was twenty-three, Malloy remembered.

"Coffee?" he said.

She shrugged.

"You went swimming?" she said.

"Yes. It was very cold."

"Am I cold?"

"No, you're not cold," he said. "You're sure you don't want coffee, Franca?"

"You were thinking about home again," she said flatly.

"Yes," he said. The coffee was bitter, and made steam in the morning chill. The sound of the sea had receded and he could no longer hear the buoy. Away off a truck backfired. He saw his briefcase, with breviary, rosary, credentials, all of it, standing impatiently at the door, like a sentry arrived to release a prisoner.

"Thinking is a dangerous pastime," she said.

"And you're too intelligent."

She lay back, laughing throatily, her hands jammed behind her head. Dark tufts of hair showed under her arms. Her round dark breasts heaved when she laughed.

"Padre," she said, "if I were intelligent I would not be here."

"Neither would I."

She rose slowly from the bed, wrapped in the sheet, shaking her long hair free. Her naked feet made a padding sound as she moved across the room. For a moment she looked out at the cold shore. Then she lit the incense pot under the picture of the Virgin. The house was dark. She touched him, guiding him in the darkness, moving him.

He made love to her in the incensed room, listening to the gulls and the awakening beach, on Holy Thursday in the morning, before leaving for the Vatican.

CHAPTER 2

Rail felt trapped. The cushions of the limousine were wheezing and slippery and the driver's Italian cigarette smelled like burning dung. He opened a window and hot wet air flowed around him. He wondered if his feet would soon begin to stink. The disturbed countryside around the airport raced past: gas stations and soft hills green with spring, ruined buildings and weathered old barns with hay piled in back in the shape of huts, and farmers talking to children in yards while chickens scampered among them all. It did no good: Rail hated it all. It only made him wistful for the places he had never been, for the polished oak study in Connecticut that he had furnished in his mind, with logs charring on a snowy night, and the smell of food beyond the doors. The world was too disorderly; this great purring Cadillac on this road was hemmed in, surrounded, in flight before the ant people, in their hundreds, thousands, millions of buglike little cars. The little man beside him did not stir. Rail was sure that he also did not sweat.

"Driver," Rail said, "driver, do you speak English?"

"No sir, yes sir, a little, sir."

"Stop somewhere. I want something to eat, something to drink."

"Yes sir. We come soon. Trattoria. Down the road."

"What do you want to stop for?" the little man said.

Rail didn't turn. He did not like to look at the little man. He reminded him of an asp.

"You don't have to eat with me, Harwell," Rail said wearily. He was tired of Harwell already. Seven hours from New York was too much. He took a blue-trimmed silk handkerchief from his pocket and tamped at the tiny blisters of sweat on his brow. His hand moved in a precise, almost feminine way, like a dowager powdering her nose.

"This wop shit is poison," Harwell said. "You know, there have been scientific studies. Rats won't eat white flour. They turn their noses up at it. Rats! They've really studied this thing. White flour is not organic. It's the truth. And that's what these people eat three times a day."

"I'll take my chances, Harwell, I'll take my chances."

"Just remember the body stores up toxins," Harwell said. "It could take you years to get them out of your system."

Rail sighed. "Yes, Harwell. I'll remember that."

The limousine slowed in the clotted, midmorning traffic, and pulled up before a battered stucco building. A sign identified it as the *Trattoria Napoli*. The driver got out.

"Driver," Harwell said, "are you sure this is all right? It doesn't look like it's very . . . elegant?"

The driver was squat and powerfully built, like a retired welterweight. He had two black bars for brows. They climbed his forehead together. "I go with you, sir?" he said.

"Let's go into Rome," Harwell said. "This place could poison you, and what would you do then?"

Rail stood for a moment in the dusty driveway, rubbing the handkerchief inside his collar. The breeze died, a wave of exhaust settled around him, and Rail felt as if a clammy envelope of gassy wet air had been dropped on him from the sky. Perhaps Harwell was right. At least in the car, with the window open, the air moved.

"Driver . . ."

"The food is very good, sir."

"Well, if you come in with us, I suppose . . ."

He saw movement behind the restaurant window: a young girl with dark eyes, olive skin, and a promise of breasts beneath a white blouse.

"Come on, Harwell."

Rail's body seemed to squish as he walked, as if he were encased by some rubbery sack filled with water. The trousers of his dark blue suit held their crease, the shirt collar was unwilted. Yet the great bulk seemed to be forcing its way out of its cloth bonds. The little man looked at Rail with distaste. The man must weigh four hundred pounds, he thought, all of it poison. He walked behind Rail, picking his steps with neat, dandified movements, and wiped the tips of his polished loafers on the back of his trousers before entering the restaurant.

"Very nice," Rail said.

The restaurant was small and cool, with candles jammed into wine bottles on white tablecloths, and bare whitewashed walls. A faint smell of damp concrete reminded Rail of prison. A door opened in a corner and the young girl, wearing an orange apron, came across to greet them at the door. Someone was washing pots in the kitchen. It was otherwise quiet.

"We'd like to eat," Rail said, making a scooping motion with his hands.

The girl smiled. She had yellow teeth.

"Explain, please," Rail said to the driver. The driver translated and the girl led them to a table near one of the two windows. Rail could smell dried sweat coming off the girl. She was thick-set and heavy-breasted, with a face still wrapped in baby fat, and down on her upper lip. Lovely, Rail thought. Good fierce peasant stock. He wiped his face with a napkin.

"You look like you're gonna order *her*," Harwell said.

Rail smiled.

"You *can't!*" Harwell said. "We got work to do. Besides, she looks like a wop Viva Zapata."

The menu was plain; Rail ordered a salad, a plate of fettucine, a small steak with three fried eggs, and a bottle of Frascati. Harwell asked for a bottle of mineral water. The driver excused himself and went out to the car.

"You see, Harwell, you simply don't enjoy yourself enough," Rail said. "Food is one of the few earthly pleasures, one of the few ways a man can approach divinity."

"Food is fuel," Harwell said. "You keep the body pure the way you keep a car pure. You don't put sand in a gasoline engine, do you?"

The fettucine was served, and Rail wrapped a small mound around his fork, making sucking sounds as he ate. Harwell looked out at the limousine. It was a 1966 Cadillac with Rome plates.

"Who sent the car?"

"Don't ask questions," Rail said. "It doesn't matter."

"Look," Harwell said, "all I want to know is whether you arranged it, or *they* arranged it."

"Why don't you eat something, Harwell? You can't look like a little boy all your life. How old *are* you, Harwell?"

"Twenty-nine."

"Twenty-nine!" Rail laughed with his mouth full, snorting as a strand of fettucine dropped on his napkin. He poured the wine as if it were Coca-Cola. "You know, Harwell, that's obscene. Twenty-nine. Good God, I'd bet that young barracuda back there thought you were nineteen. There's something unnatural about it, Harwell, unnatural! You look like a chorus boy!"

"I stay in shape," Harwell said. "Is that a crime? What difference does it make how old I am? As long as I do what I'm supposed to do."

The girl brought a fresh beaker of wine, and Harwell saw the muscles twitch in Rail's face. Beneath that sleek, fat, pudding face, there were still muscles.

"I can live to be a hundred," Harwell said. "I don't carry an ounce of fat on me. I don't smoke. I don't drink."

"Do you at least, for God's sake, screw?"

"My sex life is entirely adequate," Harwell said.

This was another reason Rail hated him: he spoke like a kid reciting a catechism, with every response memorized so long ago that it had at last become rote. It bothered Rail, because it said more about the questions than the answers.

"The secret is in what you put in your mouth," Harwell said. "White flour, very bad. White sugar, very bad. Too much fruit gives you an excess of vitamin C. Liquor is out. Too much meat is no good, and especially swine. You know why you'll die, Rail? You'll die because you sit there pushing all that shit down your throat."

"Now, now, Harwell, don't get vulgar," Rail said. He wiped the last of the tomato sauce from the plate with a piece of roll, and exhaled softly as he poured more wine. His body shivered slightly. "God always punishes the vulgar first," he said, "before the pious."

Harwell smiled coldly. "Listen," he said suddenly, his voice dropping to a murmur. "Why did they have us picked up together, for Christ's sake? That doesn't make much sense."

"Yours not to reason why, my boy."

"But they might remember. . . . The chauffeur out there, he might remember. This girl here. . . ."

"Harwell, your fasting is going to the brain. Just don't worry. It's all being taken care of."

Rail heard the kitchen door open and turned to watch the girl bring the steak and eggs. Perfect, he thought. Tender, vulnerable, arms like rocks under the baby fat. I could take her to a riverbank and read poetry to her on a field of ferns.

"Do you speak English, signorina?" he said.

She seemed confused, looked around for the driver, then shrugged and giggled. Her tongue darted out over her upper lip when she giggled.

"These wops don't speak anything," Harwell said. "Not even wop."

"Hush, Harwell!"

"It's the truth. I read it in a book on the plane."

The girl was blushing and didn't seem to know where to put her hands. She was about eighteen.

"Er . . . *parlez vous inglese?*" Rail said.

She shook her head. "No, signor," she said, flushing. Her voice was guttural.

"Harwell, you're not doing anything. Get the driver."

"I'm not your pimp, Rail," he said.

Rail's gray eyes hardened in the pampered face. "I said get the driver."

Harwell slid the chair back, scraping the tile floor, and walked across the restaurant to the door. The driver had the hood up and was staring into the engine. Rail watched him from the window. The steak was overdone and thin, and one of the eggs was runny, but he kept eating. The driver closed the hood and came in. Harwell stayed outside, leaning on a fender, sulking, examining his lacquered fingernails.

"Tell this girl I will give her twenty thousand lire if she comes to my hotel tonight," Rail said.

The driver's eyebrows flickered.

"Go ahead," Rail said, without looking at the driver. "Tell her."

"Sir . . . in Rome, there are many girls who—"

"I want this one."

"I don't know if she—"

"Ask her."

Rail watched the driver go into an alcove near the kitchen. The girl was sitting down, reading *Oggi*, a picture magazine. The driver leaned over, whispering, nodding in the direction of Rail. The girl looked up, put her hand to her mouth like a character in a bad opera, stole a glance at Rail, then slammed the magazine down and went into the kitchen.

"She says it is impossible, she is not that kind of girl, sir."

Rail shrugged. He wiped the plate clean, finished the wine, and tapped his fork against the water glass. The girl came out, cleaned the table, and hissed something in Italian at the driver. The driver left. Rail smiled up at the girl, at her dark eyes and trembling mouth.

"*Café?*" she said.

"*Sì, sì, café.*"

Rail took a deep breath, exhilarated by the full solid feeling of the food. He hated airplanes. The food tasted like plastic, the way the stewardesses did. Someday, he thought, I will buy my own plane, with a deep-freeze and double ovens and a private chef and double bed and mirrors on the ceiling. One good contract could actually do it. He finished the coffee and called for the check. He put three thousand lire down for the bill and then took two crisp ten thousand–lire notes from his wallet. He tore them neatly in half and wrote on one of them: *RAIL, HOTEL EXCALIBUR ROOM 634.* He slid them under the plate.

When he reached the car, he could see the girl bending over the table, examining the torn notes, and slowly bringing her eyes up to look at him. The driver put the car in gear and they left in a swirl of dust for Rome.

CHAPTER 3

M alloy no longer felt heat, did not feel the threat of the coming summer furnace, nor the black gabardine habit glued wetly to his back, nor the damp angry tangle of his shorts. He was beyond discomfort. All of that had been left behind, with everything else, in the dark rich murderous earth of the Vietnamese highlands. It was like an umbrella left behind at a party; you were reminded of it only by others.

"Father," a French voice said suddenly. It belonged to a woman in her fifties, short, wearing thick spectacles and a dress the color of tea roses. She was carrying a red Michelin guidebook to Rome, and there were dark splotches of sweat under her arms. Malloy stopped.

"Yes?"

"I need something to drink, Father. Some water."

"Yes—well, walk into the piazza toward St. Peter's," he said. "Stay to your left. There are two fountains, but the one on the left has the best water."

He could see pigeons in the shade of the Bernini fountain, drooping and flawed in the heat. High above, a helicopter from a radio station whirled angrily. He saw a lone dark pigeon bank behind the red pagan obelisk plundered from Nero's Circus, then descend murkily, flailing the thick air in diminishing circles, like a vulture. Beyond the great dome of St. Peter's, the sun struggled against a sky heavy with unshed rain. It might yet rain; and his heart thumped with the thought of Franca alone in the desolation of the beach town, with the rain hammering on the iron roof.

"Father." The woman stood before him, her face a demand. Behind her spectacles, he could see no eyes; she seemed all flared nostrils and rebuffed anger.

"Father," she said again in French, "I said I need something to *drink*."

"Excuse me, madam," Malloy said, starting to walk again. "I must go. There is a fountain over there, two of them in fact, and I'm late already and—"

She grabbed the sleeve of his soutane. Her fingers were square and thick, like rivets.

"Madam, I—"

"You can't expect a *woman* to drink from a public fountain, can you?"

He hated her. It was as simple as that. He hated her for no good reason, except the mean way she grasped that guidebook like a missal, the way her stringy hair was dyed the color of marmalade, the way her face powder rolled itself into little balls in the folds of her neck. He hated the secret little rivers of sweat running down her body like venial sins. He hated the pig face, and the thick freckled hand on his habit.

"Fuck off," he said in English, pulling his arm free angrily. Then, walking furiously across the open square, he became aware of himself: the hard leather loafers clacking on stone, the sweat on his back turning to chill frost in the dark corridors beyond the porticoes, the damp puddle in his shoes. They were all the symptoms of discomfort. He knew that; yet he felt nothing any longer of the infection. Hatred cured everything in the end; it was the only true quinine for a malarial soul.

He was inside now, climbing worn stone stairs. The cardinals and the bishops had the elevators, the way the cripples did in school when he was a boy: in this army, they were officers and gentlemen, or perhaps, Malloy thought, merely cripples. The elevators went to all five floors, to the basement and to the roof. It was really a kind of school. But at least here he was safe. In this wilderness of belfries and spandrels, towers and lost passageways, crowned hats and golden keys, in this treasure house of looted tribute and long-dried blood, he felt himself at the center of a rhetorical boast. It was a boast as broad as the piazza, with its fountains that Frenchwomen would not drink from, as high and hollow as Bramante's dome. And Malloy knew finally that to be at the center of a boast was to be safe from its ability to maim.

He turned the iron key in the old door and went into the office. He had been here seven months and thirteen days, a habit of counting he had picked up out there. Except that here there would be no liberation, no joy, no spangled voyage home, no dream of peace. Home was lost forever; it had been permanently exchanged, like a prisoner of war. He was banished to the capitol, like a carpenter's apprentice in the Renaissance, doomed to help gild the ceilings. And his cell was this office without a window, a private corner of purgatory where you carried your sins with you each day in a leather-tooled briefcase purchased on a vain Monday in Saigon.

Malloy circled the office in silence. His mail lay on the green blotter of the mahogany desk, wrapped in a thick red rubber band like stage money. There were official vellum envelopes like slivers of command, and magazines from the States, and the weekly letter, in a pale blue airmail envelope, franked at the post office, as regular as piety. He knew the spidery handwriting, and the sentiments it contained, and he put it aside, beneath the black dialless telephone which sat solemnly on the desk like a skull in a monastery.

The vellum cracked as he opened the envelopes. There were no surprises. Malloy had a job that someone had done before he arrived and which someone would do when he was gone, and it didn't make any difference. It was an appendix to a vow. Mrs. Michael Brady, of Boston, Massachusetts, USA, needed a special pass for the Solemn High Mass on Easter Sunday at St. Peter's; please accommodate her. Father Richard Devlin, OSP of Los Angeles, California, USA, would arrive Thursday evening with a group of fifty-three pilgrims; please accommodate him. Nothing changed here. He performed his duties, processed his forms, a true clerk of God, presumed safe from thought and temptation. *You are intellectually arrogant*, they had told him, in that first summer of return. *You are guilty of the sin of pride.* And now his parish was a troupe of nomads, in sensible shoes and open shirts, with faces pink as boiled ham, carrying Kodaks and asking the intercession of God over the price of food and lodging. He was beyond judging anyone at all anymore, but he was sure that on the final day, his innocent flock would be condemned to eternal residence in the confines of a postcard.

The phone rang.

"Malloy here."

"You're late again, Father Malloy."

It was Carney, the Canadian, and Malloy saw his smooth white hands and falcon's face, and remembered how he smelled of lilies.

"It was the traffic, Monsignor."

"You seem to have a knack for traffic jams, Father Malloy."

Malloy thought of the sea, and the shock of the spring cold, and the taste of Franca.

"I'll have to start earlier, Monsignor."

"Do that, Father. Do that."

"Anything pressing?"

"Cardinal Maladotti wants you to handle something for him."

He felt like a junior executive talking to an efficiency expert from the corporation. "Do I have to see him?"

"No, Father Malloy. I'll come down."

He hung up, and Malloy sat on the high hard-backed chair, thinking of the ride in, and the six young men he had seen on racing bicycles, laughing in the wind, their legs like spring steel, filled with blood and audacity, shooting past the cream-walled villages and the bald wiry grass, heading for the sea. They had passed each other in a fraction of time, under the expressionless sky while the sun spun away beyond the clouds like the steel wheels of their bikes, and he had saluted them silently because they were alive and not dead, and that was a small triumph at nineteen.

They were children, unmaimed; they had nothing to do with this room carved from old stone. On one wall, some ancient cardinal stared down, his agate eyes peering with disapproval from under the folds of his flesh, a mole like a signal of corruption on his chin, his skin cracking and dry like the varnish on the frame. Malloy was sure the old cardinal had a nose for heresy as some people have one for wine, and that he would have sent the bicycle racers to eternity in a storm of flame. He had almost certainly done so to the painter. On the other wall was the Pope, the Vicar of Christ on Earth and Bishop of Rome. Malloy could not decide which he preferred: the old anonymous cardinal with his burnt-sienna hair and his scarlet aura of linseed oil and murder, or this aggressively ascetic little man with the long nose, weak chin, and well-lit halo. In the old days you could always blame the court painter for the gloss of papal piety; there was no excuse now for that blurred smile and that high-key image of sanctity. That face, Malloy thought, came from looking at mirrors.

He smelled the lilies.

"Come in, Monsignor," Malloy said.

"Father Malloy. Good morning."

Carney glanced at the opened envelopes. If it had been anyone else, Malloy thought, I would have offered him a drink.

"You've been working," Carney said. His voice was like paint peeling on a baptistery wall.

"The usual thing," Malloy said. "Pilgrims, visitors, the usual. Chores, as always."

"Chores?" The eyes were like those of the old cardinal, prepared to pounce at a show of weakness.

"After all, they are chores, Monsignor," Malloy said. "I do not object to them. I do them as best I can, and as a matter of fact, I sometimes enjoy them. You tire after a few months of speaking Italian. I assure you, I lose no souls." He smiled tamely, thinking: None except my own. Carney was looking at the photograph of the Pope. The falcon face bobbed and nodded, bobbed and nodded. "It's Easter," Malloy said. "They all want seats on the altar rail."

"I have one more for you."

Carney slid another vellum envelope from inside his habit. This one was edged in scarlet. Malloy watched Carney's hands; they were white and tapered, with fine lacquered nails, and seemed almost detached from the arms. Malloy wondered what they had done for a living in the snows of Canada. The right hand smoothed and creased the envelope, then stopped and held it while the left melodramatically cracked the waxed seal, and moved inside like a spoiled boy working a virgin.

Carney moved back a step to read the message he already knew by heart. He's farsighted, Malloy thought; and the odor of lilies faded slightly. He had worked in the Vatican for fourteen years.

"You are to call a Mr. Rail at the Excalibur," Carney said, reading from the deckle-edged card. "He is a publisher. He is also a very good friend of Cardinal Maladotti. You are to assist him with anything he might need."

"What about these?" Malloy picked up his handful of visiting Americans, and spread them in his hand. It's infectious, he thought. I'm trying to make my hands into dancers, like his. Except that I'm holding a middle-class flush, and he's caressing power.

"I'll have Father Dongan deal with them," Carney said. He became suddenly very brusque and businesslike, stuffing the deckle-edged card back in the vellum envelope and handing it to Malloy. He turned to go out, and stood for a moment in the door. "Oh—and Malloy?"

"Yes?"

"Do keep in touch, old boy."

"Yes, of course."

Carney's mouth moved laterally, like a stain. "Save the beach until Holy Week is over."

The door closed, the latch clicked shut. Malloy stood there, the impacted wad in his chest moving against his rib cage, searching his pockets for matches, wondering if Carney knew, wondering how long it was since he had been in what they still called a state of grace.

CHAPTER 4

S he would keep out the light, shutter it away, seal off the day. Nothing would penetrate. No sun, no birds, no rolling sea, no burning glaze from the empty beach. Franca lay naked under the sheet, damp with sweat, breathing the incensed air, legs stretched wide, luxuriating, filled with her man of God. He was a hostage: stolen from God, she thought, and you've taken him and his pained jarring damaged flesh, filled with the rush of him. She had read once in a magazine that the seed lived for twenty-four hours; so she would have him there, spread out over the walls of her insides, for a full day. No light would search him out, nothing human flush him away. Now she was waiting for the rain. She would lie there through the damp empty day, and lunch on wine and cheese, and wait for night. He would be back in the dark, and they would eat and make love and sleep, she and her man of God with his hard holy cock, and she would be safe. If now he bored her, there was at least no danger anymore.

She heard movement beyond the walls, down the beach, and the sea brushing the receding sands. Voices rose, murmurous and muted, and fell away like the sea. She hoped they would go away. She turned over languorously, with the silken pillow under her, and drowsed into a half-sleep: filled with filigreed walls and tendrils of bougainvillea and bursting summer flowers purple as doom, and sighing winds and the green soft sucking roar of the sea. Movement was slippery and undulant, colors moving behind a viscous filter, wet. Then the walls fell away and she was alone and naked in a barren garden with a low black, spiky iron hedge. And away off, on a steel-gray horizon, she saw a man with a diseased face, dressed in black, his features rotting and putrescent, wet, moving like a dancer in a slow-motion film, waving some object, coming toward her across the damp earth, shouting words she did not understand, the object as familiar as blood. He reached out toward her, the movements now jerky as a marionette's, but they did not touch. She slid away into the damp marshy ground, her legs running and wet, waiting for him to undress. But the shirt made a splattering sound as he tried to take it off, and beneath the trousers she saw a rotting thicket of blood and grass and thorny stumps, and he moved and shook and bumped against the iron hedge and bumped against the iron hedge again and bumped again against the hedge.

And Franca woke, damp, the pillow hot and wet. There was someone at the door.

"Sì?" Franca said. She felt her face puffy and swollen from sleep, and the sheet around her chilled in the breeze.

"Hello," the voice outside said. "Is anyone home?" The woman's voice was slurred, dark, probably American. Franca cracked open the door. The woman was about thirty-five, with a blowsy blond head, and too much lipstick, carrying a glass.

"I'm from next door," the woman said. Her Italian

was slurred but correct. "I've been here a week and I thought we should get acquainted. I'm Mary Wilson. May I come in?"

She was moving in past the door, her head glowing like the sun, bringing daylight and everything else with her. Stay out, Franca thought. Go away. Stay out. I don't want anyone here. This is mine. I don't need anyone else. Out.

"Nice," Mary Wilson said. "Very nice." She was in: dressed in black slacks and a tight green silk blouse with the top three buttons open, displaying soft freckled breasts. "What's that smell? Is something burning? God, when will the sun come out?"

Franca moved backward, the sheet wrapped tightly around her. She reached into the closet, while the woman with the slurred voice inspected the beach house with the sniffing thoroughness of a dog entering a new home. Franca found the loose-fitting shift in the splashy yellow colors that Malloy had bought for her, and thought about how she would easily kill this woman for a small excuse. She pulled the shift over her head, letting the sheet fall to the floor.

"Is there anything you need?" Franca said. She never knew how to handle these things. She hoped her voice was cold enough.

"God, I could use some coffee," Mary Wilson said. "I thought I smelled coffee. I've just moved in, you know, just today, and I don't have anything in the house. They are supposed to bring food and the rest of the things this afternoon." She said: "Do you speak English?"

"A little," Franca said, thinking of gray flesh and waiting under the lamps off the Via Vittorio Veneto in spring, waiting for cars. Learn English, they told her. It's good for business.

"God," Mary Wilson said, "I wish I could spend a month talking English. Just English, twenty-four hours a day. You don't even know it but it happens to you; you don't even think in your own language, do you know what I mean? You get homesick for it. You listen to the BBC on the shortwave at night and read too many American magazines and when you get drunk you talk too much. I haven't talked English for three and a half months."

She took a drink from the glass. It smelled like rum, and there was no ice, and Franca thought: It must taste like gasoline. She lit the gas stove, and filled the small saucepan for the coffee. Perhaps, she thought, I can give her the coffee and keep quiet and she will go away, and someone else will come here in a station wagon and take a cabin at the far end of the beach and she can sit and talk English through the day.

"I've been here six years now," she said. "In Italy, not Fragene. They told me that Rome was the place, *la dolce vita*, all of that. I thought I would get into films, and I did for a while. I was always the blond American in Rome for a good time, and sometimes I was a Swede. They were always small parts, but I thought they would get bigger. I lived with a producer for a while. An Italian. He told me he would do everything for me. He was going to buy me a villa and an Alfa Romeo and make me a star of the international cinema. But he was a lying bastard. He was married, I found out first, and then he went bankrupt." She said: "Then I met Googie."

Franca stared at her; she had seen those heavy dark

false eyelashes somewhere, blinking quickly, younger. She couldn't remember where. She saw black roots in the blond hair.

"You know what the movie business is?" Mary Wilson said. "It's sucking cocks. That's all it is. That's all I discovered. If they asked me to write my life story, it would be one page long. How I found love and adventure at the business end of a cock." She said: "The Americans are the worst. It's terrible to find out that kind of thing about your own people. I mean, aren't they satisfied with straight screwing? They must not get enough straight screwing. They all want you to eat them."

The water was bubbling, sending steam into the chill air. Franca spooned out the Nescafé and poured the water over it.

"It's instant," she said. "I hope you don't mind."

"Oh, I don't mind at all," Mary Wilson said. "What did you say your name was?"

"Franca."

"Franca. Francesca. Googie and I had a maid once named Francesca. She was from the north, Trieste, somewhere like that, and she worked for us for seven months. She made the best hangover cure I ever tasted and then she got knocked up by a plumber and we never saw her again." She said: "That's the way it always ends up for women, isn't it? We end up with all the dirty shit. Me and Francesca were the same in the end. I've had my insides carved up so many times I can't even have a kid anymore. There's nothing there. It must be like the inside of a rubber ball. Big deal. Now they have the Pill. If they had it then, it wouldn't have happened like this." She said: "At first I used to cry. I used to think I wanted

kids more than anything else, that I wanted them because they would be all mine. Even though Googie was
married. I would have his kids anyway. Then I thought I
would have to adopt a kid. But I don't worry about that
anymore. I just worry—you're too young to understand
this yet—I just worry: am I tight enough? Can he feel being in me? Can he feel me squeezing him when he goes
in? Or is it like putting it out the window? That's all I
worry about." She said: "There's nothing else, is there?"

Franca thought of Malloy. She wished she could love
him. Even though he bored her now, he was better than
all the others. She wished she could love him. Malloy
was something this poor foolish woman would not
understand.

"Do you have a man here?" Mary Wilson said. "I
have one, but he's not here. He says he'll come as often as he can. He's always away on business, in Milan,
in New York, in London, in Germany. Why don't you
take me, I ask him. He says that business is no place
for women. He's so goddamned busy. When I first met
him, he bought me a beautiful apartment in Vigna Clara,
up in the hills, no gas fumes, with a beautiful view. It
was really beautiful. Now he just wants me here in the
house by the sea." She said: "All he wants is to come
down when he feels like it, for a fast suck of my tits and
a quick screw. Well, I'm not satisfied with that. He's in
for a surprise, Franca. I'm telling you. There's plenty of
men around a beach in the summertime. He's in for a
surprise. The dirty shit."

She seemed suddenly exhausted, and slumped into
a cane chair in a corner. She drained the rum with one
hand and felt the coffee cup with the other.

"I can heat that for you," Franca said, hating her own voice as she said the words, knowing she was allowing her in permanently with her glib kindness and her manners.

"Oh, no, no, don't bother. I'll drink it like this."

She swallowed the cold coffee in a gulp, and sat there limply. Franca felt the wind blowing beyond the door, and knew the rain was approaching from the sea. She looked at the exhausted woman—red paint peeling from her toenails, the blackening roots and the used-up hair, the brown tobacco stains on the fingertips, the high heels lying under the chair, the swollen feet—and thought that, yes, perhaps she was right. They used you up and threw you aside and walked on. It would not happen to her.

"Would you like some wine and cheese?" Franca said.

"Yes. That . . . would . . . be . . . lovely." The voice seemed to come from the distance of the rain, and Franca thought: I hope she does not fall asleep.

"Have you had any sleep?" Franca said, cutting a wedge from the roll of cheese.

"I don't sleep much anymore," she said. Something flickered in the face; she seemed to come back from wherever she had gone. "You really don't need much sleep, do you? A lot of famous people don't sleep more than four or five hours a night. I read once that Bernard Gimbel—he used to run the biggest department store in New York—he only slept four or five hours a night." She said: "It sounds right, doesn't it? I mean when you're screwing you don't think about sleep, do you?"

Franca handed her a water glass filled with wine. The woman sipped it, made a face, then took a gulp.

Then a gush of wind took the door and it slammed against the wall with a crash. The woman dropped the glass. Franca closed the door, sliding the bolt shut, and then saw the wine spreading on the wooden floor. Malloy, she thought, would say it was the color of Lent.

"I'm sorry . . . I . . . do you have a rag, I'll clean it up, the noise scared me . . . I'm so sorry."

The woman was on hands and knees, but Franca brushed her aside, sopping up the wine with paper towels. She didn't care about the wine, but now she wished the woman would leave. It was all she had, this room, with the windows closed, and now something alien had walked into it.

"Would you like to go to a party?" the woman said suddenly.

"I don't go to parties," Franca said. She dropped the wet towels into a garbage bag.

"It's tomorrow night. Googie is throwing a party. He throws the most fantastic parties. That's my friend, Googie. He's a count. Do you know him? Count Rienzi? His wife is a bitch. I wish you would go with me." She said: "It's important that someone go with me."

"I have a man," Franca said. The words sounded strange to her. "I don't have to go to parties."

"Well, bring him along. The more the better," she said. "You'd both enjoy it."

The woman drained the last drops of wine from the glass.

"You see," she said, "if I go alone, they'll laugh. I can't stand the laughing anymore. I can't stand walking into a place and feeling like a whore. Do you know what I mean?"

Franca thought of a leering bellboy, bringing drinks to a whiskey-swollen tourist in a room overlooking the Spanish Steps. Get out, she thought, I don't want you here.

"They laugh, they always laugh," the woman said. Her mouth trembled. "They think I don't see them, but I do. It's like you're a piece of property, an animal on some farm somewhere. They laugh now because they know he's pulled my tits for years and now they're drying up, and he's looking around for something else to play with. Some kid. Some kid like I was when I first showed up."

"I'll think about it," Franca said.

The woman was up on spindly legs, sliding her feet into the high heels. "Oh God, I hope you can come."

"Try to get some sleep," Franca said.

"You're a friend, a real friend."

"I'll talk to my man."

"Oh God . . ."

The woman kissed her on the cheek, and then went out, trudging unsteadily through the sand between the houses. A gray wall was coming across the sea, flattening the earth, bringing the rain. Franca closed the door as the first gusts hit the beach. She took off the shift, and lay in the gray light, smoking a cigarette, listening to the monotonous assault of the rain.

CHAPTER 5

M alloy moved through the slanting sheets of rain, pushing the small car down the Via della Conciliazione. His mind was filled with tombs. Before him, under the dripping awnings of the shops, there were tourists standing bitterly with their shopping-bag cargoes of plastic Christs. Seminarians in sandals and thick black robes trotted heavily through the rain, like a military squad made up of stout Victorian ladies. The traffic slowed, then stopped, and scraps of language drifted through panels in his memory, moving and fading, and then becoming suddenly tidy, like the movement of the traffic itself. *O God, forasmuch as without thee we are unable to please thee. . . . If we say that we have no sin, we deceive ourselves, and the truth is not in us. . . . Enter not into judgment with thy servant, O Lord, for in thy sight shall no man living be justified.* The rain beaded the windshield. He hoped the car would not stall.

The wipers peeled the water back before him, and for a moment he saw two young Americans—were they students or pilgrims?—crossing the street. Their young faces were marred with desperation. He wished they would come up to his window and ask him something, anything. And then they were gone again in a sheet of water and steam. On his left, a green and black cab detached itself from the trapped pack, moved swiftly past him, then skidded to a stop. A blond girl with a bulbous German nose and pendulous breasts sat in the back, shouting, and smearing lipstick on her mouth. Malloy wondered how Franca knew about the rain.

He was out of the traffic without knowing it, the car driving him, moving in the tide along the bank of the Tiber. It was funny: he had always seen Italy all gold and weathered brown; it turned out to be Hadrian's Tomb standing like a section of an old tunnel set on end, and the Palace of Justice gray and bleak, like a courtroom sentence of ten years to eternity. It was all muted and sticky; the sky was a sheet of steaming lead, and away off he could see the rain coming in a vast blur, washing and battering the city, spattering the dead gray surface of the river.

It was not much river, he thought, as the traffic slowed, and he stared out at the skirls of water moving across its surface. And then Malloy thought of that other river, piling down from Tibet two thousand miles to the west, and the way it looked that first time from the plane. He had slept most of the way from Guam. There were five Australian soldiers in the front of the plane, getting boisterously drunk and singing Irish songs in the dark, and then it was suddenly daylight, with land ahead. The river was below, a wide umber-colored worm, feeding incestuously with the delta. There was no movement, no boats or sampans, no inhabitants: just the million panes of reddish tesserae spread out across her mouth in the dawn, and the China Sea waiting in ambush. The Australians went silent. The country seemed abandoned, in some terrible moment of final suspension, and then he saw white puffs in the hills to the north, and he knew that somewhere that morning, men were dying. It was the river he always remembered afterward: secret, bloody, powerful, pushing men and blood and history before it, unmoved, beyond defeat, a main traveled-road fed by the monsoon and those distant unseen mountains with their silvered peaks. No wonder some of these people thought Victor Hugo was a saint. The Mekong was sacramental, altering everything it touched, unalterable itself.

The traffic stopped completely at the entrance to the Ponte Cavour. Horns blared; the rain pelted down. A young boy with hair plastered to his skull by the rain hawked the first edition of *Paese Sera* from an oilcloth cover. They were bombing Haiphong again. And he thought about that night: the four of them, alone in the darkness, under the fluted trunks of the mangrove tree, leeches dropping from the branches above, no water left to drink, cut off, afraid of betrayal by the eerie brightness reflecting off the tiny mirrors of the still water. They were listening to some movement behind them, hoping it was animals moving on land, staring out through the tangle at the vast expanse of the river. Everything was wet. Water slid down the trunks of the trees. Something pinged across the water and vanished. Everyone waited for the hunters. "Jesus motherfuckinchrist," Shaw said. "Jesus motherfuckinchrist. Jesusmotherfuckinchrist." Malloy told him to shut up. "Up your ass, Father. Up your fuckin' ass." Jennings smacked Shaw in the face. "Shut up, you black bastard. They're out there."

And they were out there all right. Malloy could hear voices, some cracking movements, and then smelled something cooking. The hunters were making breakfast. For the moment they were safe. Shaw whispered: "Get it the fuck over. Get it the fuck over." Jennings put a hand over Shaw's mouth and Shaw pulled away. And then the hum of the voices stopped. Malloy still heard movement, but no voices. Something was pushing against foliage, making a slapping sound. It was over; there was no refuge, except the river. Malloy tried to pray, and then the machine guns started hammering. *Brrrrrr-AP! Brap. Brudarap.* Shaw was up, his eyes white in the black face, shouting jesusmotherfuckinchrist, come and get me you motherfuckers, come on you cocksuckas. A burst ripped him open. And then Jennings was firing like mad and Malloy felt fear sliding through his stomach, and he forgot Shaw and forgot Jennings and forgot Rustin, and he was crashing through the swamp, the bottom slimy, his head going under, grabbing a slippery root, up again, under, thinking he would drown, making for the river. And then the rain started to belt down as he came from under the tree roof, and there was nothing left but the hammering of the guns and the torn voice of someone screaming: all of it braided together, the guns and the rain and the artillery away off and the fear and the screaming.

"Get it moving!" someone shouted. "What is it?"

The car horns were jarring and insistent, and he put the car in gear and moved at their command across the bridge. The rain had slackened, and he drove up the Via Condotti, and into the Piazza di Spagna, where tourists stood on the Spanish Steps like members of a high school graduating class. The traffic stopped again. A horse dropped a pile of steaming dung onto the glistening cobblestones. The tourists stood smiling in the rain, and he saw the photographer now, with a young boy holding an umbrella over his head. Traffic again. The Via Sistina, shops and loud dresses and young women. How far am I from the beach? He went into the Piazza Barberini, with its wild neon frieze guarding the rooftops from the sky. It was almost lunchtime; the traffic was thin on his side of the street now. He climbed the hill, past the airline office and the American Library. There were cops outside the American Embassy, dressed in slick black raincoats, and the counters at the newspaper kiosks were still covered with plastic sheets. Down the street was the Church of Santa Maria della Concezione, with the picture of the Archangel Michael killing a dragon, and the walls of the chapel in the gloom, covered with skulls. Four thousand of them were there, Franciscan friars, dead and gone forever, grinning down from the walls, like guarantees of damnation. He wondered if anyone knew their names, or if anyone but priests and scholars ever saw them. He took a right at the Excalibur and went down the street looking for a parking place. A whore with powdery yellow hair stood in a doorway, her hands jammed in the pockets of a beige coat. He looked at her. She was the only person on the street. She caught his glance, took her hands out of her pockets and cupped her breasts, like an offering. Then she stuck out her tongue. Malloy laughed.

He parked the car on the next street and walked back in the rain. He thought about coming home that time, and the three days in Bangkok, staying in that strange bare room in the hotel with the blue pool in the garden. The hotel was filled with soldiers, big men in sports shirt and peeling skin and very short hair, all of them, like him, survivors. They drank all the time, and in the evening the hotel was noisy with laughter, bottles falling over, high-pitched squealing from the women. The man at the desk had a round, pouchy Oriental face, and when he saw Malloy leaving that first day, he smiled in amusement. A priest in Bangkok; it was like a nun in a whorehouse. And yet the city that first day had the feeling of peace. No uniformed troops; no jeeps; no burnished machine guns at the ready. It was like peace. He changed the collar for a sports shirt. And that night, alone in the room, he dreamed explosions and horror, and awoke shaking and walked out into the thick warm air. The city was deserted, the blackness of the broad open boulevards broken only by an occasional taxi cruising with a red light in the window. He could not guess what lay behind the doors of the shuttered store windows; the signs were all in some alien script and he realized that until now, the West had not touched Thailand. It was the virgin of the Orient.

He could not remember now why he walked into that building. Perhaps it was the light. Perhaps he had come to understand that sin was a celebration. Perhaps it was just loneliness, and not wanting to go back to the hotel. He wasn't sure even now whether he did in fact go in, or whether he had imagined it. He remembered hard light in the front room, the smell of dampness and water, a girl with a royal-blue dress, slit to the hip as it was in every bad Orient movie he had ever seen. Was this Nancy Kwan or France Nuyen? Was he William Holden? Had he wandered into a whorehouse or a cathedral? The girl gave him a card. He could not remember the name of the place, but it boasted of *Vitamin D Soap*. Yes. He wanted some Vitamin D Soap. Oh Lord Jesus, protect me. A girl in a green smock, broad nose, and a gap between her teeth came out from a side door. They went upstairs. There were hard blue lights everywhere. A long aisle of cubicles. Laughter somewhere. They went into a cubicle. She started unbuttoning the sports shirt, but he finished the job. He placed his trousers on a hanger and covered it with his shirt. Beer? she said in English. Yes. When she was gone, he slid his wallet into one of the shoes, and plugged the shoe with a sock. A glistening white bathtub dominated the room and he remembered a long metallic snakelike shower hose and a table on wheels covered with a sheet, like something from a hospital. The girl came back, and slipped off her smock. She wore no bra, and her breasts were tiny, with hard dark nipples. She wore black cotton panties. She ran the water, testing it with her hand, while he sipped on the beer. He tried not to look at her. Then she motioned him into the bath. She had square flat hands and rubbed his back and his shoulders with soap, sudsing and massaging, and saying something he did not understand. He closed his eyes, and felt her strong hands raise his leg, gripping his feet and rubbing soap between his toes. Her hand ran up his legs, and he tried to remember the Latin words for those muscles she was gently squeezing. She gripped his penis hard, rubbing it with soap, up, down, all slippery and warm, and gently touched his testes, and sent the hand under for a further probe. His eyes were still closed and he felt his back arching upward, seeking contact, the penis packed and hard. And then the hand was gone, a tease or an advertisement, and she was showering him gently, and handed him his beer, and with his eyes open she still had the gap between the teeth and the broad flat nose and away off he heard someone groan. Later, drying on the table, she finished it, her mouth a lusting vessel, no tease, without remorse, accepting, taking without question, and for that moment those seconds, he was out of himself at last.

It was feeding hour at the zoo. He saw them sitting out of the rain in the plexiglass enclosures in front of Rosati's on the sidewalk of the Via Veneto. He knew most of them now, and they probably recognized him. Richards had cataloged their sins for him. That was Richards's job. Nobody bought his novels, but his newspaper in America always took his stories of adultery and failure and drunkenness. Richards had pointed out Hawley, the blacklisted director, who used that forgotten political sin as an excuse to stay in Rome and not test his mediocre talents; Kaiser, the pretty actor with the coal-black hair and the California face, the narrow hips and waist, one of the forgotten boys of 1953 Hollywood who had come to Italy to make Westerns and was breaking up with his third wife at the age of thirty-four; the writer with the hawk face who had not had an article accepted in an American magazine for eight years and supported himself by translating dialogue from Italian pictures for dubbing into English, and running crap games on the side. They were talking to the stringer for *Variety*. At the other tables, there were kids with American sports jackets on vacation; the fat countess with the diamond earrings; Italians reading *Il Messagero*, the respectable morning paper; two homosexuals in sandals, sunglasses, and cerulean-blue dungarees. The waiters moved among them, bringing the cappucinos and the omelettes. All the Americans were reading the Paris *Herald Tribune*.

Malloy walked into Doney's, in front of the Excalibur, and sat on the veranda. A waiter with a dry, corrupt face took his order, and he sat for a while, waiting for the rich sweet coffee, watching the noon crowds walking the wet streets. A middle-aged man tried to sell him a Paris *Herald*, but he didn't want to read about any of that anymore. He watched two Scandinavian girls walk by with three small, blue-haired young Italian kids behind them. A woman in her fifties with washed steel hair sat down at the next table, ordered a double martini, and asked him for a light. He gave it to her.

"How are things at the Vatican?" she said brightly. "I hear that Sistine Chapel is just wonderful."

"It's marvelous," he said, and took out the Quasimodo and started to read. It was the only way he had ever learned to stop conversation. Strangers always thought priests were reading prayers.

> *Ognuno sta solo sul cuore della terra* [he read]
> *trafitto da un raggio di sole;*
> *ed e subito sera.*
> Each alone on the heart of the earth,
> impaled upon a ray of sun:
> and suddenly it's evening.

He looked up and saw a fat man crossing the street. He knew it was his man.

CHAPTER 6

Naples was the color of blood. All the buildings were covered with the sticky sun. The volcano was red, the boats in the harbor were red, the lettering on the poster was red. Harwell wondered if blood had a taste. It was probably sweet. He had seen dried blood once, on the sidewalk of a street three blocks from where he was born. It looked like chocolate. It must be sweet.

Why was it so noisy? The goddamned guineas. Always with their mouths. They really are inferior, he thought. No wonder their armies always lost. No strength of will. They didn't fight because they were soft. They liked talking too much. They liked bad food. They liked women. Every guinea he had ever seen chased women. He remembered Ralph. They used to call him "Fire Down Below" in the old neighborhood. He had a car. That's why the girls liked him. He would drive around in that gold Hudson with all those little girls. They would park near the factory with the windows steamed up. We got him pretty good. Harwell remembered Ralph's bloodied mouth, where the front teeth had cracked off at the gums. That was one guinea bastard who wouldn't fool with white women anymore.

The room was very big. But the man who ran it wasn't a guinea. He was a spic. He was talking spic when Harwell came in to register. He knew what guinea sounded like and he knew what spic sounded like. The guy who ran this place was talking spic all right. It was cheap though. About two and a half a night. He would only be there four nights. He could last it out.

Harwell thought about his room at home. He wondered about Charles. For a moment, his heart tripped. He thought about the time Charles was arrested in the St. Marks Baths. The cops were like that. Probably a gay cop, at that. Oh Charles.

He unzipped his trousers, lying on the bed. He switched on the night light. It was afternoon, but the shutters were closed and the light was dim. Charles was the one who stayed with him the longest. Charles was strong. He loved going out with the club on Saturdays and shooting in the woods in Jersey. That was the best time. Shooting in the woods. Charles.

Guineas were Catholics. But they were bad Catholics. They had no faith. You had to have faith. Maybe there was no God. He would find out why. Naples was the color of blood. He remembered hitting a bird at three hundred and fifty feet one time in Vermont. The club had gone together. It was the best time, even better than Jersey. They were all up early, cooking breakfast, and then drilling, and hiking through the woods. That kind of life made a man hard. Hiking, and wrestling, and shooting. It was almost as good as the barracks. We got Ralph pretty good, that guinea bastard. We taught him not to fool with white women.

But women liked men like that. Ralph had a car. But some of the others had cars too. They liked him for something else. The guys used to say he ate them. Maybe he did eat them. He thought of Ralph in the backseat of the old Hudson parked beside the factory, with his head between Barbara Colfield's thighs.

She is probably fat now. A fat bitch with five children. She probably married some dockworker. Some drunken Irish bastard. At least the guineas didn't drink. She had nice blond hair, but she was the kind of girl who let herself go. It's probably dirty blond now. She wasn't laughing at anyone anymore. She was probably in some kitchen, picking her nose, with a kid with shit in his drawers on the floor. The house probably had linoleum on the floor. And oilcloth in the closets. He thought of the deep rug in the apartment on Bank Street, and the warm sliding penetration of a Friday night.

A horse clattered by in the street. What could a horse be doing there? Then it was gone. He heard cars coughing in the street, and the sound of high heels sticking the pavement. It was too early for that. What time was it in New York? Do you add the seven hours or subtract them? There were Communists in Italy. He had read that somewhere. Millions of Communists. He wondered how the Church allowed that. Catholics couldn't be Communists. But these guineas were bad Catholics. The Pope was nothing. He was just another politician. Him and Johnson and Khrushchev. They were all the same. He was nothing. A politician.

He heard more high heels in the street, tapping, tap tap tap tap tap tap tap tap. Then they were gone. Why was Jayne Mansfield dead? Because she deserved it, that's why. He thought of her naked beside a pool, with the pale shimmering skin. I screwed you, Jayne, and you never even saw me. Next to the pool in the sun. Front and back. I gave it to Carroll Baker too, and Tina Louise.

Tina Louise had a red beard between her legs, and she screamed for mercy when I got on top of her, with her arms and legs tied to trees in the woods of Vermont. I pounded it right into her guts. It was the best weapon. He thought of Barbara Colfield's thighs.

The room smelled of wood. It was very hot. He remembered the guy they called Tarzan in the old neighborhood. He did it to niggers. Every Friday night he went to Times Square and paid for a nigger. It was disgusting. The club should have followed him. They would have killed him and the nigger girl. They could do that. Roger had once stomped a man to death on the Bowery. He was never caught. Roger was a real killer. He wondered where Tarzan had gone. Probably married to some kike.

Kikes were the worst. They were weak. That's why they went into the gas chambers. The Leader was going to get them all. Right back in the gas chambers. People who didn't fight didn't deserve to live. Survival of the fittest. He saw his mother's face and smelled something cooking in the kitchen in the old neighborhood. Candles and seders. I'm a Christian, Harwell thought. I'm a Christian. You must be strong.

There was a fountain down the street. He saw it coming in the car. It was the fountain he saw in *Three Coins in the Fountain*. Debbie Reynolds was in that picture. He saw it at the Orpheum. In the balcony. He didn't know why he had never done it to Debbie Reynolds. Maybe she was too clean-looking. But she married kikes. How could she let those kikes touch her? He thought of Barbara Colfield's thighs. He had done it with Ursula Andress. She had a hard strong body. She was not a cow like Blaze Starr. The guys in the neighborhood liked Blaze Starr.

She had round boobs, but compared with Ursula Andress, she was a cow. Once when he was young he did it to Ava Gardner. She was too old now. He never did it to Sophia Loren, not even when they printed those pictures of her bare boobs in the first movie she made. He thought about Ursula Andress.

He heard more horses going by. Naples was the color of blood. He opened the case beside him. It was beautiful. Long and beautifully oiled. It was German. The Germans knew how to make these things. He ran his hand idly along the barrel. He reached down with the other hand. In Vermont, there were rough Army blankets and the woods smelled like mint. Ursula Andress. The Germans made these things better. Charles. Your square hard pecs. Your clean perfumed armpits. Your powdered hole. Your tight sack, bursting with strength. Men must be steel. Men must be weapons, like this beside me, with its polished barrel and wooden stock. Hold me. Sliding, pulling, the insertion of a Friday night, the warm pillows, hold me. Tits and a torn hard stomach and blood, ripping, and pulling, tied to the trees in Vermont. Tearing again screaming, beg, you cunt, beg. Oh Harwell! No more, Harwell! Beg!

He bit his lip and turned on the bed to spill it onto the hardwood floor. Outside another tourist horse-car was tap-tapping down the street. He lay back, drowsy with the heat and the afternoon, and tamped his brow with the edge of the sheet. I'm in Rome, he thought. I'm in Rome. He touched the barrel of the rifle. In a minute, Harwell was sleeping, dreamless.

CHAPTER 7

"You don't mean to say, my dear Father Malloy, that you deny, or even doubt, the existence of God?"

"I don't deny it. I'm a priest of God."

They had been there forty-five minutes, with Rail ordering most of the menu. Malloy thought: You look like a sedentary jellyfish, the sort of man who did not grow older, just larger. Malloy noticed the fat spreading Rail's legs apart under the table. The talk had been morose and dull: the humor of Pope John, the great progress of the Council, the elimination of the guilt of the Jews. It was a lot of talk to put out, Malloy thought, just to obtain tickets to the Easter Sunday services.

"But in some respects, my dear father, it is easy to understand those apostates and heretics who claim that the nature of God is malignant," Rail said. He was eating a spinach omelette.

"It seems that way at times," Malloy said. "You could certainly say that about man." And thought: Malloy, you glib bastard. You are sitting here, and discussing these things like a panelist on an educational TV show. But at least once you saw God in the evidence of a billion suns; now the best His artistry could produce was men. Malloy sipped the oily-sweet coffee.

"Why do priests remain priests?" Rail said. "How

can they surrender so much of themselves? It's a wonder and mystery to me, Father."

"You don't have to call me Father."

"Forgive me," Rail said. The spinach omelette was gone, its traces congealing on the plate. "But as a layman, I would say from personal observation—entirely unscientific, mind you—I've taken no Gallup poll, ho ho—I would say that more men are leaving the priesthood these days, wouldn't you say so, er, Malloy?"

"I have to go." He pushed the chair back, making a sound like coal grating against stone.

"Father, Father, forgive me," Rail said. His eyes moved toward Malloy, then away, searching out the waiter. "I *am* too inquisitive. You see, in my business I spend much time with priests. That is, we see each other across desks, or in the mail. Why, Cardinal Spellman was a dear friend. He sent me an autographed photo two Christmases ago and it hangs now in the most honored place on my office wall. But I have never really *known* a priest. I have *wanted* to, because they are, as I say, great puzzles to me. I have been a convert, you see, since 1937. You know what they say, that converts are like reformed drunks: they have steel consciences. Unfortunately, I have never been that way, my dear Malloy, and I suppose I shall serve my time in purgatory. If I had been a better Catholic, I should have been a priest, I suppose. If only the *tempo*ral world had not been such a grievous temptation."

You would have been a cardinal too, Malloy thought, selling votes at the councils, making your relatives bishops, peddling mite boxes to the poor. And said: "What exactly is your business, Mr. Rail?"

"I'm a bookseller, you might say," Rail said. "Oh, nothing big. No best sellers. No Shakespeares or Miltons. Nothing too terribly commercial," he said, his lips pursing in distaste, as the waiter removed the omelette plate and deposited a thick slice of veal in a wine sauce. "I publish religious books."

"Oh?"

"Yes," Rail said. "Biographies of the saints. Stories of the great popes. Our book on Pius XII was a great success, and I must say that John XXIII is even outselling him. But it's nothing big, mind you. It's not like publishing the *Baltimore Catechism*."

"I suppose not."

"My favorite saint was St. John of the Cross," Rail said. "He was a great poet, a great, great poet, a true mystic and martyr, a soldier of God."

"Why don't you put out a book called *The Wit of St. John of the Cross?*"

"Ho ho, Father Malloy, you are a funny man," Rail said. "*The Wit of St. John of the* . . . ho ho ho."

Malloy could feel the rain coming again, gathering strength beyond the hills. He watched the street. The inhabitants of the zoo were in motion again; they had crossed from Rosati's to Doney's, hoping for sun, but now, with the breeze coming wet up the Via Veneto, they were calling for checks and moving back across the street to the shelter of Rosati's plastic cage. The cab drivers were looking up, and shouting animatedly to each other, but Malloy could not hear them. There seemed to be more cops assembling in front of the American Embassy.

"Excellent veal," Rail said. "The Italian cuisine is execrable, but they occasionally manage to do things with an inferior meat."

"You should see what they do with money," Malloy said.

"Father, I do believe you are a cynic."

"Is there anything else I can do for you, Mr. Rail? I'll have the tickets delivered to the Excalibur before five, but I must be going."

"Yes, yes, the tickets," Rail said. "You understand that I must be at the services tomorrow. It wouldn't do if my friend Cardinal Maladotti didn't see me there."

"No, that wouldn't do," and he thought of how Maladotti's eyes burned, and how he smelled dimly of burnt cloth.

"What *is* happening down there?"

Rail was looking past Malloy at a mob coming up the Via Veneto, chanting something that neither could understand. The mob was a dark anonymous color, but Malloy saw some faces, all of them young, and cardboard signs sticking over their heads like the banners of a medieval army. The signs were about Vietnam. The police locked arms and made a human fence, two deep, before the American Embassy's shuttered gates. The mob came like a wall, then stopped, facing the police, with an alley of enmity between them. The waiters started taking the chairs in from the sidewalks. In Rosati's, the inhabitants were standing for a better look. Then a short young man with a black raincoat broke from the mob and slammed his poster at the line of cops.

"What is it?" Rail said. He looked nervous.

"They're protesting against the war."

"They must be Communists," Rail snapped.

"No," Malloy said. "They're just students. They're just young. They just want the killing stopped."

"Communists," Rail said flatly, chewing on a piece of veal.

The police were smashing everything in front of them now. They had long white bats in their hands, and Malloy saw a girl struggling and then being grabbed by the hair and twisted and then falling and the bats going up and down, up and down. There was a siren blowing somewhere, and then the rain arrived, heavy and pelting, and they grappled in the rain. A van pulled up; police piled out like men from gunships, crashing into the crowd, and then the students started running, cursing behind them at the police. One ran past Doney's, with a thin rill of blood running down his face, and for a moment their eyes met: the bloodied young man with the blood going pale in the rain, and Malloy in the dry safety of the verandah at Doney's. The young man shook his fist: "No balls. Capitalist priests. Imperialist tourists. No balls. No balls." And then he was gone, sprinting for the safety of the Borghese Gardens. In front of the American Embassy, three cops were kicking a lone marcher who was facedown on the street in the rain.

"Thugs and hoodlums," Rail said. "The world is being over*run*, Father. These thugs and hoodlums and Communists are overrunning us!"

"It would seem," Malloy said, "that the only person being overrun at the moment is that kid lying in his own blood over there in the gutter."

"He asked for it," Rail said. "If they think they can take the law into their own hands, then the law must deal with them firmly. All we have to protect us, my dear Malloy, is the law."

Rail was settling down again. He had finished the veal, and his eyes searched for the waiter.

"Well, I really must go."

"If you insist, Father," Rail said. "But we must chat again. Most stimulating, most stimulating. There is no Mass on Good Friday, is there? Just services. Well, I shall see you there tomorrow. Perhaps we might even have lunch and do some sightseeing. I suppose you don't see much of Rome, being a priest." He chuckled obscenely. "But I'm sure my friend the Cardinal would not mind if you decided to spend some time showing a poor lay bookseller the sights. It's my first time, you know."

"I don't think I can make it."

"I'll talk to the Cardinal about it."

Malloy took six hundred lire from his pocket to pay for his coffee. Rail's hand caught his wrist. Malloy thought: Shaw's mouth.

"No, no, *no*, my dear father. This one is mine."

"I insist . . ."

"It's mine," Rail said. He sounded like a real cardinal now. "I shall see you tomorrow, Father. Goodbye."

Malloy was dismissed: just like that. He walked out into the rain. There was a thin knot of people in front of the Embassy gates, and a crowd across the street staring blankly. Malloy pushed through the cab drivers in front of the Excalibur and crossed over for a closer look. The street was littered with discarded signs: all about peace, all of them violent. The blood was gone in the rain. Cars pulled over, and moustached men with pins in their lapels leaped out and started barking orders at the police. A newsreel crew piled out of a truck. The police looked surly. Malloy saw pale faces moving in the windows of the Embassy: secretaries, second-rate diplomats, adventurers, spies. Inside the compound, a Marine in full-dress uniform stood at the door, his gun at the ready. The gates were locked. In front of the crowd of journalists at the gate, he saw Richards.

"Frank," he shouted. "Frank!"

The cops looked at him. The journalists were arguing and shouting.

"Frank, over here! Frank Richards!"

Richards turned. His glasses were spattered with rain, his thin gray hair flat against his skull. He slid out of the crowd, took Malloy's arm, and saying nothing, moved across the Via Veneto and through the crowd of spectators. They stood in the vestibule of the Ambassador Hotel.

"I saw it," Malloy said. "A kid rushed out of the crowd and bashed a cop. Hit him with a poster."

"What time, Bob? Do you know?"

"I don't know exactly. Maybe half an hour ago."

Malloy described what he had seen. Richards took no notes.

"I'm trying to get in to see the goddamned press officer," Richards said. He was drying his glasses with his tie. "You'd think it was the goddamned U-2, instead of a mob scene. The goddamned Marines wanted to shoot us. I asked them if we could at least get out of the goddamned rain. Just let us into a goddamned hallway or something. No. Against security. They would have no comment to make anyway. Shit. Wait here a minute."

Richards walked across the street, and pushed

through the knot of newspapermen. He shouted something through the gates. The Italian police moved in closer. One of them grabbed Richards by the arm. Richards pulled his arm away. Richards and the policemen stood arguing. Richards took out his wallet and showed the cop his papers. The cop studied them in the rain. He turned and said something to the other cops. Then they all moved in, holding the batons in two hands before them, and started pushing the journalists into the street. The Italian photographers pushed back. A baton came up and went down. Richards stormed back across the street.

"The hell with it," he said. He walked like a lot of people from Chicago who Malloy had known: pigeon-toed, on the balls of their feet, like jockeys or prizefighters. "You eat? Let's get away from these sons of bitches before I get myself arrested."

They walked down the hill, past the USIA Library, toward the Piazza Barberini. The rain thinned, then stopped.

"Relax," Malloy said.

"Yeah, yeah, I know. But these sons of bitches . . ."

"You just don't like cops."

"Did you ever meet one that shouldn't be in jail?"

"Did you ever meet a cardinal who shouldn't be in hell?"

"Does a bear shit in the woods?"

They took a cab to Piazza del Popolo. That was Rosati's South, but there were never any tourists, and the menu was in Italian only. Everyone looked like Marcello Mastroianni, even the waiters, and the Italian movie industry collided with the journalists there, the way the

Americans in the movie business collided with the tourists on the Via Veneto. The café stood out on the square; there were no sidewalks; you drank and looked out at the vast square with its absurd obelisk and its fragment of a palace. The tables were deserted when they arrived, except for two young women in blond hair and dark glasses who were trying quite hard to look like Monica Vitti. They are all trying to look like Monica Vitti this year, Malloy thought. Except Franca.

"You ready for the big day?" Richards said casually.

"Easter?" Malloy said. "It should be all right. I've got nothing to do, except ferry some fat clown from the States around the sights. If the weather holds, they could charge admission at St. Peter's Square and feed Southeast Asia."

"My friends in the restaurant racket say pilgrims don't carry cash."

"We accept Diner's Club."

The waiter brought two beers. Malloy thought: I've been here two dozen times and never visited the twin churches in front of me. They remind me of the opera house in Saigon. And thought: Richards is about the only person in Rome I can talk to. Perhaps because he is an atheist and believes only in money and himself.

"How is she?" Richards said.

"She's all right."

"Good," Richards said. He didn't say anything else. That was why Malloy liked him. He never said too much. They drank the beers slowly, then paid the checks. Richards called for a cab. Up the hill, Rail's table was empty. The chairs were back on the sidewalks in front of Doney's. Down the street, three young journalists stood in the wet gutter facing the troops of the police. The faces were gone from the windows in the Embassy. The cab stopped where Malloy had parked his car.

"I probably won't see you until the big sacrifice is over," Richards said.

"Probably not. I'll call you next week."

"Don't eat any wooden Christburgers," Richards said.

The cab went off toward Richards's office. On the way back to the Vatican, Malloy wondered who Rail was.

CHAPTER 8

The sand was cold from the rain. Above her, the sky ran and pitched and moved again. The seabirds were gone. She was alone. Franca tried to light a cigarette but the matches were pulpy from the dampness. She leaned on an elbow and looked down the beach. Nothing moved in the cheap villas and shuttered shops. The sand stuck to her arm as if glued.

Once she thought the world was round: it was what they had taught in school, all those nuns with starched faces and barren hearts. But now she knew that the world was flat. If you went far enough across that table of sea you would fall into the void. There would be no real horror. You would simply vanish into the emptiness, and every other life would go on. It meant nothing. That was the truest lesson one ever learned: the lesson of nothing. You were nothing and God was nothing. If you went off the edge, you would be free. In the dark void, you were beyond contact.

Away down the beach, she saw a ball of rain pounding its way through the small cluster of shops and villas. It would arrive in a few minutes. She lay back and closed her eyes. In minutes, seconds, the rain would come crashing against her, washing and attacking, bringing the solitude of assault. She trembled in the chill, and then heard the roar of the unleashed rain. She lay nailed by the water to the sand.

CHAPTER 9

I t had been a terrible day, Rail thought. The chauffeur moved the limousine past monuments and memorials, through blocks of faceless concrete housing for the poor. It was a day devoid of grandeur, he thought; a day just like these shabby little principalities around me, with their sullen flags of wet wash. He had not slept; he had tried, all night tossing and stretching in the darkened room; he had placed a cloth mask over his eyes to keep out the light. Nothing had worked. There was something about the jet airplane, he thought, that destroys natural balance. He saw a vision of himself, unrealized and sad; it was the vision he had had as a young man, thirty years before: in pressed white duck, on the deck of a steamer going through the Red Sea. Women with floppy hats and sensible shoes leaned against the railing, melancholy for England, bound for India to see husbands who were living in colonial outposts and writing histories of tea in the slow afternoons. Ah! Rail breathed heavily; a sigh. That was travel. Journeys had beginnings and endings then. One had a sense of moving through time and space, of conquering distance, of bringing the mind evidence of adventure. And there was comfort and pleasure: first-class cabins, dressing for dinner, Somerset Maugham in the book bag.

Alas, all mystery is gone, Rail thought, except that

which you create. The car passed a dull street of hamburger shops, coffee bars, a movie house, all glowing luridly in the gathering dark. He remembered the places he had dreamed about in childhood: Sarawak and Java, Borneo and Tahiti. I have never seen the Southern Cross, he thought, and his mind filled with palms at dawn and the jungle. Africa! In that Africa, planes had one motor and crashed in the forests and were never seen again. Stanley and Livingston. Sir Richard Burton. Those were men. Men beyond vulgarity. Men of endurance. He thought of Maria Montez and her ivory skin and pouting lips and how the men who fought for her love went fishing in the still blue waters of the Pacific. There were places still undiscovered then: no ship ever passed; no airborne geographer gave them a dot and a copy of *Time*. In those places, the white man was always Thomas Mitchell and he was God and King, drinking palm wine and entitled to enter the finest women. It was all civilized now, Rail thought; that is, vulgar and corrupt, and I never tasted it when it was pure. Now the French were testing the atom bomb in Tahiti.

"We have believed the beautiful, false stories," Rail said aloud. "Fed on the faiths that after childhood fail . . ."

"Eh, signore?" The driver looked around, a smear of moustache and dark eyes.

"Nothing, nothing," Rail said. "Move on."

He waved the man on. Nobody read Ernest Dowson anymore. An ancient priest was caught in the glare of the headlights and was gone. Rail thought about Malloy. He would get nowhere in the Church, Rail thought. He had a tough-guy veneer, and he was vulgar. He was a third-rate functionary, an assistant to a prince, and he spends his time sneering at lunch. He knew the type: Irish, from a drunken family, half of them in prison and the other half in the priesthood. Spent his youth eating baloney sandwiches and sipping Campbell's chicken noodle soup. Still, there was something about Malloy that didn't fit the type. There was something hard there.

The car was climbing now, and the buildings were thinning out, along with the air. He smelled open land, trees, earth. He could see Rome spread out behind him: lights blinking on in a thousand apartments, ribbons of light where the main avenues were, a dark smear for the river and another for the Borghese Gardens, and over everything, the dome of St. Peter's, white and imposing, demanding submission. The road was lined with cypress trees, and as they turned one blackened corner, Rail saw a light in the window of a crumbling farmhouse. It was yellow and warm, and Rail imagined its master writing with a goose quill in a ledger and blotting his thoughts with sand. I should have married, Rail thought, I should have had a dozen wives and three dozen children, and lived on a great farm with serfs in the fields and log fires in the living room, like Tolstoy. Rail felt depressed, and then, with a loosening of the bowels, he was afraid.

I will die, he thought. Now I am alive: that is, my heart beats, oxygen feeds my brain, blood flows through my veins. But I will die, unknown, in a high dark street. I am going now to seal this monstrous thing. I cannot turn back. I am only a small cog in a great machine. But I know now that I will die and all I ever really wanted will have eluded me. Who was that man with the candle in his window? I shall never see his face and he shall never see mine. It was impossible: he felt the way he had

once as a boy, walking into the central library in Cleveland. There were too many faces, as there were once too
many books. If I had any curiosity left I would go back.
I would turn the car around, and stop and talk to that
man. I would ask him about his children and his dreams
and his taste in music, and I would make an appointment with him for dinner. It would be foolish; it would
be gross sentimentality; the man would think me mad.
Perhaps I am.

Beyond the rise, over the hill, he saw a dull glow,
like the distant burning of a house. That must be the hotel. Another great plastic cavern, Rail thought, made by
American money, staffed by American Italians, its every
room filled with Americans on their way somewhere else.
He wondered if any of them in any of those rooms were
thinking about death. It was unlikely, he thought. Americans believed in money and copulation. They didn't believe in death anymore; the word had been banished; it
was something that happened to other people, and they
were only concerned now with being good *and* greedy. If
they thought more about death, they would think more
about food. Rail's stomach suddenly ached; his bowels
loosened again, with regret and excitement. He thought
about the pressed duck at the Tour d'Argent in Paris.
The ortolans at the Grand Véfour. He swallowed hard.
There hadn't been a great American stomach since Diamond Jim Brady, Rail thought, except possibly for mine.
The car turned into the main gate.

"Don't stop at the front door!" Rail said.

The black cap and the moustaches turned, but the
eyes were blank.

"Stop here! Right here! I want to get out here!"

The car stopped suddenly. Rail lurched forward. An attendant in battered cap and long brown coverall coat walked over, as Rail opened the door and got out.

"You need help, mister?" he said.

"No, er, yes, would you tell this man to wait for me over there in the corner?"

"Sure."

"Thank you, thank you."

Rail slipped the attendant a hundred-lire note. His bowels loosened again, with fear. I don't want to look conspicuous, he thought. They will follow every trail, every inch of it. The driver is from Milan; he won't matter. But I saw the first driver today outside the Excalibur. The attendant was from Rome. He spoke perfect English. He was one of the smarter ones. He might remember a fat man in a parking lot. And then where would I be? Rail brooded as he crossed the darkened lot to the lobby. There were too many inferior people, that was the trouble. Both of those men were younger than I; they were obviously inferior, in intellect and taste and desires; yet each would live longer than I will. It was dreadful. Rail looked at his watch. It was seven forty-seven. He had thirteen minutes. It would not be right to arrive too early. They might think I was nervous.

He walked into the lobby. There were Americans everywhere, all wearing cardboard badges with their names lettered across the face. He looked casually at the Scheduled Events case. There it was, the lead listing: the American Medical Association. It couldn't be, Rail thought. He could not have traveled all those miles to find himself surrounded by a gang of conventioneering quacks.

". . . That's really funny, Dr. Morton . . ."

". . . So the resident said . . ."

". . . And I said that if a heart transplant worked, the next thing they would start doing was penis transplants . . ."

They were all around him, and Rail hated them all. He thought of all the thousands of dollars he had spent in his life on little bottles of colored pills. He remembered the furnished room in Newark that time, with the frayed carpet smelling of feet and the pubic hair floating up out of the drain when he ran a bath at the end of the hall. He had covered the top of the night table with pills that winter, and the summer afterward, and the winter after that, and none of them had done anything for him. Pills were for people like that horrid little creature Harwell.

A tall man in a double-breasted black silk suit was staring at him. It might be the house detective, Rail thought; and suddenly his stomach fell, and he remembered flight, pursuit, capture, public shame, and the names you used in the second-rate hotels, and the knock on the door in East St. Louis and the cold verticals of a judge's face, and iron, and pissing in a sink in a high tier. I will never go back to a place like that again. I had done nothing truly wrong that time; but his mind filled with whips, net stockings, blonds with black fur, and horses. I must not look conspicuous, he thought. And drifted into a cluster of doctors waiting for elevators.

". . . The fees were not terribly high . . ."

". . . The Colosseum . . ."

". . . That was the road to socialism, I told him, and it was a road our profession . . ."

". . . His wife got under the weather, and we said . . ."

Rail was crushed against a menu in a plastic case on the wall of the elevator. It was in French, Italian, and English. I must try the squab, Rail thought; and his stomach felt like a great empty barrel. He thought about the girl in the tavern on the road from the airport. I should not have been so conspicuous, but perhaps she will come. I must go back early. The air-conditioning in the elevator was out of order. ". . . The electricians are out on strike and so are the garbagemen . . ." The elevator stopped at every floor, and never emptied. One set of doctors got out at one floor and others got on at another; sweat ran into Rail's eye; he licked his lips and they were salty. The doctors were all alike: tall with distinguished hair, like the people in liquor ads. Or foremen of juries.

For a moment, Rail thought of staying on the elevator, not getting off at the fourteenth floor, just taking it to the roof, and coming back down, and walking out through the lobby into the night and taking a taxi to the airport. What they wanted him to do was monstrous; there was no other word for it. He imagined going away, and then his mind took him to the Excalibur to see if the girl had arrived, and she had, and they went north to Cortina and Lake Como and into Switzerland and lived happily ever after. Yes, he would leave Harwell to his mock-turtle soup and his sauerkraut juice and his weapon. He would leave this meeting, and all it could mean. The car stopped at the eleventh floor; doctors got off, doctors got on. And then he thought of all the places he had never seen, meals he had not eaten, women he had not purchased. The trick was money. It was the ruling tenet of the modern faith. He did not want to accumulate money, like other Americans. He wanted what it could buy. Happiness and consolation, and places where nuns did not beat him in the night, where he was his own father and his own mother, where he owned and ruled all.

He stepped off the elevator on the fourteenth floor, looked at the arrows on the wall plates before him, and turned left, enjoying the luxury of the thick rich carpet. That was it: I shall live a sultan's life, all carpets and pillows and oiled women like odalisques and soft dark grace. It was only a business proposition, after all. One must look at such matters coldly. Pragmatism: that was the word. When it is over, I can wait a year and sell the business and live abroad.

He stood absolutely still in front of room 1430. I can still turn and leave. I can still go to the airport and leave. He knocked. The door opened silently, and Rail saw a man with a tanned face, hair gray at the temples, wearing a dinner jacket. For a moment, Rail thought he had made a mistake. The man looked like one of the conventioneers. But he looked past the handsome face, and in a far corner, he saw the hawk nose, the mask of rimless glasses, the scarlet cloak, the decaying body, and the voice—"My dear Mr. Rail, do come in"—and he stepped into the suite, with the black wall of glass at the far end and the lights of Rome sprinkling across it, and his heart was filled with doom.

CHAPTER 10

Evening seeped into the tiny office. It was like a dark yellow fog that had slid under the windows and around the bed and into the water lilies when he was sick that time with malaria. The dark was harmless, but the fog had taken the shapes of faceless men and smelled of decaying jungle; it came at him to choke and smother, licking at his face, fouling his tongue, blurring the edges of the room, enveloping everything, poisoning the clear water in the white ceramic bowl beside the bed. One moment he had been clear-headed and cool; and then the chills came, and behind them the fog, and he was screaming for help that never came.

It was dark now. The Pope's hard angular face on the wall receded into blackness, along with the long-dead cardinal. Malloy heard steps in the marble halls, faint and distant, then growing stronger, clacking with the sharpness of expensive leather, then fading away toward the elevators. Doors closed, locks were loudly turned: the clerks of God were going home.

Malloy laughed softly in the darkness. I am losing my grip, he thought. I am thinking again about the word *home*.

He had learned finally that he had no home anymore, and even the memory of the old one was blurred and murky. There was only a succession of barren rooms, twenty years of barren rooms, and none of them had been home. In the seminary, the hard northern winter rushed through the cracked walls and the ill-fitting windows, and none of them had protested. They were only boys; they did not protest, because of fear. They were afraid of themselves, afraid of pleasures and softness, drummed daily with the need for mortification and denial. But they were afraid also of punishment, of retribution, of the vengeance of God. God, after all, controlled the winds and the rain, and everything had its purpose. I believed in God then, Malloy thought, as I have never believed since; I believed in heaven too, the way I have come to believe in hell.

Malloy snapped the head off a wooden match. He lit a Camel, sucking in the smoke. He had felt nothing move in his chest for three hours. Once, he would have lit the match and then crushed the cigarette in penance. That was an act that came with belief, like the silence in the barren rooms. When one believed with every fiber in God, one could also believe in sacrifice. One lived in discomfort, and felt its shabby pressures at every moment, because discomfort could be offered as penance. One shivered and groped for a corner of warmth, and offered the night to the Virgin Mary, or a sick aunt, or the souls in purgatory. It was easy to do as a boy; as a man one encountered hell more easily than one tasted heaven, and discomfort was only an identity card.

Malloy turned on the light. His hand shuffled papers: a third carbon of the form admitting Mr. Rail to all Masses and ceremonies as a guest of the Holy See; letters from three travel agencies advising of the arrival in June of six planeloads of pilgrims, via Shannon and Lourdes;

a memorandum advising all staff that during the Holy Days they must surrender the privilege of saying Mass to visiting priests. It was like working in a brokerage house, Malloy thought; I have become a customer's man.

He heard more footsteps in the corridors, less emphatic, more a shuffle. Then he heard the murmured voices, gruff and whispered, of the *sanpietrini*, those arrogant little men who had lived on the grounds for generations and cleaned the altars and the offices, and gossiped darkly about the secrets of the Vatican. It was always gossip of sex and money; there were probably no other true subjects. They would tell you about Pius XII and Sister Pasqualina, the Bavarian peasant who had become a nun and stayed with Pacelli for forty years, and lived with him in the nineteen rooms of the papal apartments. They would tell you which of the visiting cardinals were gay, which one had fallen for a countess, which member of the Pope's family had made a killing on the stock market and which of the College would be the next pope. They had been doing this for centuries; they would do it for centuries after all those present were gone. Malloy's door suddenly opened.

"*Scusi.*"

A bent, aged *sanpietrini* stood at the door with a dust mop in one hand. "When will you leave?" he demanded.

"When I feel like leaving."

"You will not have a clean office."

"I don't care."

"Don't talk like that, young man."

"Get the hell out of here," Malloy said in English.

"What?"

Malloy stood up.

"I said, get the hell out of here or I'll wrap that broom around your neck."

The *sanpietrini* understood. He sniffed haughtily, muttering in Italian about the Americans and their mothers, and slammed the door. That, Malloy thought, is a good man.

He could hear bells ringing somewhere; it was seven. There was still time, but he no longer had anything to do. I have become a clerk at last, Malloy thought. This must be what marriage is like, sitting in the office, wasting time because a wife wants precision, and one should not come home too early or too late. Tomorrow I shall guide Rail around the city, as directed; I shall meet him at Mass, as directed; I shall coddle him and protect him, as directed. I should really take him to that spot in the Pincian Hills near the Aurelian wall, behind the convent of Santa Trinitá. That was where the villa of Lucullus once stood, and Lucullus was the patron saint of gluttons.

Malloy put the cigarette out, and stretched, enjoying the unslipping of muscle, the cracking sounds in his back, the blood pumping a little faster. Then he looked again at the letter.

My dearest Robert, Well, I have not heard from you for three weeks and I hope that you are not sick or anything serious. You know I worry and pray for you especially that you dont get sick again like in Los Angeles. I do worry about you, Robert—
(2)
It is so lonely here since your father died. I won't be in this vale of tears long. I am prepared, so I dont worry about it. I see Father Ahern at Mass every morning and he always

asks about you. I think your vocation made his life happier
as it made ours. Old Mr Kurtz the

(3)

caretaker at Holy Name died. You remember him, don't
you. Janet Kelly had a terrible tragedy. Her son (R.I.P.)
was hit by a truck and died. His name was Brendan. He
was only six. The whole neighborhood went to Smith's for
the wake—some people I hadnt seen for years. It rained
for the funeral. I sent her a Mass card. I am including ten
dollars ($10) for a Mass

(4)

card from St. Peter's. Please remember his soul in your
prayers and pray that Janet has the courage and grace
to bear her cross. Surely the boy is in heaven. Mr B died
and they closed the candy store. I hear they all moved to
Florida. The RKO Prospect is closing too. No customers I
guess. They are making it into a supermarket, at least

(5)

that's what Mrs. Devlin said. You remember her? The ca-
shier? I saw her on Fifth Avenue the other day and she was
looking well. She moved to Bay Ridge. The neighborhood is
worse than ever. Drug addicts everywhere and more Puerto
Ricans and coloreds. I know you always say that God gave
them souls too, but you have to admit that they don't really

(6)

know how to live in a decent neighborhood. Some Puerto
Ricans opened a grocery store on the corner where the
cleaners was. The Pet Lady moved away and the store is
empty. Please write soon as you are always in our hearts.
I hope you are happy in God's work, and that God is with
you during Holy Week. Pray for me.
Your loving Mother

She had written to him everywhere he had ever been. The handwriting had thinned now, and grown shakier with age. But the concerns and the tone remained: the piety, the charting of the neighborhood which meant so much to her and so little to anyone else anymore, her own isolation and loneliness, her pride in her son's career in the Church. It didn't anger him anymore. He didn't even try to understand. It was just another phenomenon, like snow on mountains or lichen gathered on sea rocks.

For an hour, he had tried to remember who Janet Kelly was and what she looked like, but it would not come. He remembered only a burgundy-colored coat and thin bird's legs and a gray chipped tooth. He supposed he had gone to school with her; his mother always wrote to him about people he had grown up with, and could no longer remember. He wished he could explain to her that Janet Kelly was just another piece of that time and place, part of the home he had not lived in for twenty years, a name in a letter. Even the people he thought he remembered were no longer certain; what he knew was that all of them were still fifteen, the age he was when he had left. The only one he really remembered was the one called Kathleen.

An hour before, pity had made its cheap move, as he tried to picture the girl's grief, the child's broken body, the waiting room in the Methodist Hospital, the small coffin in a crowded room in the back of Mike Smith's, with the visitors smelling of cheap wet wool on a wet spring night. But he fought it down; he was certain that it had been shabbier than his memory could imagine.

He hated the death of children, but their deaths were a subject for the Grand Inquisitor. Mutilation was worse. And he had seen them in the hospitals in Vietnam. Row after row, acre after acre of them, stunned and silent, their eyes betrayed like wounded wolves, with blistered faces, scorched hair, pus oozing from the sores where the phosphorous bombs had hit them, the medics in green doing what they could, and the whine of aircraft somewhere close by, flying on to mutilate more of them. That was sin. That was when he understood it for the first time. He remembered the young medic in the field hospital near Da Nang, treating a boy whose face was gone, saying, "You'd better pray for him, Father. He's going to live." And adding: "I hope he never falls in love with a beautiful girl." Hell was inhabited by the sinned-against. He beat back pity, and realized that the closing of the Prospect was sadder, because that big ugly building with its mock-Persian arches and 1920s walls and hard seats and angry soda machines and balcony for lovers had at least given someone laughter. He pocketed the ten dollars, put the letter in the drawer, and went out. He did not lock the door.

The halls were deserted, and yet they seemed violent with action. Satyrs, nymphs, fauns, sphinxes fought each other across the walls in a tangle of painted vegetation and vines. Through a window, he saw the façade of a Vatican office building, its tawny color altered to a puce green in the hard light. Beyond the buildings and the Leonine Walls was the city: two million people moving through a scape of roofs, domes, cupolas, campaniles, and ruins, among oleanders, cypresses, and evergreen oaks. He felt like a visitor, as he had from the beginning;

of those millions, he knew exactly two. He went down the worn back stairs. There was a service elevator that was always in service, but he needed the exercise.

The stairs were empty. He felt suddenly light, and as he hurried down the three flights, a song moved through his mind:

She had a dark and a roving eye
And her hair hung down in ring-a-lets
She was a nice girl
A proper girl
But, one of the roving kind . . .

Jesus, Malloy thought, if Maladotti could hear that song, he'd have me excommunicated. He tried to remember the rest of the words, but they were lost with everything else. Guy Mitchell was the singer and he remembered a stoop in the evening and a crowd singing until the neighbors shouted from the upper floors. And now I'm in Rome, the Eternal City, the Holy See, with ten dollars in my pocket to ransom the soul of a dead child.

He emerged into the cobblestone street at the back of St. Peter's. The streets were dry now, and he saw a cat move through a pool of hard light, heading toward the gardens. He moved with a combination of stealth and bravado, a true Italian cat. His father had probably died and decayed beside some ruined pillar in the Forum, lying on its side in the grass and the poppies; the second generation had made it to the Vatican. Malloy suddenly hoped that the cat was a female; that it would play lasciviously among the fountains in those

carefully tended gardens where youth and women had
been forever banished, where old man followed old man
in walks through the rows of ilex and chestnut trees,
dreaming of God and sin.

All of it was now too familiar. When he saw the
lights at the Vatican radio station on the hill, his mind
saw the squads of determined Jesuits broadcasting the
Word in Bulgarian, English, Hungarian, Russian, and a
dozen other languages, but seldom in Italian, because
Italy was secure, and therefore lost. He saw an old man
lolling in the shadows of the railroad station, that ghastly
sepulcher of white marble, without ticket window, luggage locker, bookstore, or cafeteria. The tracks ended
at the steel door of the Leonine Walls. No college girls
in camel-hair coats stopped here with snow melting in
their hair, for a weekend of football and love. The sun
had given Italy an unquenchable passion for melodrama.
This was a railroad station built for choirs.

This was what it had come to: all the hours under
lamps in cold rooms, dismantling verbs and the sub-
junctive, sweating over scholastic syllogisms and the
histories of dead princes, years in virtuous dull towns,
sliding grates between himself and the faithful with
their endless catalogs of missed morning prayers, and
stolen quarters, and sins of impurity, Father; and five
Our Fathers and five Hail Marys and the Act of Contri-
tion later. All those hours had come down to escorting a
fat man through Rome, while Shaw's eyes burned their
accusation from the mangrove swamp, and you folded
a ten-dollar bill in your pocket and thought of thin legs
and a burgundy-colored coat.

"Hello, Father Malloy."

The figure emerged from the shadows beyond the street lamp: black, tall, thin. It was Carney.

"Good evening, Monsignor."

Malloy looked into the hard gray eyes, but there was nothing beyond the surface; no clue, no signal of knowledge or intent. Carney's soutane hung loosely; the scarlet piping looked like slices of blood in the light.

"And how was your day, Father Malloy?"

"Passable."

"Passable?"

"I survived."

"You, of course, met with Mr. . . . ."

". . . Rail?"

"Yes. Rail. Of course you did. I saw your memo. He received the tickets you sent him?"

"I sent them. I assume he received them."

"Ring him first thing in the morning to make sure," Carney said. "And you will be taking him around tomorrow, won't you, Father Malloy?"

"Of course," Malloy said. They strolled around the back of St. Peter's. The streets were busy with priests and chauffeurs and visitors with polished shoes. A long line of young people walked three abreast toward the St. Anne's Gate—the choir brought in for the Holy Days to replace the tape recorder.

"Mr. Rail is an important Catholic layman," Carney said.

"So you told me."

"You don't think much of him, do you?"

"I don't care one way or another," Malloy said. "If he wants to see Rome, I'll show him what I can. For me, Mr. Rail is a duty."

"Like all your other duties?"

"No," Malloy said. "I no longer think everything is a duty."

Carney was silent for a moment. Malloy noticed that the smell of lilies had worn off.

"You were a Pope John man, weren't you, Father Malloy?" Carney said suddenly. The eyes peered at Malloy.

"What does that have to do with Rail?"

"It has to do with your general attitude, not so much with Mr. Rail. Your resentments, your cynicism, your—"

"I never thought of popes being members of a ball team."

". . . hardness."

"It's not a contest, Monsignor."

"Still," Carney said, "I'm curious. What do you think of the present Holy Father?"

"He's doing what he can," Malloy said. "It's a tough job. He's been good on the war. What can I say?"

"It's good of you to *lower* yourself to be so *humble* about the Pontiff," Carney said.

"You asked me," Malloy said, "I told you. With all due respect, Monsignor. Actually, I was always a big fan of Adrian VI."

Carney's eyes squinted.

"His name was Adrian Dedel," Malloy said. "He was the son of a shipbuilder from Holland, and he was elected in 1522. Rome hated him. He hated Rome. He detested pomp, he detested flattery, he cut off patronage to merchants, poets, painters, and other prominent Catholic laymen. He lasted a year and then he was poisoned."

"My, my, we're very bitter tonight, aren't we?"

"I didn't mean to be."

"Adrian VI is, after all, a bitter taste, isn't it?"

"I suppose I really like him because he was the last pope who wasn't an Italian."

Two German seminarians cut across their path, dressed in flowing red cassocks. Say what you will about Italians, Malloy thought, they have good eyes. They called the Germans *gamberi*, for crayfish, and that's what they looked like.

"Can I drop you anywhere, Monsignor."

"Thank you, Father Malloy. I'm staying at home with my breviary for the Holy Days."

"I'll probably see you tomorrow, then. I've parked my car in Italy."

"Just a minute, Father."

Malloy thought: Here it comes. "Yes?"

"Be careful with Mr. Rail. He is a great favorite of the Cardinal's."

"Yes, he told me that himself."

"Do you have a guidebook to Rome?"

"Somewhere."

"Read it tonight," Carney said. And added, with curled lips: "If you have time."

Then Carney was gone, fading into the darkness. Malloy walked out through the gate, nodded to the guard, and came out in the great square. Perhaps he doesn't know anything, Malloy thought, but I'm certain he does. The hell with it.

Red taillights moved around the square, slowly, like retreating insects. Groups of tourists stood in the play of the fountains, blessing themselves with the water. Two Japanese men took photographs. The obelisk was bathed in white light, and he saw a couple standing at its base, staring up, but holding hands. Thank God for the fountains, Malloy thought. The obelisk was bloody plunder; the colonnades, stretching away in the dark and never touching, were loneliness. But the fountains, with their warm mossy stone and audience of foreigners, were some fragment of normalcy. Just once, he thought, I would like to dive into them.

He passed out of the Vatican and found the car. It was parked in Italy; everyone in the Vatican talked of Italy as another country, as if Mussolini had made the Italians legitimate and imprisoned, instead of the clerks of God. It was, like all else, another piece of fiction, with the virtue of being amiable. A sheet of paper was stuffed in the windshield wiper. It was a call from the Communist Party of Italy to protest the infamous capitalist war in Asia, and the outrage at the American Embassy. Well, Malloy thought, they had the handbills out faster than usual; they must have a double agent at *Osservatore Romano*. He crumpled the paper and threw it into the street.

When he reached the highway, Malloy removed the collar. He saw lights like pinholes approaching, growing larger, suddenly becoming a sheet of dazzled light, then leaving him blinking in the darkness as he pushed the car on. He gripped the wheel tightly, enjoying the luxury of power and speed; roaring, racing, a bullet fired toward the sea. The silence seemed to shout from the fields and hills. He went past crumbling ruins, through a narrow stretch fenced with leaf-covered hedgerows. Once he saw a lonely pillar standing alone in a field, marking some forgotten purpose or hope, like the headstones in a French graveyard he had once seen sinking into the dark rich earth of Vietnam. And then he smelled the sea.

The scattered lights of the town were off to his right, like a smear of burning candles. Malloy slowed as the highway dwindled. The streets of the town were empty; the rain had evacuated them for the day. Tomorrow is Good Friday, Malloy thought, and I wish it were all past. He did not want to hear the demand for marmoreal silence, or see the black theatrical costumes enact the drama, or hear the mumbled words stumbling toward reverence. He did not believe in any of it anymore.

He could hear the sea now. It came in a long roar. He parked the car and started walking clumsily through the sand. A glass wind lashed his face. There was no light in the window and Malloy felt the approach of the incense and the shutters and the long silences; it was as if the house were advancing on him; it might be the most terrible crypt of all. He swallowed hard as he reached the door, and looked around at the deserted beach. She opened the door before he knocked, and beyond her he saw the soft light from the hurricane lamp, the color of dawn.

"Roberto," she said.

"Yes."

"I'm so happy you are home."

Again, Malloy laughed.

GOOD FRIDAY

Q. Why do you call that day "good" on which Christ died so sorrowful a death?

A. We call that day good on which Christ died because by His death He showed His great love for man, and purchased for him every blessing.

—ADVANCED CATECHISM OF CATHOLIC FAITH AND PRACTICE

Men tire of evil, and of good they sicken.
—Niccolò Machiavelli

CHAPTER 11

Rail awoke in the bright air-conditioned room, saw the carved plaster cherubim hovering hollow-eyed in the corners of the ceiling, and shut his eyes in pain. In youth, he had seen himself as a future boulevardier, sitting at cafés in Paris in the spring, reading the *Journal de Genève*, or the *Frankfurter Zeitung*, or *Le Temps*. At the next table, John Gunther would be talking to H.R. Knickerbocker; they would be sipping *anis*, and talking about Masaryk and Maniu and Salvemini, about Danzig and the Polish Corridor, about all the now-forgotten names once murmured discreetly in schloss and garden, embassy and cafés. It was a role he loved even more than the role of worldly traveler in the South Seas. But it would not happen; he would die alone, unknown in a high dark street. And he shut his eyes tighter, repeating the latest litany of his days: spaghettini, stelline, rigatoni, mezzani, tortellini, agnolotti, rechietti, fidellini. Pasta short and pasta thin, pasta long and pasta thick, pasta smooth and pasta ridged. Pasta in brodo. Pasta with butter. Pasta with cheese. Noble pasta. Vulgar pasta. Pasta.

He opened his eyes again. The cherub was staring at him. For a long moment, he stared back. But that baby angel with its fat creased legs and golden painted hair was remorseless. Rail closed his eyes. His hand inched across the sheet. The sheet was damp. The hand moved

more, on its own, making an independent reconnais-
sance. Rail tried to place the bed and the dampness in
some sequence, but couldn't. That hand was in command of his thinking. The bed was damp, but empty.
Rail sighed, relieved, thinking: I must surely have the
clap. At the very least.

Spaghetti, lasagna, stelline, rigatoni, mezzani, tortellini, yes, Alfredo's. Yes. He had gone to Alfredo's and
sat in the garden under the umbrellas, where the film
stars played in the evenings, with the waiter taking the
order from the whore across the table. Alfredo's, with
great mounds of fettucine: butter and cheese and violins
and wine. It was almost as he had imagined it. Except
that the girl wore too much rouge and had bad teeth and
was no longer young, and the tourists talked too much,
and he had finished and then remembered a meal he
had once in Paris, during a three-day booksellers' convention, where they served spaghetti à la Lucullus, with
foie gras and truffles in Madeira sauce; and Alfredo's
had not seemed such a deal. I have the clap at the very
least. Rigatoni, mezzani, fidellini.

The girl from the tavern on the highway had not
come; he knew then that he was truly doomed. She
would have been freedom. She would have been flight,
possibility, the correct fork in the road. But she had not
come. I suppose I was repulsive to her. But she did not
understand: I could have loved her well. I could have
given her old-man love, fat-man love, yes, oh bleeding
virgin; real love on a bed of silk with carnations scattered
tenderly upon your dark hard-nippled milk-bursting
breasts. I should not have tried to buy her. It is a disgusting habit. I should have taken her to a riverbank and

read poetry to her on a field of ferns. She had not come, and instead, in the swirl of wine and fear and whiskey later, I mounted an aged whore with a straw-colored head, and dark swirls of black hair on her back, and flattened breasts as the brassiere came off, and hair, and a voice like cheap perfume, her hands moving like blue-prints, straddling the bed, mouth and hair, a vast cavity devoid of mystery, or conquest, or magic, or fear.

Just once in my life I would like to make a virgin bleed.

Rail jumped from the bed, wrapped in the sheet against the cold breath of the air conditioner, and stepped into the bathroom. The floor was covered with bottle tops. He switched on the light, reached past the swollen hillock of his stomach, and examined his penis. It was shrunken and seemed to cower before his inspection. He squeezed it, pulling forward. He felt nothing and saw nothing. He poured a half-inch of red mouth-wash into a glass and filled the glass with equal parts of hot and cold water. He squished the mouthwash around his teeth, spat it into the sink, and then gargled the rest. It takes a week for the first signs to appear, he thought. I should have used a rubber. He brushed his teeth fiercely, and then drank four glasses of ice water.

Suddenly he remembered the Cardinal's waxen face, yellow as a dying rhododendron, yellow as butter gone bad, yellow as the scum on the rim of soup: smoking Turkish cigarettes in an onyx holder, with black leather shoes, crossed legs, holding the arms of the chair like a prince, and his dying eyes lurking behind rimless glasses, talking about the Jews and the Communists and the heretics and, of course, The Contract.

Rail's stomach suddenly went oily and gassy and

he felt hard chunks pressing against his throat for release, bending his body with their pressure, and they were suddenly before him in a roar, his body contracting and expanding, the dark soft chunks splattering the sides of the wall and the floor, dark red stains drifting down through the water. And again: and drifting down through the water. And again: spewing everything, his stomach emptying, while coils of intestines pressed upward like imprisoned snakes, and his rectum quivered with panic. And then it was over, and he stood there, crying, the sheet fallen into the dark soft chunks on the floor, the room blurred from the tears in his eyes, gasping for breath.

I should have taken her to a riverbank and read poetry to her on a field of ferns.

Rail staggered to the bed, still crying, and fell heavily on the damp bottom sheet. He shivered in the cold of the air conditioner. I must take deep breaths of cold air. His mouth was very dry. I must not panic.

It was too late even for panic. Rail knew that. I have become a perhaps, a should, a possibly. Yes. Perhaps I should not have been drawn in deeper and deeper, if I had not dreamed so much. Possibly. He pulled a wool blanket from the bottom of the bed and drew it up to his chin. The blanket was damp too. I cannot even remember if I came. He closed his eyes.

And again he was in the room with the black rectangle against one wall, with the city lights like gunshot punctures in a strip of black foil. He was drinking a martini. The two other men did most of the talking. He became conscious at that moment that he had stepped into someone else's story and someone else's sin.

"He must not leave the room."

"He won't. He has strict orders against that."

"How do you know he will obey them?"

"He enjoys obedience."

"Nevertheless, I'll take precautions myself."

"If you see fit to do so, Eminence."

"He has the rifle?"

"He has the rifle."

"You will rehearse him Saturday. I have the guide here, with the doors and the exits and the positions."

"Thank you, Eminence."

And the other one, smiling ironically, drinking Scotch, slim, swathed in evening clothes, going later to a fashion show with his American wife; smiling and nodding silently. Rail felt the perspiration on his brow and scalp and in his crotch.

"You don't seem too happy, Mr. Rail."

"Oh, I'm not unhappy . . ."

". . . But you have been thinking."

"Well, I *was* thinking, and it's just that, well, you see . . . I was thinking that it can still be stopped."

"It cannot be stopped," the Cardinal snapped, looking at no one, addressing the world. "It is God's will."

And hoping they had not seen it, had not located the fear and the flight lurking in his own eyes: the weakness, the softness, the admission of the inability to truly act. The desire to finally say no, I'm through, I don't want your dirty catechism, I'm taking a cab to the hotel and packing my bags and leaving forever. The desire to beg them to temper the act; to slide a fluid into a poisoned draft, served in a cut-glass cruet, with medical bulletins later; not this audacity; not murder most foul. He had felt himself shrinking and afraid, no longer a fat man of impressive bulk, but a man saying to himself: If it were over, if it were Monday, if it had been done or if it had failed, if I were on my way to the north, to the clear pure air of the mountains; it would all be easier then, and I would be a whole man again.

"When do you see him again?"

"Tomorrow evening in the Borghese Gardens."

"Stay away from the *pensione*."

"Of course."

"Don't make yourself conspicuous in any way. No rows, no drunkenness."

"If it were possible, I would not like to see that degenerate at all."

And the other one smiling in his evening clothes, rattling the ice in the expensive Scotch: "Mr. Rail, you worry too much. You should relax. Find a girl. Have a night out in Rome. Enjoy yourself."

And the Cardinal's face, yellow, waxen, with rimless glasses, not hearing, not stirring, smoking his Turkish cigarettes: mad with sin and years and power. He was beyond enjoyment, or its suggestion, or its spoken condemnation. His spare ascetic frame was his only sermon. He seemed suddenly to tire, to be captured by hours, boredom, ennui; and he waved Rail away. The Count took Rail's elbow and showed him to the door.

"Tomorrow night," he said softly, slipping Rail a card. "My house. A little entertainment. You should find it quite droll."

Perhaps. Possibly. Rail got up from the bed to turn off the air-conditioning, his head filled with the shark's grin of the Count's good night, and then the fear was rising in him again, his bowels loose with it, remembering he was to tour Rome with that Father Malloy and wondering what time it was. On the bowl, the room filled with his evacuations, he stared at himself in the mirror on the door. Poor fat bastard, he thought. You're a poor fat hopeless bastard.

Finished, he called room service for breakfast and the time. Good: Malloy would not be there for two hours. Malloy. Maybe Malloy was a solution. I was a Catholic once, a bad one. Perhaps I can talk to him. Perhaps I can ask him for a kind of absolution in advance. Perhaps, possibly, should. He lay on the bed, waiting for food. Once he got up and closed the door to the bathroom. Then he lay under the wool blanket, his eyes closed against the angel's stare. Stelline, rigatoni, mezzani, tortellini. I haven't even looked at my wallet, he thought, and I don't care what the whore took.

I should have taken her to a riverbank and read poetry to her on a field of ferns.

He sobbed quietly for a long time, alone in the cold room, abandoned. Then the food arrived, and he got up to answer the door.

CHAPTER 12

Richards breathed in the deep rich smell of the coffee percolating in the corner, writing B-copy and waiting for the call from Firenze, the photographer. He liked the feel of the old Royal, with its battered black housing and worn brass keys, its machine-gun staccato as he typed. Its noise filled the office like the smell of the coffee. The Royal was not some tin toy like an Olivetti, designed to be photographed or given at graduation to children who would never use it. It was a machine, as hard and dependable as a drill press. It was perfect for the sort of journalism he did; it eliminated its user, its qualities as a mechanism overpowering what it produced. It was the greatest of all whores, giving equal service to murderers, thieves, cardinals, and dukes.

The reference books were stacked neatly on the table against the far wall, with strips of yellow paper in their pages marking the dry facts which Richards would later convert into a 1,500-word feature story for the Sunday paper, a think piece for the syndicate on the changing papacy, and three more days of hard news, filled with purple stretches of rite and ritual and a bogus sense of awe, to be topped later with the handout from the Vatican press office.

Firenze would permit the photographs, as he did for every permanent correspondent in Rome. Richards hated him: hated his suave manicured manners and his urbane air, his name-dropping and God-dropping, his corruption. But neither he nor the other correspondents had much choice. Firenze was a one-man monopoly, a robber baron in the old style. His father and grandfather had been official photographers to the popes, and the job remained in the family; he was a kind of commercial baronet. His grandfather had begun by photographing the Zouaves who protected Pius IX from the Piedmontese; he himself had topped them all by photographing Pacelli in the midst of a vision. His photographs were not good: dry and dull, lacking passion, wit, and even the charm of bad taste. But he knew how to behave and he was well organized: every seminarian in Rome had his picture taken at one time or another with the Pope, and Firenze's files bulged with photographic histories of every man who might ever make it in the bureaucracy of the Church. Firenze even owned the only press helicopter allowed in Rome, and rented it at high rates to TV networks and the magazine boys. He was beautiful. He would not even make the photographs himself; but for three hundred fifty dollars he would get another photographer admitted as an assistant. Richards hated him and needed him. It was part of being a professional.

The coffee was ready and Richards stopped typing to pour a cup. The office was as close to a home as Richards had ever had, and the walls were a collage of his recent life: bullfight tickets from Barcelona, a yellowing copy of the first page of a now-dead paper in New York, when he had interviewed the bandit Salvatore in Sardinia; pictures of Che Guevara, Jack Kennedy, and Brendan Behan; and the colored photographs of the two girls he no longer knew, with their hair long and straight now, breasts forming beneath the prim school uniforms, the background of volcanic rock, and the high hard light of the great mesa.

Today he was writing B-copy because the ceremony would not take place until late afternoon; he had his bargaining to do with Firenze and he would have to stroll three blocks to the embassy at noon to see if the Communists pulled off their demonstration. He was no longer young, and did not feel old, but he wondered what it would be like when he had covered his eighteenth Good Friday, and his twenty-fifth; this was his eighth and he was already tired. He had only learned how to be tidy; it was the great virtue of the professionals.

Voyagers and the untidy paid for everything; he had learned that too. He felt some affection for Rome because he had stayed there the longest, because it fed him and entertained him, and he could choose the details of his loneliness. But he did not love Rome; it had been a long time since he had loved any city. He had become a friend of Malloy because they shared common ruins; Malloy's were in New York and Richards's were in Chicago, but the ruin was complete. The last time he had been home, even the Poles were gone from Division Street, and the yard of the old house was filled with rubble, broken glass, decaying garbage, and there was an old Negro woman sitting in impenetrable silence in her black casing and organdy dress, fanning herself with the *Sun-Times*, and watching her children shoot each other with toy guns.

He had known every corner of those streets, the way all animals know their territory. He had run wild there in the years of the Depression, drinking, fighting, putting skinned hands up the dresses of girls they knew in the lots at night; and then the war had started, and they had all gone laughing to the recruiting station in the Loop. It was still possible for kids to do that sort of thing in those days. The wildness stayed with him through Army towns in the South, and into the streets of Glasgow; and then burned itself out in the deserts of North Africa, and on the beaches of Salerno and Anzio.

The first wife left him in college, in the first year after the war. He was studying journalism on the GI Bill and trying to write a novel, and seven months after their marriage she left him to go off with a bartender. He could not bear to look at the shabby furniture in the apartment near the campus, or the drying remains of the canned spaghetti in the garbage can, or the dark-blond hair she had left behind in the clogged razor in the bathroom. So he had left school, moved on to New York, and then back across the country in a wild night-filled ride; had paused in LA, and finally pushed the old Ford down across the border and into the baked wastes of the desert and up into the high mountains and on to Mexico City.

He wrote his novel there, drinking cold beers in the afternoons, sharing his bed with the thick-bodied Indian girl who had started in his kitchen and moved wordlessly in beside him in the night; she had understood his pain and his loneliness, and there had never been anyone after her who did. The novel was about the war and was accepted by a publisher and came out the week after *The Naked and the Dead*; in a month, he knew that something had come to an end. He left two hundred dollars on the table for the Indian girl, kissed her broad plain face, and left again, seeking refuge in flight and whiskey, and was washed ashore in Le Havre.

For a year, he worked on the copy desk of the Paris *Herald Tribune*, marking wire copy, watching the young men come through the town looking for Hemingway and Gertrude Stein and finding only heroin, pneumonia, and failure in the high reaches of Montparnasse. And then he met the Chilean girl with the high fine cheekbones, and the long tight spring-steel legs, and they were married when she was three months' pregnant. He remembered her eating avocados and reading Pablo Neruda to him in the morning; and two hurried trips to Spain before the money gave out. The rest of it was a blurred decade of passports and lost trunks and unpacking and packing again; New York and New Orleans, London and Dublin, Barcelona and Aix-en-Provence; there were six months in Tangiers for the second novel, eating oranges and watching Arabs selling young boys; the States again; then three months in Mexico, searching the old streets in secret for the broad plain face and the squat body, seeing them in every other girl pounding tortillas in the markets; never finding her; then another child.

The untidiness was all they had: the leases broken; the promises made to each other that this town or that country would be the great good place at last; the unpaid bills; the letters arriving in bundles at the latest set of doors; the envelopes with cellophane windows and their threats from the government; the memories of rooms never truly known and beds never fully inhabited, and the children's faces as they left again, desolated by the toys abandoned in closets or scattered across unsold rugs. They had all that. And the money he never seemed able to pay back, the assignments given and never completed, the scraps of language good only for newsstands, restaurants, and whorehouses; stained tablecloths in certain restaurants and shoes spattered with vomit in certain bars. All of that: and his lack of surprise when she left him for good in New York, taking the children and his money with her, leaving the note Scotch-taped to the mirror in the bathroom at the Hotel Chelsea. He had tried to put all of it into a novel, but it had not worked, and he had burned it and never tried again. And he went off one morning with two assignments and three hundred dollars in his pocket and kept going until he stopped in Rome.

That was eight years before; and filling the coffee cup, staring out into the bright morning at the oleander trees in the garden, he knew that Rome had never completely cured him. It was simply a place you went to when you were old or burned out. The checks came in every month, and were sliced up like bread; he sent the check for the children's school, and another check to the accountant for their insurance; and she sent him photographs of the girls every four months, and he wrote them letters every other month. The photographs were like indictments; his letters were an attempt at warmth and care, filled with serious advice, counsel, and the fanning of hopes. He was never certain if they would get to read them, but he mailed them anyway, though the girls now were only an address in a city he used to know.

She had married a Fiat dealer in Mexico City, a man she had met once with Richards at a party he no longer remembered. She told him about it in a letter, and he had not even been jealous or sorry, because he loved her once and wanted her to be happy; she had never mentioned the man again. Richards knew that the man must have supplied what he could never give her: clockwork and stability, a life of punctual meals and docile servants and orange school buses in the mornings; and money to pay cash for clothes, and no running; a life in a house where time brought true possession, where every room was lived in, where the closets were not mere lockers for swift arrivals and imminent departures, where travel happened for two weeks in summer and you always returned to the same place. It was Richards's conceit at the beginning to think that such a life had to bring her peace, because a Fiat dealer did not live in his imagination, like a writer. He now knew that what he thought was imagination in himself was only nostalgia, and whatever the Fiat dealer had given her, it was not negative. She had stayed with him, and had two more children by him, for a reason; he probably lived out front, with nothing hidden, and even if what he supplied her was a kind of wan tenderness, even if she were only the lovely display piece at the cocktail party in Polanco, even if he had his own *casa chica*, his own dark thick-legged Indian girl, it was better than uncertainty, desperation, volcanoes for breakfast and snows in the afternoon.

Richards brought the coffee to the table and placed it next to the stack of Western Union copy paper beside the typewriter. He lit his first cigarette of the morning, and slipped two sheets of paper and a carbon into the roller. He started typing, the words coming out hard and fast, precise and flat, like the victims of a drill press. In New York, they had hired his fingers, not his brain, and he worked steadily, without tiring, without thought, without care, and finally, without pain.

CHAPTER 13

Malloy shaved carefully, almost tediously, in the gray half-light of early morning. His skin was sensitive and bled easily, and as he inched the razor across his face he thought: I should have grown a beard long ago; I should have devised some dark opaque mask like an Orthodox archbishop, a face of hair and eyes. But there are times when even that kind of small act requires courage, and I did not have that, and instead blamed time. While he shaved the left side slowly, the lather on the right began to dry. He soaked the razor, lifted it carefully, trying to balance the glistening balls of water on its straight polished blade. When he looked up, the mirror had fogged over with steam. It's going to be one of those days, he thought. He wiped the mirror clear with the towel, and in its cracked face he could see Franca against the wall behind him, silent, lost in morning reverie. The smell of bacon crackling in the pan displaced the odor of soap and lather.

"What do you think I would look like in a beard?" he said.

"A beard?" She smiled.

"I'm serious," he said. "A great big black beard."

"You would look like a rabbi."

"Where have you ever seen a rabbi?" Malloy said. He placed a steaming towel on his face, letting the heat soak into the skin, almost feeling the pores opening.

"In the district, of course," she said. "They have been there for hundreds of years. You must pass it every day. You can see the district from your window, I'd bet. Or at least *il Papa* can see it from his."

Of course: the district was across the river, below the walls of the Vatican. "I'll have to go there someday," he said. "When I have the time."

"Let's go today."

"Not today. I'm working, Franca."

"Yes, of course."

Breakfast was ready. Malloy pulled on a T-shirt and sat down at the rough painted table. Franca sat across from him, silent, her flesh spilling from the black two-piece bathing suit.

"Sleep well?"

She nodded yes, dipping crackling fresh bread in the yolks of the eggs. He had always tried to be light with her, and knew that at best he was banal. He ate slowly; she ate greedily, her elbows up on the table, savoring each piece of egg, each slice of bacon. He wanted her again. The round young brown body with its damp secrets; the beads of sweat there now on her upper lip as she fed herself. He knew that other men had lived in her body before him; it didn't matter; it excited him. Somewhere in those other beds was the secret of what had happened to her. All he hoped for now was that she would survive, and he along with her. At the beginning, he had hoped that somehow he could sanctify her; if he loved her purely enough, it would bring her a kind of holiness; the silence would break; the haunted need for night and darkness and incense would be over. He no longer believed that would happen, not all of it. It was arrogance and vanity. He had never seen her laugh, and maybe that would be enough; if she could only laugh, she might survive.

"There's a party tonight," she said. "Will you take me?"

"If I can," he said. "I have to show a man around Rome this afternoon. Some friend of the Cardinal's. What time tonight?"

"I don't know. Late."

"Can you find out?"

"Yes."

"Would it be all right if I met you there?"

"I'm sure that would be all right."

She smiled. Perhaps it was the beginning of something. For the first time in weeks, she would be leaving the beach house, and it was because she wanted to leave. They seldom went anywhere, even at the beginning; partly because of the collar, but most of all because they were happiest in bed. He would laugh at her about this, and she would stare at him, unsmiling, and say, of course, and why not, as if that bed were all she had ever wanted from the universe. Outside, in restaurants they had gone to, on rides to taverns in the hills, on a visit to a lake, conversation had been difficult. Questions were idle. Answers were idle. They had solved that with isolation and banality. Malloy had even come to enjoy those long silences; they had become a habit, a kind of daily breviary into which he could read anything or nothing. Now, drinking his coffee, he knew he should have felt elated. There was some movement at last. But he only felt uneasy.

"Let's go for a swim," she said.

"Sure."

He finished the coffee, changed into trunks, and walked out with her onto the beach. It was very early, still cold, the beach empty. Franca started sprinting toward the sea, her legs supple and brown, moving gracefully across the hard-packed sand. She splashed into the surf, with Malloy behind her.

"You have to catch me," she said, and he pounded after her, the water splashing around him, then slowing to let her go on, then coming close to her again, then letting her swim on. The water was icy, but he did not mind. Franca was swimming straight out into the dark blue currents. He dived beneath her. The sea below was clear and green; he could see all the way to the bottom, and above him her shimmering body against the roof of sky. He came up fast and bumped her.

"Oh!" She lurched, thrown off stride, and went under, and came up again, and he unhooked the top of the bathing suit, and started swimming away.

"Son of a whore!" she shouted.

"Come and catch me."

He made for shore, and realized for the first time how far out they had gone. He saw the line of houses, the dusty town, the hills turning green beyond; but he could not pick out their house. He knew where it was, but in the blur, he could not tell. He was swimming alone now, conscious that she was near, but alone, the cloth halter clenched in his hand like a trophy. After a long time, he felt the ground beneath him and stood up.

He had expected her to crouch low in the water, and beg. But she stood up, walking toward him through the surf, her hands swinging at her side, unashamed, her breasts very white with broad dark nipples, soft and round and bobbing as she walked. She did not seem to care if anyone else shared either the beach or the moment. He waited for her. She was not angry. He handed her the halter, and she put her hands around his neck and pressed her breasts against his chest. Her nipples were hard from the cold water. She kissed him wetly and they walked together to the house. She closed the shutters and struck a match to burn the incense.

Afterward, she slept heavily while Malloy smoked and drank coffee. I would like to sleep, he thought. I would like to feel your full body beside mine through a chill morning. But I must go to see Rail. It is Good Friday. But I don't really care. There are many things that I don't care about anymore.

I don't care about celibacy anymore. He remembered his old iron conceit, its terrible variety. Celibacy was the worst conceit of all. The older priests described it as a strength, a sacrifice, an atonement; but Malloy knew it was a conceit, fed by young girls in confessional booths, the eyes of bridesmaids with homely faces at afternoon weddings, matrons at bingo games and bazaars. I'm old enough to be your mother, said the wife of the motel owner, her eyes filled with lust and unhappiness. But he had been taught that the body ended at the neck, and had accepted that; the rest was secret lore, the Baal cult of Canaan, the worship of Ishtar; and he remembered a manual of moral theology he once owned, arranged according to the Ten Commandments and how two-thirds of the book was devoted to the Sixth. *Thou Shalt Not Commit Adultery.* It was a matter of priorities. Later, still a boy, he had gone through a time when church spires were penises, vesical windows were vaginas, and fonts were wombs; a time when he felt mutilated; a time when he dreamed each night of petals, shells, alabaster, and flesh; and all the dark opposites.

And now he was almost free. If he could break through, if he could just make contact, he would have true communion. For communion had never been communion, but a hurried dispensation, diluted morphine for the slightly wounded. *Domine non sum dignus, Domine non sum dignus, Domine non sum dignus.* And an altar boy with a golden platter to catch the crumbs from the Mystical Body, and the faces buried in the hands in the dark hardwood pews, the mouths all stilled, filled with neither feast nor joy, but fear: afraid to move a muscle in the jaw until the body decomposed, and the taste of a plastic wafer gone flabby, afraid that chewing was a mortal sin and a sentence to eternal damnation.

He remembered the first time he saw her: only months, weeks before. There was a reception at the Excalibur thrown by an American film producer for himself; his services to the Spanish government were to be rewarded with a papal decoration. Richards suggested that Malloy should go, if he were interested in evil on its hind legs. And he had gone, to a second-floor ballroom, filled with Italian photographers, reporters, the permanent population of the Via Veneto; a trio of guitar players, tables weighted down with shrimps and avocados and crab on crackers and caviar; drinks flowing from three bars; the walls silvery; chandeliers boasting glassily from the ceiling; women with glossy hair and turrets for breasts; actors; the thin gray-haired producer himself, doing his best to look like a Mittel European arms dealer; the producer's servants; and Franca.

She was against the wall, talking to a photographer. Richards waved to her; she waved back. Later she came over, and Malloy saw the hysteria deep in her eyes, and knew he would go home with her; knew that he was tired of the desert, and the accusation of Shaw's eyes, and the ache of his body for contact, and whatever it was that was moving in his chest. He was tired, most of all, of himself; and they had left early and driven fast toward the sea, with the wind blowing and Franca silent beside him with a raincoat pulled tightly against her neck. Knowing the prescription for himself, but no longer able to pray; knowing in that part of him that was still alive that it was not a fall, it was an ascent. And he kissed her, her mouth tasting of salt, and they made love on the sand.

"You had better go," she said drowsily, from the bed.

"You're awake. That was a fast nap."

She smiled.

"Find out about this party first," Malloy said. "I don't know when I'll be back. I might not have time to change."

She walked into the tiny kitchen, washed, and slipped into the bathing suit. Before going out, she smiled again, standing close to him so that he could smell her, and himself in her, and the sea.

"I'll be right back," she said. And then: "It was fun just then, in the sea."

"It was," he said.

Away off, he heard the first blare of the car radios, and the town coming awake. He washed again and dressed for his appointment with Rail.

CHAPTER 14

Harwell heard bells ringing, horses tapping on the cobblestones, water gurgling, music coming from a radio above him, people shouting across alleys, an airplane passing overhead, and someone knocking at his door. He went to the door but did not open it.

"Who is it?"

"Señor, your breakfast . . ."

"I don't want to eat."

"But it is included in the cost of the room."

"I said I don't want to eat."

He heard the heavyset man shuffle away down the tile halls. Then Harwell went to the windows and opened the shutters. The street was filled with taxis, noise, and tourists climbing out of polished horse-drawn carriages, glistening in the sun. I am going out, Harwell thought. I don't care what Rail said. That fat bastard said I must stay here, I can't be seen. But if I stay here I'll starve. I can't make it with this slop they serve here. Fuck it. I'm going out. Somewhere here there must be a health-food bar. Somewhere there has to be a market with fresh food and vegetables, maybe even herbs. I can't stay here. They'll poison me.

Harwell dressed quickly, zipping up the light-blue jacket, brushing his hair carefully. He placed the weapon in the suitcase and then put the suitcase on top of the mahogany clothes closet. He looked at himself again in the mirror. Then he stepped into a room that served as a lounge for the third-floor *pensione*, and locked the door behind him. A television set stood gray and cold on a cane table. There were cane chairs at the bamboo table, and a cane crucifix on the wall. The other walls were covered with travel posters: Havana, Mexico City, Key West, New Orleans, Miami, Acapulco. There were no travel posters for Rome. The poster in his room was the only sign that Harwell was in Italy—and that was for Naples, not Rome. This guy is a real weirdo, Harwell thought. The telephone rang as he reached the door.

"Señor Harwell," a voice said, "it's for you."

Harwell saw the heavyset proprietor holding the phone, his hand cupped over the receiver. The man was almost bald, with shiny strips of gray hair combed over his dark head. His eyes were always watery, and Harwell thought: You're weak, mister, you're one of the worms. Harwell took the phone.

"Hello."

He heard breathing.

"Hello? Hello?"

There was still no answer.

"Talk, you son of a bitch, talk!"

No answer.

"Hello?"

He heard a click.

"Dirty sons-of-bitch bastards!" Harwell shouted. He held onto the phone, shouting into its dead ear. "Dirty filthy *schweinhund* bastards!"

"Señor . . ."

"Shut up!"

"Perhaps . . ."

"Shut the fuck up! You ignorant spic bastard!"

Harwell slammed the phone down, and walked to the door. He stopped and turned around.

"And don't make up my room!" he shouted. "I don't want your hands touching anything there! I know your kind."

And he was gone.

The balding man stood in the silence of the lounge, amidst the cane furniture and the travel posters, and thought: Fuentes, as soon as you can, you will go back. You have fled enough. You have drunk from exile long enough. Fidel was right about the Americans. Fidel was right, and you were wrong. As soon as you can, you must go back. He sat down heavily in an easy chair. No, I will not clean your room, gringo. I will no longer prepare your food. I will sit here and I will smoke a bad cigar and drink bad coffee from North Africa and dream about palms blowing in a late-summer breeze and the girls in starched dresses walking along the Malecón in the evenings, eating ice cream cones, and the orange rinds floating in the debris of the harbor, and my old house with the crickets in the yard and the blackbirds making noise in the first light of morning. I will think about Cuba. I will not think about young gringos with hard eyes and filthy manners. As soon as I have the money I will go back. I was wrong.

CHAPTER 15

Going through the streets, with Malloy beside him driving, the muck and sweat and turmoil of the city changing into quiet streets, villas with hanging gardens, narrow lanes, high lush trees; seeing that, and a young boy playing with a red plastic ball and a girl in a hip-hugging yellow skirt and an old man playing dominoes with another old man in a public park; seeing them, and the ruin of an ancient wall, and the weathered face of an abandoned fortress, and a flower bursting from a crack in a pavement; smelling spring in the high clear air of the hills; climbing higher, and seeing dandelions spattered in the scrub overlooking the sea, with Castel Gandolfo standing timeless and clean in the sun; knowing that the heat was gone, at least for this day, and that his suit would not crumple and go fuzzy; and everywhere seeing fountains, with water spurting, playing, soaring, gurgling, flying, drizzling, and blowing in the wind; at that moment Rail wanted desperately to live.

"Do you dream, Father?"

"Yes. All the time."

"I've found that as you get older, the dreams get worse."

"Well," Malloy said, "maybe it's not the dreams. Maybe it's the dreamers."

"Maybe," Rail said. "Maybe."

Malloy was driving aimlessly, up and down streets and hills, out around the rim of the town. Rail did not object; he had told Malloy that he wanted to see the "real" Rome, not some collection of monuments and old stones. Malloy had laughed. He did not know what the real Rome was, or the real Vatican, or the real Church, or the real anything. So he had started driving, letting the car take him where opportunity and chance decided.

"I used to dream of many things when I was young," Rail said. "I had my eyes open, I knew I was awake, but the dreams still came."

"All of us did the same."

"But I used to dream grandly."

"There's nothing wrong with that. Everyone wants to be Babe Ruth, Al Capone, or the heavyweight champion of the world. That's all right."

"No, it isn't," Rail said softly.

"Why not?"

"Those dreams can destroy you, that's why."

Malloy had noticed the change in Rail when he picked him up at the Excalibur. The sense of command was gone from the voice; he did not seem quite so sure of himself; and he was no longer sweating. Malloy was sure that the night had gone badly for him, but he was not at all sure that he cared.

"Perhaps this is the dream," Rail said. "This journey through sun and air. These villas, these flowers, these people . . ."

"Mr. Rail," Malloy said, laughing, "I believe that deep within you beats the heart of a poet."

Rail smiled thinly. "Or a sinner," he said.

"Or a philosopher."

"Or a dying man," Rail said, and looked off at the fields to his right, where heather and flax were sprouting in broad bands in the afternoon sun.

"Want me to open it up?" Malloy said, gunning the engine for emphasis. Before them the highway stretched away to the north, four lanes wide, straight as a ruler.

"No," Rail said. "Please don't."

"You don't have to worry," Malloy said. "It's a good car, a good road, and no traffic."

"Thank you. But I'm afraid."

"All right."

"You're younger than me," Rail said. "You don't have the fear of death."

"Everyone's afraid of death."

"But you at least have the consolation of God."

Malloy laughed. "Mr. Rail," he said, "you really haven't known any priests, have you? Let me tell you something: priests are men. Their consolation, as you put it, is not any better or stronger or warmer than yours."

"Perhaps," Rail thought. "I don't know."

And Malloy thought: Neither do I, my fat friend. That's what it comes to. I don't know about anything anymore. The only certainty was that there were no certainties. Except death, and that was a mystery no one had yet penetrated. And he thought of Shaw's eyes, and how he came up on the far bank of the Mekong, safe, not knowing where he was, his face caked with mud and slime, the chaplain's insignia lost in the river tide, panting and exhausted, knowing that he had run. And the cowardice had shriveled and chilled him, and he had lain there in the mud with his heart beating furiously, the machine guns silent, knowing that all of them were dead or dying and that all of them had died better than he ever would. Shaw had been crying for help: from the rain, from his country, from aircraft, from friends and strangers, from politicians and old girls and unborn children and from God; he had been crying for help from the girl at home whose photograph he had shown him once, the girl black and smooth and young, with her chest bared to the waist, looking shy and uncomfortable and embarrassed, a girl who did not pose for strangers, but who had sent Shaw that photograph as the truest message she could send, a message without words, a message saying that Shaw should make that extra effort, breathe that extra gasp, fight for that extra inch, stay lower, run faster, fire quicker, be braver. Because at home she would be there black and warm and moist in his bed, in the black privacy of all his nights and days. "Is it a sin to have this picture, Father?" "No, it's not a sin." Shaw had cried for help, and of course, no one had answered, and Malloy had run. And somewhere in those jungles, in the malarial forests, in tunnels, in sandbagged fortresses, in the back streets of tiny hamlets, in fields where rice no longer bloomed, somewhere in the snare of mines and spent shells and poisoned sticks, in that place of death falling from high altitudes, of jelly scalding children, of ruined schoolrooms, demolished churches, blinded women, somewhere a young guerrilla was carrying the picture of the young black girl. Those breasts bared in love, those sweet black offerings, those promises and warnings, had surely become a trophy of war.

"Can we . . . er . . . stop somewhere?" Rail said.

"Sure. You hungry, or have to go to the can?"

"I could eat."

"So could I."

They climbed higher into the hills, leaving the Roman suburbs in the distance. It was cooler now, and for the first time Rail worried about a chill. I know I should not worry about such trivialities, he thought. I know I shouldn't. I should worry about my soul. But perhaps I will live. I want to live. I know that now. I want trees, roads, wind, rain, I want onions, garlic, tomatoes, mushrooms. I want breasts and thighs and teeth and buttocks. I want them all of my days. And motor cars and the decks of ocean vessels and cafés in Paris in the spring; and hills and valleys, sisters and brothers, children, hair and mouth, and the pyramids along the Nile. I want. I want to live. I want the steam fogging the windows in a kitchen, and cheeses tied with waxed cord, and sprigs of parsley and basil and sage, and honor and obedience, and cinnamon on French toast and hair in the heather and my heart in the highlands. I should have taken her to a riverbank and read poetry to her on a field of ferns.

"How about that place up there?" Malloy said, and high above them, perched on the edge of a distant hill, Rail saw a low white building, bright in the sun, surrounded by clumps of evergreens. Yes, Rail thought, a white fort in the sun, with trees on guard like cavaliers. I do not want to die alone, unknown in a high dark place.

"It looks wonderful," Rail said quietly.

Climbing through the back roads, with the dust rising behind them, Malloy was positive that something had happened to Rail. The day before, he was prepared to hate him. Now, driving together, on a day of dazzling sun, and chickens scattering before them on a dusty country road, on Good Friday when his brow should be black with mourning and gratitude, he had begun to like him.

The road came into a small town, with old men in caps and snowy moustaches standing in the afternoon stillness. The shops were all closed, no newsboys hawked their wares. A cop in white helmet dozed on a bench. Malloy thought: It's almost like peace.

"What a lovely town," Rail said.

"It is," Malloy said.

"It's like a movie set, or a book, or . . ."

"Want to get out and stroll around?"

"No," Rail said. "I might want to stay."

"You can get out if you want," Malloy said. "I've got plenty of time."

"No," Rail said. "Let's go on."

"I know what you mean."

The car passed through the town, and onto another road, more winding now, with the white restaurant still above them as they climbed the shoulder of the hill. Through holes in the screen of trees, they could see the town dropping away below them. He knows what I mean, Rail thought. I wish he did.

The road ran above the restaurant, and they took an even narrower branch downhill again, the blacktop turning to gravel. Malloy parked on a flat concrete ledge on a gloomy terrace below the level of the restaurant. The ground was damp with old rain, lack of sun, and droppings from the trees; cigarette packs lay crumpled in the undergrowth; the concrete was cracked. You're never completely surprised, Malloy thought; it's not as pleasant here as it was climbing the mountain.

They walked out into the road, and circled back to the entrance. A fat woman in a dark blue suit sat at a small table in the foyer, writing numbers in a book. They walked through a door at the left and into a long bright terrace, with white walls and white tablecloths, and one wall made of glass against the wind. It should have been brilliant, but the memory of the dark underbelly beneath seemed to have followed them through the door. There were no other customers. A waiter with a young face and an old man's docile manners ushered them to a table near the glass wall.

"Lovely," Rail said. His voice was flat. He too seemed to have tasted the dank of the parking area.

"Yes," Malloy said. "Do you want a drink?"

"Let's have wine," Rail said, with a hollow cheerfulness. "A good bottle of the best."

"The house wine in these little trattorias is as good as any," Malloy said.

"Yes, yes, the house wine."

Malloy ordered a bottle of the house wine, and they looked out over the valley, green and ripe with the promise of summer. They could see houses clinging to the sides of hills, and a sliver of stream, and the red tiles of the town, and a flock of white birds moving against the bottle-green shade of a hill. The waiter brought a shallow basket of fresh bread and a plate of curled butter on ice. He did not go through any elaborate ritual with the wine; it had already been uncorked, and he placed the dark umber bottle on the table and left. Malloy poured.

"Why is this place so empty?" Rail said.

"Who knows? It's late. Maybe everyone has eaten.

Maybe they've all gone to Rome to see the Pope tonight. He's doing the stations of the cross on the Palatine Hill. I don't know. I don't really know."

"I can't go to the ceremony tonight. I've got a business appointment."

"That's all right."

"Which way is Rome?"

"Out there, past the hills," Malloy said, sipping the wine, not pointing. "That's the south. I figure we're about fifteen, twenty miles north of the city."

"And past Rome? What's there?"

"I haven't gone very far. I drove down to Anzio once, with a friend who was there during the war. But I haven't been very deep into the south. I hear it's bloody awful."

"Poverty, starvation, that sort of thing?"

"Exactly," Malloy said. And melodrama, knives, rape disguised as marriage, dust, sunsets, and Africa.

Rail ordered the food: an avocado salad, a plate of shrimps, spaghetti in brodo. The same, Malloy said, and more wine and butter. The young waiter bowed creakily.

"Anzio," Rail said, letting the word out softly, savoring it, looking out across the hills to the south.

"You should drive down there sometime," Malloy said. "It's filled with fine words, umbrellas, souvenir hawkers, and the dead."

"The dead?" Rail felt a chill.

"Row after row of fine white crosses, all of them forgotten. You should drive down there some morning."

"I don't drive."

"You don't *drive*?"

"I don't drive," Rail said mournfully.

"Congratulations, Mr. Rail," Malloy said. "You must be the last nineteenth-century American."

Rail's face flushed, and he sipped from the wine, and started talking rapidly. "I don't do anything, Father," he said. "I had what is now called a deprived childhood. I had no money. So now I don't drive, I don't swim, I don't ski, I can't play tennis, I can't play golf, I can't ride a horse or a bicycle, I don't understand football, I've never been to a baseball game, I can't play handball, I can't fight, I can't sail a boat, I can't dance, I can't swim . . ."

"You said that already."

"I hate supermarkets and plastic and TV dinners and motels and office buildings and flying in airplanes and The Beatles and miniskirts and cellophane . . ."

He seemed ready to go on and on, building in pitch and desperation. But the waiter arrived with the food, and Rail stopped. His face was white; his eyes were watery. Malloy stared at him, but Rail looked away.

"I'm sorry, Father," he said after a while.

"For what?"

"For that outburst," Rail said, his lower lip slack now as he rolled the spaghetti against his spoon.

"That?" Malloy said. "What the hell. You just talk like any average, driven American," Malloy said, and thought: Please don't call for help; I have none to give. I have only my bedside manner. Nothing else is intact. The insignia vanished in the Mekong tide.

"Father . . ." Rail paused, chewing abstractedly.

"Yes?"

"Would you hear my confession?"

"Come on, Rail. Things can't be that bad."

"I'm afraid, Father. I'm afraid of dying. I haven't been to confession in four years."

"Well, I suppose you can hold out for a while."

"I'm afraid of dying."

"Don't be."

"I can't face death in a state of mortal sin."

"Eat."

They were quiet for a long time. Rail never looked up. He sat there eating mechanically, dryly, and Malloy realized that this meal was not like the meal the day before. This time Rail was eating for fuel, not pleasure; he even seemed to have shrunk, to be less gross. He finished the spaghetti, but did not wipe the sauce with his bread.

"Have some more wine," Malloy said, tipping the bottle.

"Thank you."

He sipped the wine. Clouds were moving across the sky, their shadows soaking the hills and the road and the red tiles of the town.

"We'd better go," Malloy said.

"All right."

Malloy called for the check. He scanned the addition automatically, and tucked one hundred lire under a glass for the waiter. They got up to leave.

"It's getting cold," Rail said.

"Night comes faster in the hills."

Rail pushed his hands into his pockets. "Have you ever been to Cortina or Lake Como?" he said.

"No."

"I'd like to go there someday," he said glumly. "I'd like to watch the young people ski."

"Why don't you go on the way home?"

"I'd like to. I really would, Father. But you know . . . Business . . . One gets tied up."

Malloy paid the fat woman at the little table. She took the money and gave him change and never looked up.

"Friendly, wasn't she?" Malloy said.

"A true Italian."

"No," Malloy said. "A true Roman."

They got into the car. Rail made a wheezing sound as he sank into the seat. He tried to fasten the safety belt, but it would not reach around his stomach. Malloy backed into the road.

"Let's see where this road goes," Malloy said.

"Yes, yes, that's a good idea. It's too early to go back." And thought: Too early to go back, to meet in the darkness of the Borghese Gardens with that murderous little asp with his filthy habits and his armor of obscene health; too early to go back to the baby angel staring from the ceiling; too early to shower and change and powder one's self for the Count's little entertainment, or the shabby disasters that will surely follow. He would not hear my confession; it was in his voice and his eyes; he will grant no absolution; he is as implacable as God.

The road curved and narrowed in descent, and at one point seemed only a trail. The trees were dense; they saw no human movement. Malloy thought: Good ambush country, and I wonder if there will ever be space to turn around. In the dells it was very dark, and the sky appeared in patches, mottled with shreds of dark cloud. Then quite suddenly they were around a bend, and the lake was before them.

"My God!" Rail said. His voice was hushed like a man in a cathedral.

The lake was dark and blue and empty, hemmed in on all sides by steep shrub-covered cliffs, and pine trees in the clefts. At one end of the lake there was a stucco restaurant standing beside an unused boathouse. In front of the restaurant, a group of young Italian soldiers in greatcoats lolled in the cool breeze, drinking beer.

"Let's have a beer," Malloy said.

"On top of the wine?"

"Well, you can get a liter of red."

Rail mumbled an agreement. They parked and went into the restaurant. There were more Italian soldiers inside, some eating spaghetti, others drinking wine or beer, all of them kidding or laughing. Rail looked forlorn. They were funny-looking soldiers, Malloy thought, but they were the best soldiers in the world. They understood that the only way to end a war is to stop fighting it, to go home to wives, warmth, pasta, children, gardens, and wine.

"They make me feel old," Rail said.

"Come on, Rail. You're not very old. Cheer up. You should see some of the people in the Vatican. Hundreds of years old."

Rail sipped his wine; Malloy swallowed his beer.

"Father, you must hear my confession."

Malloy sighed. "Look, Mr. Rail. I'm the worst priest you could have asked," he said quietly. "Don't you have a priest at home? Isn't there a confessor at the parish church? Someone up the street from your office? I'm only a clerk. Believe me."

"I'm afraid of going to hell, Father," Rail whispered.

And Malloy thought: So am I, so is the earth, so are those young men in the brown bulky uniforms around us. Rail's sleek fat face now looked strained and flabby. If I could, fat man, I would tell you that I am in a state of what is laughingly known as mortal sin. That this is Good Friday and there are no confessions. But most of all, that I don't want to share your pain. I've had all that; I've heard all the varieties of pain in the last twenty years, and I've given all the advice I know how to give and all of it was bad. I've told wives not to sleep with their husbands if they didn't want children. I've told boys that masturbation would send them to hell. I've told young men that drinking and laughter did not honor God. I've told young girls that they should not let their young heroes touch them on the breasts, that they should think of the Holy Virgin, that they should go to daily Mass and communion, that they should wear miraculous medals and make novenas, that they should take showers, preferably cold, that they should above all go no further, that the boys who did what they were doing did not respect them. And all the things that were worse than that. I've heard all the anguish and sorrow and pain that I want to hear in my lifetime. I don't want your pain, Rail. I've got my own.

"Father," Rail said, trying to break the silence across the table, "do you really think that sins against the Sixth Commandment are the worst?"

"No."

"No?"

"Murder's worse."

"Then you would understand about . . ."

"It's getting dark, Rail. We'd better go."

CHAPTER 16

Harwell was lost but did not care. He had met with Rail, received the documents, the map, the instructions. And now he wandered the Roman streets, avoiding bright piazzas, choosing dark alleys empty of people, where water tinkled in small sinister fountains, and garbage lay in wet piles against the walls of the buildings. He did not look at any churches, but sensed the presence of their gargoyles hovering in the dark. There was no moon. He was cold, and very thirsty.

Once he stopped and bought a newspaper in a tiny stall. A headline said, "Pope Washes, Kisses Feet of 12 Boys from 8 Nations," and he threw it away in disgust. He should be a king, Harwell thought, and he acts like a slave.

He knew that he could never find his way back alone, that he would have to take a taxi, that each new turn brought him farther away from the *pensione* and into unknown regions, but he was not afraid. He had conquered fear, he thought; he had mastered it by confronting every horror; he had never run.

Rail could not give him orders, he thought; only the Leader could give him orders. Rail thought he was using me, but it's me who's using him. I am here because I alone can execute the thoughts of the Leader. In the barracks, the Leader had sneered at him; they would make fun of his drawings of gas chambers, his threats of violent destruction. But when he was finished in Rome the world would know his strength. He would make even the Leader look like a mere John the Baptist.

He imagined the scene in the barracks, the others sitting in the kitchen eating Corn Flakes and water, and the TV playing, and the Leader upstairs with the dirty laundry on the floor of his room, pecking out his messages on the old typewriter, sealing each message with the spit of his own tongue; and then the screen going dark and the announcer coming on to announce what happened and all of them jumping in the air in outrage, all of them screaming about the Communists. And only the Leader understanding, because he was the only one there with any brains, explaining calmly that it was not the Communists, not the Russian Communists. It was the Jews. And then all of them piling into the truck for a trip to Woolworth's for cardboard and felt-tipped marking pencils and the posters, and then a trip to the White House, with the Leader calling the police first and telling the Jew organizations, and then all of them picketing in the fine brown uniforms, the polished boots, the thunderbolts, the clean hard faces, the posters driving the Jews nuts, right out of their diseased minds, and the Leader being interviewed and telling the world what had really happened.

And only I will know.

And only I will sit and bide my time and wait to strike with the truth.

Occasionally, Harwell would emerge into brightly lit squares with neon signs, and young men walking with their girls, and policemen standing around, and automobiles poisoning the air; he would watch them in their innocent folly, understanding their ignorance of the way the world was going, despising them for it, enjoying his secret. And then he would walk on, down darker alleys where no one else was brave enough to go.

Often, his mind filled with great shapes of formless horror lurking in the darkness; he clenched his fists and his jaw and waited as he walked, but no one dared to spring.

I fear nothing, he thought. I've seen them all, and conquered them all: the dog-faced devil with the silk ladies' bonnet peering from behind the china closet, the rat in the treasure chest dripping with slime, the man with the tin hat eating a child's brains with a golden spoon, the Jew demons drinking blood with cherries from a soldier's dry skull. Who else had met the orange man with the green globe and his army of moth-winged insects? I have. I was strong. I've seen the dagger raised high and become an adder, the cunt become a bowl of worms, the Maltese cross hung from the horse's cock. Even in the barracks they had to admit it. Even the Leader used to say: Harwell has heart. He walked on, through alley and street, thinking about the dead dog decaying on the ark curtain from the synagogue, black men inserting steel rings in the rectums of Nordic virgins, salamanders with crossbows, fish heads with silver helmets, and swans blowing evening flutes. None of them would sail through the high humming white of the final tunnel, because they were weak. They did not know that you must save yourself by destroying.

Once, he saw three willowy young men with black pipe-stem pants and velvet coats emerging from a taxi.

They were giggling and talking Italian. I wish I knew just a little of this degenerate language, Harwell thought. All I have is this goddamned dictionary. I could talk to those men, to the handsome one. But the three men walked into the recesses of a courtyard, and he saw a door opening with a burst of talk and music. Then there was a sudden silence, and they were gone. It's a degenerate language anyway, Harwell thought. Only the northern countries have pure languages. Not even American was pure anymore, with all those spics and guineas and niggers, chipping away, chipping away.

He walked on. That fat bastard, he thought. That fat bastard Rail. When this is over, I'll settle with that cocksucker. I'll do some job on that fat sloppy face. I'll sink one right into that sweaty gut of his. Right up to the elbow, and then I'll stomp him, hear the bones crack, see his nose splinter, let him beg for mercy, and then break his teeth off at the gums the way we did to Ralph. I'll leave him on Barbara Colfield's doorstep. She'll probably think it's her old man. Home from the job in the usual condition. Rail has some nerve trying to tell me what to do. Who is he to tell me what to do? Who the fuck is *he*? Fuck him. Fuck him where he breathes, man. Him? *It* is a better word. Fuck *it* where *it* breathes.

Harwell started to laugh and then caught himself. He remembered how the Leader looked when he laughed. When the Leader laughed, he looked weak. They won't be laughing when this is over. And it's the first act, just the first act, and the rest will be terrible. The world will have to stop laughing for a while until it's purified.

He heard footsteps behind him. His throat was very

dry. He stopped at a store window on the street corner and looked around. There was no one there, only a long silent row of parked cars. Probably an echo, Harwell thought, an echo. But if they try to jump me, let them try. It will be the sorriest day of their lives.

There was a neon glow ahead of him, another square, more people, a fountain, automobiles. Harwell walked toward it, his step becoming more military, holding himself more erect, hearing march music in his head, clack, clack, clack, clack, thinking if only I had had the chance to march under the Arch of Triumph in Paris in 1940, my life would have been complete.

A movie theater was emptying, and Harwell pushed through the crowd, bumping, angry, ready for a protest. None came. A young man with blond hair walked past him, with an arm around a dark plump girl. He looks like Jerry, Harwell thought. Good old Jerry. Jerry was very clean, especially around the barracks. He even shaved twice a day, and had gold hair like Lawrence of Arabia. Jesus, he was dedicated. He even called one of his kids Horst Wessel. Harwell liked it when Jerry would talk about the Jews. Jerry would put gas chambers at the end of Long Island so the smell would go out into the ocean. He would put electric wires up their asses and down their throats until they touched and then he would throw the switch. All the Jewish broads would be gang-banged to death by the nigger prisoners, one after the other, hundreds of niggers banging them until they bled to death or drowned in come, and then they would cut the niggers' nuts off and bury them alive with the Jew broads' bodies. Jerry was something else. Harwell liked the one-way tickets to Africa Jerry printed up and carried around with him. He used to paste them on the A train before it went up to Harlem. Jerry used to call the A train the African Express. He used to carry this bar of green soap around with him too. With the letters written on it in German: *Made from Finest Jewish Fat*. Jerry was a real card.

Harwell marched on alone. I've gone miles, he thought. It's good for you. Keeps you in shape. Anything to stay out of that room with its sobby-eyed spic owner outside the door.

I need some water.

None of these people knows who I am, he thought. I'm moving among them and they don't know me. They don't understand what I've done, and what I'm going to do. They don't know about the woman with the helmet of giant blue grapes, who kept a white mouse as a pet in her mouth, and stored weapons in her cunt. She tried to get me that time, leading me to her in the fields, but I resisted. She wanted me to stick flowers up her ass while she played a golden harp. None of these people know about her, and how I had the strength to walk away from her.

He saw a light at the end of the dark street. I have to get a drink of water. He took out the dictionary. There it was: *acqua*. He repeated it to himself: *acqua, acqua, acqua, acqua*. The light spilled out onto the sidewalk from the coffee bar. Inside, three men sat at a table, and another in a white apron stood behind the counter. Behind the man in the apron there was a huge espresso machine, and off to his right, another counter with a glass face, filled with sandwiches, bread, cheese, ham, and meat covered with tomato sauce. The men did not look up when Harwell walked in. They were all watching television.

"*Acqua*," Harwell said.

"*Acqua? Che cosa di—*"

"Just *acqua*," Harwell said. "Plain *acqua*."

"*Acqua minerale?*"

I'd like to kick your face off, Harwell thought. The man reached down and took a bottle from under the counter. The bottle was small, clear, and covered with a very detailed label.

"Yeah, yeah, give me that."

"Ah," the man said. "*Acqua minerale.*"

Harwell put one hundred lire on the counter. The man pointed at a spot behind Harwell. A woman was sitting beside the door on a high stool at a small counter. Harwell had not seen her when he came in. The man was pointing to her, talking Italian.

"Pay her?" Harwell said, holding the hundred-lire note, touching his own chest and then pointing at the woman. "Me . . . pay . . . *her?*"

"*Sì sì sì sì*," the man said, still smiling.

Harwell walked over, gave the woman the note. She shouted in Italian, the counterman shouted back, and she gave Harwell a receipt stub and twenty lire change. He left the receipt. No, no, the woman said. She held up the receipt stub and pointed to the counterman.

"You mean now I give it to *him?*" Harwell said.

"*Sì sì sì*," she said.

"Aaah," he said. "*Then* I drink the water."

"*Sì.*"

These people are out of their fucking minds, Harwell thought. He gave the receipt to the man, the man smiled, pushed the bottle forward, then turned around to watch television again. A glass of water is a major production, Harwell thought. We'd better get the gas ready for the wops too.

He sipped the water slowly, his eye wandering to the television screen. There was a crowd of people on the screen and a lot of torches, and someone on a litter that bobbed above their heads. An Italian voice came from the set, talking softly. There were thousands of people on the screen, and Harwell felt a fleeting longing to be with them, to be a part of them, to be cheering, to be leading them. They were all parading under a large arch, and then the camera angle shifted, and the arch was in the distance, at the bottom of what appeared to be a long hill. Then the camera zoomed in for a close-up and Harwell put the glass down softly on the counter.

"È il Papa," the counterman said, turning and addressing the small coffee bar. "Ecco."

The others nodded. They looked bored.

It was him. Harwell stared at the blurred hard face, the mitered hat, the stark chasuble. The television commentator talked on in Italian, in a hushed voice. The Vicar of Christ on Earth. Torches bobbed in the background. It would be easy, Harwell thought. You could do it right there. It would be easy. The tide would turn. The traitors, the soft, the liberals, the Reds, the mongrelizers, the Jewboys; all would be turned back. And this was the worst of all. Harwell walked quickly out into the night.

He had reached the river. He heard water slapping against stone. I must find a taxi soon. It's time to be going back.

He crossed a bridge, heading for a glow of lights at the other end. He could see a line of tiny taxis in the square, with lights climbing a hill behind them, and the roofs of houses falling away toward the river on his right. There was no traffic. He entered a clump of trees beside the walkway as he came to the end of the bridge. Something moved in the shadows. A husky voice, cheap perfume.

"Signore . . ."

"Who's that?"

"Ah. Nize. That's nize. American. You like a fuck? Rosa best fuck in Rome."

She was standing closer to the road now. There were penciled eyes where her eyes should have been, and heavy orange lipstick. She was wearing a pink wool coat. Harwell stopped. She opened the coat and began massaging her huge breasts. She was about forty.

"No," Harwell said. "Get away from me!"

"How old are you? Twenny? Twenny-two? Young boy need good fuck."

She came closer, and Harwell stood there watching her approach. She opened her mouth and made circular movements with her tongue. Harwell started to move away, but she was next to him. "Rosa best fuck in Rome." She had her hands on his waist, up and under the zippered jacket. Then she had his penis in her hand, squeezing it softly through the trousers.

"Hah!" she said. "Good. Good. Very strong. Very good. You very strong young boy. You come my house? Not far. Cheap."

They climbed into a taxi, and traveled down dark streets to the right. Harwell did not look at her. At least she knows: I'm strong, and this will add to my strength. This will make me stronger. He thought about the steam room of the St. Marks Baths.

The cab stopped at a faceless two-story house, with an entrance leading into the street. Harwell paid the driver, who winked at him when he climbed out. At the top of the hill behind them, more cab drivers sat at another taxi rank, talking to two cops with white gloves. They went through a door, into a dark hallway, and up some stairs, one flight. The house seemed somehow familiar. There was some smell, some feel to the place that made Harwell remember something buried and terrifying. They went into a large room with red velvet curtains, a low yellow light, mirrored closets, and a great brass bed. He undressed quickly, sitting on the bed, watching her in the mirror in the yellow light. She had monstrous breasts, the largest he had ever seen, too large, sloppy, overflowing the brassiere. She did not remove her brassiere or panties, and then with a yellow smile she was on him, her bulk heavy on his hard small body. He unhooked the brassiere and felt the loose spreading breasts against his chest, and he reached down and peeled back her underpants. He looked to his right, and saw his own face, and the great spreading buttocks, their black gash, and his penis standing large and erect. He thought of Barbara Colfield's thighs. And then she was moving down his chest, sucking at his skin, with small bites and pinches, moving down, and then suddenly she was up, huge and vast. Her hair messed and falling, holding his penis, shaking it, and laughing.

"*Mamma mia*," she said. "*Un ebreo!*"

"What?"

She smiled at him, playing softly with his penis now, looking gently at him, like a mother.

"You Jew," she said, pointing at his chest. "You Jew, and *mamma mia*, *Rosa* Jew," she said, pointing to herself.

"No," Harwell said. He felt his penis start to soften in her hand. "I'm a Christian. I'm not a Jew. I'm a Christian."

But she moved down again, greedily, not hearing. Harwell thought about Charles, and Barbara Colfield's thighs, and Ursula Andress, and a small boy on a lawn outside a hotel in the Catskills, beating at a big man in white shorts, striking at him, trying to kill him for what he had seen. And feeling fear in him, and then vengeance rising in him, rising to strike, as the woman worked over him with practiced solace, experience, gratitude, and love. When she turned over on her back, and he moved up the bed to grip the wooden headboard, he knew what he would do.

In the street, he thought he would be caught. He could hear her coming down the stairs behind him, bare feet pounding against wood, tears, disgust, outrage, all coming down after him, and he saw a dash of something white at the top of the hill. I cannot allow them to catch me. I cannot fail now. He ran down the hill, as she came out into the street, her anger and betrayal echoing off the walls of the silent houses. Harwell felt good as he imagined her standing there in a torn nightgown with her old lady's face, her insulted mouth, wiping with a towel at the brown steaming mess on her chest and neck, screaming in Italian to the cops and the cab drivers about the American, screaming to anyone who would listen. They would come after him, all right, and he looked behind him and saw figures running, a blue blur, movement, something white, headlights blinking on. Feet were drumming on pavement. There was shouting. And I'm not afraid, Harwell thought, and his heart was pounding, and pain made a move in his side, and his legs bunched, and grew heavy, and kept moving. I cannot be caught. So on he ran; across one street, down another, a left here, a right there, hunted, looking for an opening in the endless canyons of walls and shuttered shops, and still they kept on behind him. Vengeance was mine. I cannot be caught. But his head was swelling, the legs rebelled, he was certain he would drop.

And then he was in a dark street leading to the river, and the street was suddenly brilliant with light, and a car was behind him, then passed him and stopped. The lights went out. The car was long and black, not a taxi, and there did not seem to be police inside. Harwell stopped running, and started circling warily to his left away from the car. Maybe it's her pimp. Or her husband, or Jesus Christ, *her son*. He was suddenly quite terrified. Well, if he's looking for a fair one, I'm ready. I paid the bitch. Or I meant to pay her. She insulted me. Well, I'm ready. Come on. The door of the car swung open, but no one stepped out.

"Come on," Harwell said, raising his hands. "Come on, I'll give you a fight . . ." But his teeth were chattering and the pain was spreading in his side and his legs felt encased in rubber tubes. He heard the sound of running in the distance, and a woman's shout. She would tell them. She would tell.

"Get in," a voice said from the dark interior of the car. "Get in. Right now."

The voice sounded English and had command in it. It had leadership. Harwell walked to the door and climbed in. He saw a large man with wide shoulders and yellow hair sitting against the far window. Jesus, Harwell thought, a Nordic warrior. The car sped away.

Chapter 17

Malloy turned off the main road into a lane fenced by high, hidden trees. Electric candles in discreet frosted globes marked the way. For two hundred yards, gravel kicked against the mudguards of his car, and then the road became smoother and quieter. From the road, nothing had indicated that the house even existed; suddenly, it was before him, all stone and glass, lying low and hidden, like a cardinal's private fortress. A cluster of yellow lights burned a greeting above a bronze-studded oaken door. Malloy had his windows open, and heard a meld of noise drifting across the night: fugitive Latin chords entwined with the insistent thump of a rock band; a door slamming; sudden laughter punctuating the steady hum of many people. A dull muted brightness rose beyond the wall to his right. Several uniformed Italians were planted in the flagged walkway before the entrance, and as he got out of the car, he could smell pine, dirt, paint, and the hard machined dampness that goes with a swimming pool. One of the uniformed Italians handed him a slip of paper, asked for the keys, and drove Malloy's car into the darkness. He felt conscious of the Roman collar, hesitated a moment, and went up three steps, grasped a bronze lion's face, and knocked.

The door opened, and he saw a tall, neckless, thick-shouldered man with yellow hair and a pug's mashed nose. He was wearing a tuxedo and holding a clipboard with both hands. His eyes looked as if someone had washed socks in them. The eyes looked at Malloy's face, and then down at the collar, and then up again. His head never moved.

"Nime, please."

"Malloy. Father Robert Malloy."

The man ran his fingers down the third page of his list, his lips moving in silent concert with his fingers. He looked up at Malloy.

"No Malloy here. Sorry." He started to close the door.

"Just a second," Malloy said. "I'm invited. Look at the end of the list. I was added today."

"Sorry, mite. No names, no hadmittens. That's me orders."

He flipped the pages abstractedly, not really looking at them. Well, Malloy thought, it's a new style in British butlers.

"Nothing 'ere. Better move it."

"Would you please page the Count?" Malloy said. "I'm sure there's just been a mix-up. Someone's waiting for me in there."

"Impossible. Nime, please?"

There were people behind him: a girl with an iron laugh, tall and dark-haired, on the arm of a man with a toothbrush moustache who looked like an out-of-uniform French general. The British butler nodded to them, checked their names with an elaborate gesture, and stepped aside. They went past him into a long hall where a woman in a blue maid's uniform took their coats.

"Look, mite, you can't stand around here."

"I'd like to leave a note."

"I ain't your secretary, mite. You'd better clear out. In about ten seconds. Or I'll have the coppers 'ere to help you."

Malloy heard gravel kicking against mudguards, doors opening and closing, thumping with the luxury of money. The hell with it, he thought. It's not my scene. He turned to go.

"Father Malloy!"

She was in the hall behind the butler, frowzy and heavy-bodied, with a curl coming loose in her hair. Mary Something, from the beach. She had a low-cut dress on, a blue-and-white medallion bouncing on a gold chain between her breasts.

"What are you standing there for?" she said. "Aren't you coming in? Franca's inside already."

"I'd like to come in," Malloy said. "But Kid Ironhead here won't let me."

"I got me orders . . ."

"Oh, George, don't be so ridiculous. Father Malloy is an old friend."

"But Miss Wilson . . ."

"He's a *priest*, George. Did you ever hear of a priest crashing parties?"

"'Ow do I know 'e's a priest? They got more R.C. collars in this bloody town than they got motor cars. 'E could be just a bloody imposter."

"Let him in, George."

George stepped aside. Mary Wilson took Malloy's arm.

"Thanks."

"Oh, Googie has such trouble with staff," she said.

Her voice was hard and hollow. "They get to be like those doormen in New York, always acting like it's *them* that live in the penthouse."

"Excuse me, Miss Wilson. We've never met." He held out a hand awkwardly. "It is *Miss*, isn't it?"

"Mary. Just call me Mary."

"Thanks then, Mary."

"Oh, I know all about you, Father. Well, a *lot* about you. I see you at Fragene a lot. That Franca is a sweet girl. Lovely. Very quiet."

Malloy didn't answer. He looked around nervously, as the maid took his coat, realizing that a small snake of vanity was working in him: he hoped that no one thought he was escorting Mary Wilson. The bouncer remained at his station at the door, his head jutting up from the tux like a giant yellow rivet. Malloy heard car doors slamming, but the only music was drifting in faintly from outside, like a band playing at a neighbor's house.

"Where's the party?" Malloy asked.

"Oh, the whole *house* is the party. There's dancing in there," she said, pointing at one door, "and gambling in there. Why don't you wander around and get a drink or something while I go find Franca?"

She went through a door, into another hall. Malloy caught a glimpse of framed etchings, prints, antique guns in a polished case, but no people, no party. He tried the door on his right.

It opened into a large room with plush red carpets on the floor and paintings in baroque frames on the walls. Two men in small red jackets worked with silent precision behind a bar. A flamenco guitarist strummed vacantly in a corner, dressed in an Andalusian costume that was too tight. A roulette table stood in the center of the room, with an elegant French-speaking croupier orchestrating the game. The players were studious and distracted, staring at the purring wheel. There was only one woman among them, someone Malloy had seen in a movie once, with a straight thin nose, piled red hair, lush breasts, and a long white gown. Her face was harder than he remembered it and he was sorry: she was a lovely guerrilla in that picture, until Richard Widmark shot her for treachery. Against the far wall, a French door opened onto a patio, with the blue-green shimmer of a swimming pool beyond.

Malloy asked one of the bartenders for Scotch and he nodded in understanding. The painting behind the bar was a Caravaggio, or someone very much like him: a fleshy Neapolitan girl disguised as a Madonna, holding an impossibly huge child in her arms, while two peasants who were supposed to be Joseph and Mary knelt in awe before her. The Madonna's head was circled by a slice of halo, but Caravaggio had brought it off. It was as simple as plainsong, Malloy thought, except for the melodrama of the light. When the Scotch arrived, he took a sip and edged his way around the room to stand before a wall of Russian icons, waiting for Franca.

"*Messieurs, faites vos jeux.*"

Chips murmured against chips, bodies went stiff with tension: the roulette game was in high gear. A small Italian woman in uniform came by with a platter of plump fresh shrimp. Malloy speared one with a toothpick. The roulette players never looked up.

"*Rien ne va plus.*"

People drifted into the room: a boyish man with lavender sunglasses and white hair; a squat man in a sharkskin coat escorting a razor-thin fashion model; an Italian lawyer with a stubby gray moustache who had made a million dollars from rich American Catholics by arranging their annulments from the Congregation of Rites; three American actors who were too rich to squat with the inhabitants of the zoo on the Via Veneto; a Dutch theologian with a gray face, smoking a cigar; the correspondent from *Time;* and a number of men with tinted glasses, smooth hands, pinkie rings, and elegant manners who ruled Italy through the Christian Democratic Party. A few heads turned when an Italian lady journalist arrived, wearing a bright purple dress that showed most of her small breasts, smoking cigarettes from a silver holder. She had become famous for her interviews with the high and the mighty, a life work that was helped by a small gift for malice. She was with a tall American who looked uncomfortable in a badly fitting tuxedo. She talked at him all the way out to the patio. Malloy didn't see anyone who even looked like Franca.

"*Deux cents, à cheval.*"

The guitarist stood up, bored with his own musings, and went to the bar. He arrived at the same time as Malloy. He had a fat soft face and a Zapata moustache and he nodded sadly, after ordering a rum and tonic.

"*¿Habla usted Español, Padre?*" the guitarist said.

"*Sí, sí. Un poquito.*"

"*Bueno . . . ¿Puedes ayudarme?*" He wanted help too, Malloy thought. Everyone wanted help. The guitarist talked on. He had come to Rome eighteen months before. His wife was part of his act, but three weeks ago she had gone off with a waiter from a restaurant in Turin. They had four children. If he killed her, would it be a sin in the eyes of God? Malloy told him the old tired sermon about Mary Magdalene. Take her back, give her another chance. He didn't seem quite satisfied, and Malloy thought: If you were, you'd be stupid.

"*Bueno, Padre, gracias,*" he said, raising his glass in a toast. "*Salud . . .*"

"*Pesetas . . .*" Malloy said.

"*. . . y amor,*" the guitarist said, looking very sad, carrying his guitar with him to the pool. Health, money, love; the Spaniards had at least learned that lesson from the Arabs, Malloy thought. If the guitarist had been a Mexican, he would have added *death*. They all ignored God in the equation.

"*Vingt-neuf; noir, impair et passe!*"

Chips clattered slickly, men breathed heavily, the girl who was shot by Richard Widmark was impassive. The room was filling up. Malloy watched the door for Franca, but saw only a red-haired man with a World War I monocle, a woman with a butch haircut who walked past him talking about Robbe-Grillet in bad French, an American woman with veins showing in her nose, dressed entirely in leather. It was an odd crowd: tuxedos and monocles mixing with sandals and beards; the bohemians and the diplomats and the bankers and the painters, slices of the separate worlds thrown together, all of them using English when all other languages failed. Only the croupier maintained the forgotten mock majesty of French.

"*Troisieme douzaine, par cinq louis.*"

Some were playing their birthdays, some their ages,

some the ages of their wives or their girlfriends or the age of a bottle of their favorite wine; they were held by the numbers, locked into their rigid patterns; the wheel purred softly around, the ball plopped quietly, and it was gone again. Poor Rail, Malloy thought. He probably never learned how to gamble, either. Malloy walked out to the patio.

The night was chilly, but hot air blew from somewhere overhead, and the guests gave a good imitation of an August evening. No one had dared yet to sample the pool. Malloy heard the sound of animals somewhere, low and chattering, a sound you would hear while approaching a zoo. Walls enclosed everything: high walls of scraped red stucco, barbed with broken bottles at the top; there would be dogs somewhere, and in the daylight, without telephones or strangers, it might be very pleasant. The guests were there now, and there was no privacy. They talked at each other, and did not listen. They moved around, from knot to knot, or drifted out into the chill, walking among the dull spotlights scattered among the shade trees. That poor guitarist and I must be the only people here who are alone, Malloy thought. He thought about Rail in his prison of fat, with his gluttony and private terrors. If I were any priest at all, I would have heard his confession. Malloy drifted, hearing scraps of chatter and chewed newspaper, remembering that pity was his most dangerous vice.

". . . I said it was a disgusting war and I couldn't support it . . ."

". . . And now the Count has taken up *ecology*, or something, and he's built *cages* for these *monkeys* . . ."

". . . Simenon will be the next Nobel Prize winner. Mark my words . . ."

". . . She had tits like grapefruit . . ."

Malloy looked through the faces, searching for Franca. He wished he could talk to someone, become involved in some small talk, anything that would eat away the time. He would even like to talk to Mary Wilson. The uneasiness he had felt in the morning grew worse. It was too frail, he thought, like an Oriental bird. The old priests were right: imagination is a work of the Devil. She's probably just talking to someone and can't get away gracefully. That was it. But he wasn't convinced.

". . . If they invade the North, the Chinese will come in, and that's the ball game . . ."

". . . So I said that if he was certain there was oil in the Po Valley, I would lend him a billion lire. But I wanted to see the geologists' reports first . . ."

". . . I understand that Maladotti is planning to take all the Vatican money out of the stock market and invest it in . . ."

That was probably true, Malloy thought. Cardinal Maladotti knew about money, and you would learn more at a cocktail party than you would ever learn from Maladotti himself.

". . . We decided not to go to Greece until democracy returns . . ."

". . . But how can you preach to Asia when your Negroes . . ."

". . . I told her I would leave my wife for her, but she went off with a banjo player who was nineteen years old . . ."

". . . As the Count says, there is really no true difference between a poem and a balance sheet . . ."

Malloy did not see the Count anywhere, and he was
curious. Count Pietro Rienzi, known to his intimates as
"Googie," was one of those men he had read about in the
society columns when he had nothing at all left to read.
The society page was his own private pornography; you
went from the sports pages downhill to the front pages,
and from there to the letters to the editor. After Joseph
Alsop's latest bundle of captured enemy documents,
you were forced to the society columns for consolation.
They were more fun than the comic strips, though not
as well written. He had discovered the Count there, and
in his mind Rienzi was two-dimensional, and covered
with tiny dots like a halftone. In the papers, his life
read like a modern saga. The Count was supposed to be
one of the most important men in the New Italy, slim,
gray-haired, from a long line of nobility, but a swinger
too, a member of the jet set and all that. The family had
made millions on Brazilian coffee early in the century,
had further flourished under Mussolini, survived the
Duce's defeat the way they survived the eventual con-
fiscation of the coffee property by a left-wing Brazilian
government. After the war, with the Marshall Plan money
flowing in, the family produced the Count as its finest
modern specimen. He had gone to school in America,
worked in intelligence for the allied armies, and returned to Italy with a mastery of American attitudes and
a worship for American techniques. He started with a
publicity office, pushing automobiles and fashions, and
swiftly developed a reputation for casual sophistication,
tremendous energy, and a genius for accommodation.

He was for a long while the only Italian businessman in Rome who did not go home for lunch and a siesta. He now owned high-fashion salons in Rome, Milan, and Florence; a fourth salon in Paris, and part of a fifth in New York. He owned a piece of three automobile factories in the north, a canning company in Trieste, a sulfur plant in the south, a concrete works in Milan, a bank in Germany that catered to Italian laborers, and a hotel and a million acres in Sardinia. But he was not all money: he had translated Robert Lowell into Italian and Leopardi into English. He published a line of brilliant art books that were the best guide ever assembled to the art treasures of Italy. He knew Moravia and Antonioni, and lunched with James Jones when he came to town. He was an amateur archaeologist who had gone on successful digs in Greece, Libya, and Mexico, and written reasonably scholarly articles about his finds for the professional magazines. He was an accomplished mountain climber, an excellent horseman, and had won several international races in sports cars he had helped design himself. He had only put money into four movies, in a country gone mad on movies, and they had all been critical and box-office smashes. "I would forgive him all of that," Richards once told Malloy, "if he didn't also have that wife."

Most of the time, the wife was in the pictures he had seen of the Count: long-limbed, with chiseled face, auburn hair, graceful and sophisticated. She was an American, but had lived in Italy for sixteen years, fifteen of which had been spent as the Count's wife. She was a painter of fair ability, and had exhibitions every year in the Via Margutta and on 57th Street. She also had a Social Conscience: she signed newspaper advertisements against the war; she had marched through Sicily with Danilo Dolci; she threw cocktail parties for Oxfam and staged concerts by string quartets for Amnesty International. In all the photographs, she was gazing at her husband and three children with undoubted adoration. It was, as Richards would say, too goddamned much. She was nowhere to be seen either.

". . . I had the union in my pocket so I didn't worry too hard . . ."

". . . But, of course, the finest American novelist of that time was *not* Hemingway, but Raymond Chandler . . ."

". . . She had tits like cantaloupes . . ."

". . . I told him he would get the contract if he slipped a hundred thou in for the wife, tax-free. In her name. You've got to watch out for the kiddies . . ."

". . . When the monsoon starts, they'll come down those passes like ants . . ."

". . . I looked at him and I said, Cardinal, I said, you look terrific, and he says, My son, longevity is not a blessing but a genius . . ."

". . . I'm down to a pack a day . . ."

". . . They got to fold the whole thing up. Get back to the Real Church, you know what I mean? Abolish the Vatican State, close the Vatican School for Diplomats, melt down all those gold altars, and give it all to the poor. Otherwise . . ."

". . . They say the Pope has catarrh . . ."

The party seemed to swirl and move, carrying Malloy with its tides. He drifted out into the chill air, around the swimming pool, below the shade trees, into an area with a bathhouse along one wall and a row of animal cages along the other. In the center, a monkey cage climbed to imposing height, with a curlicued wrought-iron top like an old bandstand. People were everywhere, chattering more steadily than the monkeys, dropping glasses into the undergrowth, watching the leopard in his cage, throwing bread to the tropical birds in another, crowding most thickly around the monkey cage.

". . . The one with the gray tail looks like Frank . . ."

". . . Don't stare at them too long . . ."

". . . My theory is that Mister Hyde has won his battle with Doctor Jekyll in America, but is still calling himself Doctor Jekyll . . ."

". . . They start shooting Tuesday, after the Holy Days, if the Italian crew survives. The script is dogmeat, but they'll make it up with production values . . ."

". . . I promise you, my dear, I haven't got a tail . . ."

". . . Sullivan ought to book these monkeys. They could call the act 'Thirteen Tricks with a Banana' . . ."

". . . So now the Rauschenberg cost him twelve thousand dollars when he could have had it for five bills a couple of years ago . . ."

". . . It's very simple, darling. Antonioni is saying that modern people just can't communicate . . ."

After an hour, Malloy went looking for Franca. He pushed through an oiled oak door off the garden, into a long, paneled room, empty except for some black Mexican paintings. He tried one door, locked, another, locked. He went into the hall. The British butler had abandoned his post. He saw a flight of stairs leading to the silent bedroom landing and his stomach quickened. He tried another door and found himself in the missing heart of the celebration.

It was a cauldron, boiling and oddly private, more than a hundred people caught in some gaudy parenthesis of time: Happy Good Friday, and here's lookin' up yer dress. Malloy felt the floor trembling under him. His eyes watered from the dense fog of cigarette smoke. He was bumped, and squashed against a wall, and a woman with bare feet stepped on his shoe. Rock 'n' roll music thundered from a group of amplified young Italians on a platform at the end of the large room. It was very dark. A waiter in black uniform squeezed through the dancers, and Malloy put his empty glass down and lifted a fresh one. It was bourbon, sweet and burnt, but he sipped it anyway.

He heard no glittery facile chatter here; everything was crushed into the compost of hammering music and heads and swinging arms and music and sweat and powder rolling up into little balls on the necks of middle-aged ladies. One girl danced with her head back, staring at the ceiling, holding her dress up to her waist, showing thin legs and a triangle of sweating hair. Mouths opened in bright smiles and offerings of tongue to be answered by fevered hands. Two homosexuals tried to perform gymnastics but were denied room by a ponderous lady with a Spanish face and her sweating companion. There were no words: they were all lost or imprisoned in the music, in the great loud throbbing roar as it rushed and snarled from the amplifiers like an exercise in ferocity. Off to his left, standing silently against the bar, Malloy saw the Count.

He looked like a count all right, dressed in a dark blue madras jacket and white turtleneck sweater, holding a drink like a prop. The jacket had a lacy filigree of black running in and out of the blue; it reminded Malloy of a French cathedral. The Count was not sweating; he was standing very straight and cool, glass in hand, savoring every sip. As he inched toward the bar, Malloy saw the bartender fill the Count's glass with water. The Count was watching the dancers with patient, wary eyes, nodding occasionally to a passerby, very amused. He looked like a man who worked out: nothing as gross as heavy bags, of course, or arnica over the brows, or leather against skin, or running in the cold mornings; he stood there as trim as tennis can make you, or squash, or horseback riding, or success, or skiing, or saunas. No part of him had yet been swollen by the deadening fatty tissue of failure.

Malloy felt someone pulling his arm. He turned around and saw Mary Wilson. She was a little drunk and the medallion hung salaciously in the cleavage of her breasts, like an advertisement. Her mouth worked, but nothing came out.

"Where is she!" Malloy said.

"I can't hear you!" she said, holding his arm tightly, and pressing her soft breasts against him in the crush. The music seemed to thunder even louder. Malloy leaned closer, to shout in her ear. She had a musky smell, like decaying leaves. He asked again for Franca. She shouted back in his ear.

"She doesn't want to see you."

The music crashed and roared. *Hey. Hey. You. You. Get offa my cloud.* Bodies twisted and turned. *I said, Hey. Hey. You. You. Get offa my cloud.* Somewhere past Mary Wilson, he saw one of the musicians leaning forward, his large wet mouth hanging open, like a frame cut from a film. *Don't hang around, girl, two's a crowd . . .*

"Where *is* she?" Malloy shouted.

"She doesn't want to *see* ya!"

I said, Hey. Hey. You. You. Get offa my cloud . . .

"Tell her I want to see her!"

"I can't do nothin', Father. I talked to her!"

"Just tell me where she *is!*"

Don't hang around, girl . . .

"Come and meet the Count."

"The hell with the Count! I want—"

"He's your *host*, goddammit!"

I say. Yes. I guess. I'm doin' fine . . .

She was pulling him through the bumping edge of the crowd, and for the first time in a year, he felt the discomfort of his own sweat.

"Googie! This is Father Malloy!"

The Count smiled emptily at her, then offered Malloy his hand. It was cold. The Count's lips moved in greeting, and Malloy said he was pleased to meet him. The Count nodded coldly to Mary Wilson. Her face flushed, the muscles around her mouth flickered, and she was gone. Malloy thought: Casual brutality is the worst of all. The Count lifted Malloy's drink, sniffed it, passed it across the bar, calling for bourbon. Malloy leaned past him.

"Sorry!" he shouted. "Make that Scotch!"

"You must be an American?" the Count said, somehow making himself heard without shouting.

"Yes," Malloy said, and looked through the crowd, to see the crack of a door, and yellow light beyond, and a flash of familiar hair, a gesture, a hardening face, a memory of luxury. *I can't get. No. Satis. Faction. I can't get. No . . .* If it had been Franca, he would never reach her in time.

"Let's go somewhere quieter . . ."

"I think I'll go home," Malloy said.

"Don't be silly," the Count said. "The night is young . . ."

The Count put his drink down and led Malloy along the wall, heading toward a door at the far end, near the band. They moved slowly, as the great panting mass of hair, breasts, abdomens, of shuddering legs and stained underarms, threatened to engulf them. A fortyish woman detached herself from the mass, and blocked their way, staring off beyond the band, her tongue sliding around the rim of her mouth. *I can't get. No. Satis.* The Count was taking him somewhere. Malloy knew that. But he did not think about it. He stared vacantly out at the dancers. And then he saw Rail.

The fat man was standing against the far wall, under a dark yellow abstract painting, holding a drink. For a moment, their eyes met. Rail began to move but he was pinned by the dancers. He waved with one fat little hand. And then started moving his mouth, trying to make words travel without sound. Malloy could not decipher the words. But the message in Rail's moist eyes was clear. Malloy was moving, still looking at Rail, knowing that he was calling for help or peace or salvation, for escape, for solace, for the redemption of his soul. I can't give you anything. *Hey. Hey. You. You. Get offa my cloud.* And suddenly Rail was gone, lost in the cauldron, and a door clicked silently, and the party was in another country.

"My study," the Count said, waving his hand, and Malloy found himself in a cloistered cove, walled with sheets of dark cork, bookshelves, display cases; saffron drapes against the far wall, russet rug on the floor, large spare desk with an old-fashioned cowled lamp; all of it in earth colors, all of it muted, all of it very private. No pictures of wife or children on the desk. Only an IBM electric typewriter on a typing table, a black leather–covered couch, one chair, and a rolltop desk. In the cases, Toltec and Olmec figurines stood beside Etruscan pottery, in no order other than their beauty. The books were in the careful disarray that means they were often used; paperbacks jammed between pigskin-bound folios, art books with novels, pamphlets among worn bindings. There was another door to the right, running from floor to ceiling, guarded by a brightly colored ceramic umbrella stand filled with rapiers.

"When do you illuminate your manuscripts?" Malloy said.

"Every second Tuesday," the Count said. "I have the cellar stocked with very talented midgets I bought once in a Moroccan monastery."

"Can they cook?"

The Count laughed, and opened the rolltop desk. It was a bar. He took ice from a roughly textured bronze pot, and poured two heavy Scotches.

"You looked desperate out there," the Count said. "I thought you might want a few moments of peace."

"Thanks."

"I hate that music. It's barbaric. It's brutal."

"Well, you're the host."

The Count moved around the desk and sat down. Malloy eased himself into the black-leather armchair.

"Yes, that's true," the Count said. "But one never fully controls the details of one's life."

"You might control their volume," Malloy said.

"That's true too," the Count said, smiling. He had small neat ears and silky eyelashes. "But we all end up exercises in irony, don't we? For example, I like Gregorian chant. It is clean, it does not boast, it contains neither sentiment nor bombast. But here, in my own house, the walls shudder with this other . . . a music that is sick with sentiment, bombast, and bragging. Do you want some ice?"

"Yes. In that case, why do you do it?"

"It's expected. An image grows up, and suddenly you are ruled by the image, especially as you grow older." He moved around the desk, picked up ice with black iron tongs. "Your president is like that. He never thought of himself as a murderer until the young people started calling him murderer. After that, he becomes a prisoner of his own image, and even murder comes easy."

"That's a possibility," Malloy said. He wanted to leave, to search the house, to find out what happened to Franca and why; but he shuddered at the memory of the cauldron beyond the door.

"Opposites seem to do their own work," the Count said. He had no accent at all, Malloy thought. He must have gone to school in California. "As we sit here, the artists are in the roulette room talking and thinking and sweating about money. In my wife's studio, on the other side of the dancing room, bankers are talking about art."

"And you are sitting here drinking with a priest."

"Ah," he said. "But that is not so unusual. In my family, there were always priests. We even produced several popes, in the good old days."

"No offense," Malloy said, "but the good old days were pretty much a cesspool."

"Sentiment," the Count snapped. Now I'm certain, Malloy thought. I don't like you. "The Church has not been religious since Constantine accepted it in the fourth century. You know that, Father Malloy. You have certainly studied it. The Pope is the chairman of the board, and occasionally he is changed and the corporation changes with him. Roncalli moved the Church one way, this man is moving it another way. The man after him will move it another way, possibly. It doesn't matter. It doesn't matter that you call it a cesspool, or that I wish it would mind its business more and stay out of politics. The cesspool created the Sistine Chapel, employed Bramante and Michelangelo, built Chartres, placed the mosaics in Ravenna. That is important. The rest is sentiment."

"I wish I could be as certain of things as you are," Malloy said. The room was quiet. They sipped their drinks. The Count had been leaning back, his legs crossed; now he leaned forward, with both elbows on the glass-topped desk.

"You have a woman, don't you, Father?" he said.

"Thanks for the whiskey," Malloy said. "I've got to go."

"Don't be silly," the Count said. "I meant no offense. It's just that . . . well, it's written all over your face."

"Do you make dossiers on the private lives of *all* your guests?"

"What private lives?" the Count said. "What privacy? These people don't *want* privacy. It terrifies them. They want crowds, they want the telephone, they want houses in the American style, with lawns rolling down to the sidewalk, and no walls. That's why Americans marry so young; marriage is an invasion of privacy, a rape of the self that they welcome with screaming open arms."

"But what I do is none of your business."

"You're right," he said. "But it has its own comic insistence, like that cursed music playing in my house. It always happens to Americans in Rome. They can't hold themselves together. The women look for gigolos, and the men fall in love with whores. They can't help it. Their pasts no longer shackle them. They can be as dirty as they wanted to be in their nice little suburbs where the lack of privacy was their only restraint. Here there is little privacy either, but they are at least strangers. And in Rome you no longer care. Nothing matters *too* much, because we will die and Rome will live on." He was leaning back again, rolling the ice cubes against the walls of the glass. "Rome will live on, that is, unless the Americans destroy the world first with their bombs."

"It might happen," Malloy said. He was sitting again, and no longer felt like arguing. The Count, he thought, is playing the Old World lecturing the New. I won't argue.

"See? I knew it. That tone, that quality of *doom!* Rome has done its work on you, hasn't it, Father? You've become an American who hates America."

"That's wrong. I just don't love America anymore."

"The war?"

"The war. Other things too." Malloy thought of Rail's desperate catalog of ruined dreams, skills never mastered, pleasures never consummated.

"Do you think you will win?"

"I don't think anything about it anymore."

The Count opened a hammered silver cigarette case. Malloy took one. The Count used a box of wooden matches to light both cigarettes. They were Pall Malls.

"The Americans' problem," he said, looking past Malloy at the far wall and its plundered artifacts, "is that they think they are becoming the new Romans and they are really becoming the new Aztecs. They're doomed, prisoners of their self-created gods, oddly noble, convinced that they can only ward off this imagined destruction with blood sacrifice."

It's time to leave, Malloy thought. You're giving me a concert of your best lines, jottings from some private volume bound in pigskin, with vellum leaves. I might even agree with you; but it's too easy.

"Well," Malloy said, "I'd better go."

The Count stood up and looked at his watch. He moved around the desk, his tan looking richer in the light, and the jacket less like the colors of a cathedral. His eyes brightened.

"Wait, Father," he said, touching Malloy's sleeve. "There's a small entertainment in the next room. I'm sure you'd appreciate it."

"Thanks. I've been entertained enough."

"*This* you must see. I knew it when I saw you out there with the animals."

"No, I have to go."

"But, Father, tonight is Good Friday," the Count said. His eyes were glittery like wet coal. "In the next room, a group of specially assembled guests are about to begin a special ceremony. In there, in the chapel."

"The chapel?"

The Count flicked a wall switch that extinguished the desk lamp, and opened the door on the left. A long, windowless room lay before them, dark except for a hidden red lamp at the far end. The lamp was on the floor, blocked by a stone slab. Malloy heard a flute playing somewhere, and as his eyes adjusted, saw that the dark reaches of the room were inhabited. He saw a bare shoulder, a line of hip, hair, no faces. A door opened, and a woman in a white ankle-length shawl came out, followed by a tall faceless man in black. Malloy felt rooted. The woman climbed onto the slab, unbuckled something, and lay naked in the soft red light, with her arms straight out. Malloy thought: Thank God, it's not her. He heard mutterings like prayer, and was conscious of awkward movement in the darkness. The man in black raised something above his head and then bent forward, his elbows at the girl's knees, and leaned forward. She shuddered and screamed. So did someone in the black corner to the left, and the flute played higher, and he heard someone laughing softly beside him, and then away at the end of the room, pinned to the rough stone floor, he saw Franca. She was masked, but he knew that body more intimately than his own. And she was laughing.

Malloy pushed the Count aside, and walked through the darkened office to the dance floor. *Can't get no. Satis. Faction.* He pushed his way through the crowd, which was about six drinks louder, and came out into the hall. He asked the uniformed maid for his coat. A small girl with a tiny nose and leathery hair was also waiting. The blond British butler had not returned.

"God, *a priest*," the girl said. "You'll talk to me, won't you, Father? You'll talk to me? I keep trying to talk serious to these men. They won't listen. You ask them about Communism and they laugh. You ask them, 'Is God really dead?' and they try to assault you. Is God dead, Father? You ought to know."

"Shut up."

"What? What did you—"

"I said shut up."

Malloy took his coat and went out to ask for his car. He handed one of the uniformed Italians the slip of paper. The Italian looked at it, shrugged, and went off. Malloy could hear splashing and loud laughter from the pool. The Spanish guitar was more insistent, with a crazier timbre. He climbed into the car and drove slowly down the lane to the main road. Parked under a tree, he saw a late-model sports car. Its owner was in the shadows, bent over, heaving. Malloy turned into the main road, pushed down on the accelerator, and drove quickly and emptily to the sea.

CHAPTER 18

Malloy could not sleep. He knew Franca would not be back. She would not be back that night, she might not be back at all. He tried to read the Quasimodo, but his eyes only looked at the pages. He searched the small house, but there was nothing to drink. He made coffee and it went cold in the cup. After a while, he fell back exhausted on the double bed. In the end, he thought, all the markers were always picked up. They knew how to handle this better in the old neighborhood. You killed one woman with another woman, and walked away. You were not eaten up by mysteries, wonder, columns of figures that would not tally; you did not even try very hard to discover what had happened, because something would come along. Most of all, you did not have pain. Malloy remembered the men coming back to the camp in 'Nam, running with gonorrhea and regret, confessing to him, hoping desperately that a bullet or a mortar or a short round would not take them first. Their sins were innocent: they were not dildos, incense, mocking images of a cigar-box virgin, talk of money, the smell of luxury, dark bodies knifing into pools, dogs on the lawn, high walls, British thugs disguised as butlers, tiny ears and silken lashes, and horror beyond a teak-wood door. The horror of the evening had been smaller, because private; a shift in degree would turn it comic.

Out there, the horror had the finality of death.

And yet, he wanted her home. He did not care. He could not console himself with scraps of sermon, with Mary Magdalene, with the terrible sin of pity; his consolation could only be in possession. He wanted her back.

About four thirty he heard a car scraping on tar, an engine's roar, silence, and then the sound of someone struggling through the sand outside the door. Then someone knocked. it was Mary Wilson. She was very drunk and had lost a shoe. She nodded, stepped in heavily on the bare foot, and walked past him into the kitchen. She sat for a moment, kneading her small handbag. The medallion was gone. She looked up at him.

"I'm sorry that happened, Father. You know, last night."

"Don't call me Father," Malloy said. "How did the party turn out?"

"Rotten. All rotten. Disgusting and rotten. I know how you must feel. I'm sorry, Father."

"You need some coffee?"

"Shit."

"I've got a fresh pot."

"What are you, a faggot or something? They cut your balls off? Why didn't you go in there and drag her outta that shithouse?"

"How about talking about the Yankees, or football, or what happened to your shoe?"

"I don't care about the shoe," she said. She was trying to light a cigarette, but her hand was shaking violently. Malloy snapped the head off a match and lit her cigarette, and held the match for himself.

"Where'd ya learn that cheap trick?" she said.

"Watching movies," he said. They were quiet for a while.

"The hell with it," she said. "There's nothin' can be done about it now. You want a belt of whiskey?"

"I'll tell you what: you take some of my coffee and I'll take some of your whiskey."

"Don't be such a fucking Boy Scout, will you, Father? When I drink coffee I start singing about my mother."

Malloy laughed. He washed two water glasses in the sink and put them on the table. Mary Wilson produced a leather-covered pint with an expensive silver top. She picked up the glasses, sighted down them, then poured an inch for each of them. Her hands looked younger than her face.

"It's my fault," she said. "I never should of ast her to come. But she was nice to me. She didn't talk much, and I always thought she was a little weird, Father, to tell you the truth. But she was nice. She was, I don't know, kind of lost, like." She was flicking ashes on the floor. "But Googie's a dirty rat bastard. I should of known he was up to something. But I don't know. Maybe he seen something in her you didn't see, you know what I mean? You got to admit there's something weird with a girl who comes to the beach and don't open the fuckin' windows."

"Forget it."

"What I want to say is, I'm sorry, Father. I didn't mean to see this happen. I just wish you'd of gone in there and smacked that wop son of a bitch in the mouth. He's always playing with people's lives. Always fuckin' with people, like we were some kind of a fuckin' toy." She looked up, sipped the Scotch, smashed out the cigarette under her shod foot. "I'm sorry I curse so fuckin' much, Father. I'm always like that when I'm stewed. And you don't look like a priest without your suit on, you know?"

"Don't worry about it."

"Ah, what the hell," she said. "I've been drunk for three days: yesterday, today, and tomorrow."

Malloy laughed and took a long drink of the whiskey.

"They all went off to the yacht," she said. "Googie and some broad, and his wife and some other gorilla. They went out ta the yacht. There was a time he took me out there. He used to say he had a boat that slept twenty-four and fucked forty-eight." She laughed luridly, enjoying herself. "Jesus, excuse me, Father."

"Go on, go on," Malloy said. He didn't want her to leave. He wanted her to keep talking. "Where did they go?"

"Who knows?" she said. "Out past the three-mile limit, I guess. That way they can't get locked up for humping jail-bait. Have another. You look like you need it."

"Thanks," he said. There was spittle collecting in the corners of her mouth. He soaked a face cloth in cold water and handed it to her.

"Thanks," she said. She tamped at her face and put the cloth back on the table. "Well, what the hell are ya gonna do? Are ya goin' after her or what?"

"No."

"You're right. Why don't ya do something smart, Father? Go into a fuckin' monastery or whatever they call those places. You know, where the monks look at the skulls and things and pray all fuckin' day? That's the life.

No women to drive you nuts. No worries about money. No airplanes. No telephones. No slimy rat bastards like Googie floating around. Get out of this fuckin' It'ly. This place is a curse. Get outa here or it'll kill ya."

She seemed to shrink with the effort of talk. He noticed a soft sheen in her eyes.

"Look, Father," she said, "if there's anything I could do . . ."

"No."

"I mean I'm still a pretty good ball. I still got that. I learned *something* in the last fifteen years. If that would help, I wouldn't mind . . ."

She glanced into the other room at the bed. Malloy sighed, and looked at the glass.

"That wouldn't solve anything."

"Oh boy," she said. "Do I know that."

Malloy heard foghorns away off. The fishermen were already awake in their cottages. Their sons were unfurling the nets. It would soon be day.

"Don't you love her, Father?" Mary Wilson said. She said it softly, the whiskey voice managing a tenderness it shouldn't have been capable of.

"Yes, I love her," he said. "Yes." Yes, I did, he thought: I never measured it out with that word. I just never thought of it. But I was vain: I tried to doctor her, and she was really nursing me. Maybe she saw that I had recovered. It was just one further irony: the eunuch saved had become the cuckold betrayed. Mary Wilson reached for the bottle. I should stop her, Malloy thought, but I won't. I can't stop anyone anymore.

"Are you staying until the summer?" Malloy said.

"I can't go anywhere, Father. I don't belong."

They sat drinking steadily and did not talk for a long while. Then the whiskey was gone. The fishermen were striking out across the sea. Malloy got up and opened a window. The sea air was cold. There was no moon and he could not see the line of the shore.

"I'm gonna get some more booze, Father."

"I think I'm going to bed."

"Come on," she said cheerfully. "Stay up. I'll sing a couple of songs. I used to be pretty good, you know. I had some offers to turn pro, back in Philly. That was before I met that rat wop bastard."

"You might sing about Mother."

"Nah. I was only kidding. I'll sing 'White Cliffs of Dover.' How would that grab ya, Father?"

"It sounds terrific."

She stood up, tottering on the one high heel, took a breath, and started singing in a high cracked voice:

> *"There'll be bluebirds over,*
> *the white cliffs of Dover,*
> *tomaaaaaaaw-roe*
> *when the world is free.*
> *There'll be peace and laughter,*
> *and joy ever after,*
> *tomaaaawroe, when . . ."*

She started heaving and coughing, and put a hand on the table to steady herself.

"Bravo!" Malloy said. "Terrific!"

"I need a fuckin' belt."

"How about some coffee?"

"Nah, I'm going to get some more whiskey."

"I'm going to bed," Malloy said. He was feeling better. The whiskey started humming in his head. She looked at him again.

"If you want . . ."

"No thanks, Mary. I feel honored, believe me."

"I knew you were a fuckin' Boy Scout."

Malloy laughed again.

"Don't laugh, Father," she said, almost whispering. "I'd like to do it. I never balled a priest before."

"You collect trophies, too."

"I'm sorry, Father. It's just . . . pardon the vulgarity, Father, but you know, if I ever learned one thing for sure, it's that . . . fucking is better than loneliness."

"Ah, the hell with it, Mary. The hell with it. Let's just say good night."

She shrugged, pulled herself erect, and walked to the door on her single shoe, like a cripple. She tried very hard to look dignified. Then she opened the door and pitched forward into the sand.

"Jesus Christ," Malloy said.

He tried to lift her, but she was too heavy. He put her small purse under his T-shirt, tucked in the T-shirt, took a deep breath, and then grabbed her under the arms. Her armpits were wet. He dragged her through the sand, straining against the weight. She felt like a sack of elephants. When he arrived at her cabin, Malloy stood breathing heavily for a moment. He tried the door. It was locked. He searched her purse, but there was no key. I can't leave her here, he thought. I shouldn't care, I don't even know her, but I can't leave her here like a Bowery bum. He reached down the front of her dress. The key was tucked in her brassiere beneath her left breast. He opened the door. The cabin smelled like whiskey and dirty clothes. He lugged her to the unmade bed and let her fall across it with her legs dangling onto the floor. He put the key back and started to leave. He looked at her for a moment. Then he walked over and lifted her legs onto the bed.

Back in the cabin, he dozed heavily, somewhere between sleep and consciousness, heavy with fatigue and whiskey: and saw a ship lost in a storm, with wild and brutal seas, and an aged commander strapped in solitude upon a deck, and the sea black with the faces of the dying and the drowned, the wounded and the damned.

He came awake with the harsh glare of morning sun and the sound of distant laughter. He pulled on trousers and stepped outside. The sand was already hot. His tongue was thick and furry. He felt heavy and dull. He saw a crowd gathering, away down the beach. Two young boys ran past him, going toward the crowd, and he fell in behind them. A section of the night before came to him, and he felt the way he had once after going to the back room in Coney Island to see Jo-Jo the Horse-Faced Boy.

The crowd was swelling, and Malloy thought that someone must have landed a giant fish. As he came closer, a hum of rapid noisy talk washed against him, mixed with the tinny sound of rock 'n' roll from a transistor. He eased his way through the crowd, smiling thinly, excusing himself, feeling suddenly as eager as they were for a closer look. He stepped around a heavy woman in a blue dress, and saw that they were all staring at the body of a man. The body was large, blue-white, and naked, and someone had placed a straw bonnet over its

HOLY SATURDAY

Q. *What is Hell?*
A. *Hell is a state to which the wicked are condemned, and in which they are deprived of the sight of God, and are in dreadful torments.*

—ADVANCED CATECHISM OF CATHOLIC FAITH AND PRACTICE

Pain was to them a solvent, a cathartic, almost a decoration, to be fairly worn while they survived.

—T.E. Lawrence

CHAPTER 19

〟〟〟〟〟〟〟〟〟〟〟〟〟〟〟〟〟〟〟〟〟〟〟

Malloy gave Rail the last rites, thinking: I'm sorry, Rail, this rite means nothing to me, but it might mean something to you. He sent a fat Italian woman for some olive oil and he touched Rail's gray flesh: the eyes, the ears, the mouth, nose, and fingers, saying the only partially remembered words: "Through this holy unction and His most tender mercy, may the Lord pardon thee whatever sins thou has committed by seeing, hearing . . ." The sun rose higher; the fishermen looked on yawning; the children were racing down the beach after a ball.

You were terrified of death, my fat near-friend, and I did nothing. Malloy stood awkwardly, looking at the pile of dead gray flesh, which seemed to be sinking into the sand. The tide had worked its way to Rail's legs and burrowed beneath them. I am tired of looking at dead men, Malloy thought: dead men with tubes rammed into their noses and down their throats in hospital wards; dead men in high grass, with their faces hammered off; dead men with blistered skin. I am sorry, my fat friend, that I did nothing. You wanted the cavalry of Christ to come racing in with silver bugles and ostrich feathers; you had only a dried-up man beside you, as arid as the Sahara.

After a while, two policemen arrived, walking lumpily in the sand. A young one stared at the body while an older man scribbled in a pad. A fly prowled on the gray unmoving stomach, and Malloy kicked it away. Then an ambulance arrived, and two more men in white lifted the huge bulk onto a stretcher and grunted away with it, while the small children looked on in admiration at the policemen and their revolvers.

Malloy walked slowly down the beach. There were no ships on the sea. Away off, a helicopter chugged clumsily across the sky, circling back to the city. If I could pray, Malloy thought, I would pray for Rail. Yes, I really would. But I have prayed myself out. He came close to me, and I touched him with death, the way my kind have been touching people for twenty centuries. He remembered some words from St. Paul: "I cannot understand my own actions; I do not act as I want to act; on the contrary I do what I detest." The old bastard knew something.

He saw a gull skimming low over the water, suddenly belting his face into the water, and coming away with the shiny body of a fish. That was rough and fundamental; so was the death of Rail. The rest was like the helicopter: a contraption of wheels and tin and plexiglass, chasing traffic here and murdering men out there. The great modern bird, spitting Lucifer from its mouth in fractions of seconds. At least the gulls ate what they killed.

In the bungalow, he washed slowly and carefully, but he did not shave. The whole story is in each of us, he thought: the great peace and excitement at the beginning, when the teachers wore the birettas in the frosty dawn, and the walls of the seminary rose like battlements against the Devil; the first tentative essays into the world; the disillusion and the reading of Thomas à Kempis; and then the aridity later. The roots of the Fall came when you found it more and more difficult to close the eyes against what was really happening. In the seminary nobody talked about the old priest who kept the bees in the field and had a glassed museum of stuffed birds and put soft hands on the younger boys in chapel. No one knew that the two years of philosophy were really two years of discipline and extracted obedience; there was nothing of Ayer or Wittgenstein, no mention of Sartre or Kierkegaard; you learned to keep quiet, to submit, to have some vague quality called faith, and they gave you four years of theology after that to make it set, like the plaster in cheap statues of Christ. It did, for a while.

But you lost it a little at a time. You lost it in the parish house down the street from the other house on Columbus Avenue where the thirteen-year-old Puerto Rican girls sold themselves to pensioned men with white moustaches. You lost it in the front parlor of the Chancery when the decision was made to back the Republicans because the Democrats were agents of the Devil. The little fat prince with his sinkhole of a mind lost it for you; the first child's death lost it for you; and then the savage murdering and blood and despair of the highlands lost it for you. Cowardice stole it from you, not lust. Knowledge stole it from you, not lust. Coldness and despair stole it from you. Not lust.

Malloy ran the cold water, and drank a glass, then filled another. He knew that something was gone from him. He felt its absence on the plane coming home with the green plastic sacks in the cargo compartment. It was surely gone when the Archbishop silenced him in California, when he was made to lie on the carpeted steps and kiss the feet of a bigot whose heart was addled by fear. The something was faith.

For a while, he thought that perhaps it would come back in Rome. Perhaps in the center of the old structure, he would find out what had sent him down the detours, where men died alone of madness. But he was an American, and the Church was Italian and ancient. The old Italians shuffled about in conspiracies and tangents; he had seen all of them, smelling of unwashed rooms, faces as yellow as unhealed wounds: Masella, eighty-three; Bacci, seventy-six; Bracci, eighty-one; Valeri, seventy-nine; Testa, seventy-six; Micara, eighty-two; Giobbe, eighty-two; Morano, ninety; Pizzardo, eighty-five; Forni, seventy-three; Cicogagni, seventy-nine; Maladotti, eighty-two. They did not hate Americans; the Americans paid them. But they did not know anything else about America. The world was Italy and the only issue was the continued success of the Christian Democratic Party. Nothing else mattered: the Ecumenical Council was a whim of a pope picked by mistake. They talked prettily of ecumenism but it was only an exercise in modern art. You hired a public relations man now the way the old popes hired Michelangelo. The only important people were the men from Hambro's Bank, just in from London, or the customer's man from J.P. Morgan and Company, just arrived for a conference, or the dim man with the green glasses from the Crédit Suisse in Switzerland. They always stayed at the Hilton Hotel, because the Hilton was owned by the great real estate combine called Generale Immobiliare, and Generale Immobiliare was owned by the Vatican. They knew nothing, these old parched men; to them the modern world was Olivettis, Fiats, and Italian Westerns. It was never revolution. They just wished that the new pope would pay less heed to the war and more to the real estate business.

For a while Malloy had sought refuge in the study of art. He had prowled the great buildings, gone into deep cellars, into museums, into the high attics and rooftops, with notebook in one hand and guidebook in the other. But there was no refuge. He would follow the austere lines of the folds on the sarcophagus of Boniface VII and then hear that dead pope's voice shouting his famous edict: "God has set us over kings, to build, plant, weed, and destroy." He would see the gilded luxury of the monument to Sixtus IV, and his mind would fill with the agents of Sixtus murdering a Medici at a High Mass. He would gaze at Giotto's mosaics in the grottoes, and see a sneering Virgin, with an outer halo the color of blood drying into parched grass, and an inner halo the color of the Mekong.

Franca had been a small rescue. He had moved out of the boarding house in Trastevere and taken the house at the beach and had not thought of time or change. She was nurse and cathedral; he was sure he bored her, but she stayed on, as regular as salt tides and the bong-bong-ing of the buoys. Now she was gone. And he was the custodian of still another dead man's memory.

Malloy dressed completely and went back out into the sun. He did not lock the door, but it did not matter. Mary Wilson's house was closed and dark. He walked to the car and drove to Rome.

He asked for help, Malloy thought, and I would not give it.

The streets of the city were quiet in the baking heat. There were no signs of the rains of the day before, and nothing at all indicated that James Rail had walked some of those streets. Even the pilgrims were quiet, except for the choirs who had come to sing the praises of the Lord from all the countries of Europe. He heard someone singing an old favorite:

"Come, Holy Spirit,
Creator, come
From thy bright Heavenly throne;
Take possession of our souls
And make them all thy own."

It reminded him of genuflections, holy water, sitting in wooden pews, the smell of a censer, making your Easter duty, his mother's piety-ridden face. Then he began to see Americans everywhere: standing in the flowers on the Spanish Steps with their garlands of Leicas; posing in the poppies around the Forum; sitting in the cool of umbrellas outside cafés. Their faces were all smiling. They were the fortunate people, free of violence from strangers, protected by money and arrogance, smiling through other people's dreams. Rail was never really one of them. That was probably one reason why he was dead.

Malloy parked on a side street away from the Vatican and hurried to his office.

There were more magazines on the desk, but no letters. The office had not been cleaned. He closed the door and walked quickly down the corridor, past the bank of elevators, into the far wing. It was a visit to officers' country, he thought: the beautiful country where the heads of congregations sat in splendid isolation, worrying about the propagation of the Faith, the Oriental Church, the condition of the Sacraments, and even the building of St. Peter's. I wonder, Malloy thought, if anyone is working today in the Secretariat of Briefs to Princes? The younger men called it "Sick Bay," but it was where the power was.

He stopped at Maladotti's suite of offices, hesitated for a moment, and walked in. There was a small office and a door behind it, leading into the Cardinal's private office. Carney looked up at him through rimless glasses. His small plain desk was busy with papers.

"Aaah, Father Malloy," he said.

"Excuse me," Malloy said. "I should have knocked."

He was eating lunch. A rye bread sandwich with gray filling hung limply in his right hand. "Yes, you should have. What is it?"

"I want to see Maladotti."

"The Cardinal is not in."

"I have to see him. When will he be back?"

"He's not expected until Tuesday."

"Can you get word to him?"

"Perhaps."

"Tell him that Mr. Rail is dead."

Carney rose slowly, chewing dryly, the thin shoulders hunching beneath the soutane. He put the nibbled sandwich on top of a memo pad. Now I understand you, Malloy thought; you're a mouse training to be a rat.

"Say that again, Father."

"I said that Mr. James Rail, distinguished Catholic layman, is dead."

"Have you been drinking, Father?" He pushed his chair away with the back of his legs.

"No. I saw the body at the beach at Fragene this morning. I gave him the last rites."

Carney put his hands behind his back. "What were you doing at Fragene, Father?"

"Does that really matter?" Malloy said wearily.

"I must be sure that you are not having hallucinations, among your other problems, Father."

"Look, Carney, I was at the beach. I saw Rail's body. I know it was him because I've spent hours with him, at your direction, in the past few days. I think Maladotti should know about it. What else do you want me to say? That I'm living in sin with sixteen Dominican nuns and a pet yak?"

"Careful, Father."

"All right," Malloy said. "Forget it. I've told you. You tell Maladotti."

"Just what do you think the Cardinal can do about it?"

"Holy Mother," Malloy said. "Rail came to Rome to see him. The least he can do is find out something about the man. Does he have a wife? Does he have a mother? Or sisters? Or brothers? Don't you think that someone might want to *know*?"

Carney was quiet for a moment, then said, "Assuming that Mr. Rail is dead, assuming you *did* see his body out at the seaside, where could we check the facts?"

"What facts?"

"The facts, the facts. The location of the body. The cause of death. The usual thing."

"The cause of death, I assume, was drowning. Two cops were there, I assume from Fragene. The body was taken away in an ambulance. You might start with the police."

"Thank you, Father Malloy. I'll see what we can do."

"I'll be back a little later."

"That will be unnecessary."

Yes, it will, Malloy thought. It will be unnecessary, because I'm unnecessary. You'll check it out, won't you, Carney? After finishing your sandwich and the newspaper and a couple of decades of the rosary thrown in for your own soul. He was walking furiously down the hall. Sure, you'll worry about Rail, whose body is lying on a slab somewhere, his chest filled with seawater, being drained in silence to provide a feast for the worms. Let me know what you find out. You tell me if there is a wife or a lover, a father or an aunt. Give me their address and I'll write them a note. I'll drop the sort of note that has been my only talent. I've sent it a hundred times. I'll tell them he died well. I'll tell them he died with the consolation of God. I won't tell them anything about the trip into the mountains, or his hushed voice when he saw the lake walled off by the pine trees, or the way the young Italian soldiers were laughing over their wine and spaghetti. I won't tell them anything about that. Or about the terror in his eyes across that sweating murderous room. Or about the way he asked me for help he thought I could provide and how I denied it to him. That would be too complicated. I'll write a simple note, a note made simpler because there will be no pockets to rifle, no pictures of girls to turn over in the mud, no serial numbers to get straight. I'll just say as I always say that he died with the last rites and the consolation of Holy Mother, the Church. Then you, Carney, can handle the shipping charges, and the lawyers, accountants, and creditors can handle the estate.

Malloy sat for a long time in his office. He took the wrapping off the magazines, but didn't open them any further. He smoked three cigarettes. He started to write a letter to his mother, and then crumpled it. His body was washed by waves of fatigue. He thought he would lie down on the floor, with a book as pillow, and sleep awhile. But he didn't. He felt certain that someone would come in and see him, and there would be a row. He dozed in the chair, his arms folded across his chest, and then his mind started filling with a red glow in a dark cave, the outline of a lush body, the shock of loss, the pounding of a drummer, and his own anger surging in his blood as the music roared away. He was suddenly awake. He remembered what he was there for. He opened the desk and took out some official stationery and put it in a pocket inside his soutane. Then he went out.

When he reached Carney's office, he knocked. There was no answer. He knocked again. There was no answer. He walked in, and Carney was sitting there, peering up at him, still nibbling at the sandwich in his hand, nibbling and chewing, while the free hand scribbled in Latin on a memo pad.

"I thought it was you," he said coldly.

"Did you find out anything?"

Carney smiled thinly, and said, "Father Malloy, how would you like a transfer out of the Vatican?"

"What do you mean?"

"You're unhappy, Father Malloy," he said. "You have not been happy for a long time. You were unhappy in Los Angeles and you got into all that messy business over the war. You are here in the arms of Holy Mother Church, and you seem dedicated to debauchery and lusting . . ."

"That is all my business," Malloy said. "Mine and God's."

"You were brought here to be kept out of harm's way, Father," Carney said. "Your records show some gifts, if it weren't for the capacity you have shown for sin . . ."

"This is all very interesting," Malloy said. "But what did you find out about Rail?"

". . . And now you have taken up with a woman."

"You are really something, Carney. You are really something."

"You deny you have taken up with a woman? A woman who formerly walked the streets in Rome?"

"You're not my confessor, Carney. I don't have to discuss this with you."

"I've seen you with that woman," Carney said, rising from the chair. "I've seen the house you share with her."

Malloy put both hands on the desk and leaned over. He was inches from Carney's face. "Tell me," he said, "did you sneak up to the windows at night? Did you lie under the house and listen for signs of life? Did you smell us? Did you smell her? What did you do then, Carney, you poor desiccated bastard? Did you reach under your robes and beat your meat? You disgusting little bastard. For ten cents, I'd knock you senseless."

Carney's face went gray, and his mouth trembled as he fought for control. Malloy suddenly felt foolish.

"A report on this sinful outburst will be made directly to Cardinal Maladotti."

"That suits me fine."

"He'll have it Tuesday morning."

"With a recommendation for transfer to Uganda, I suppose?"

"If I were you," Carney said, sliding back into the chair, and reaching to nibble again on the sandwich, "I would not continue this line of discussion, Father Malloy. The consequences are . . ."

Malloy tore the sandwich out of Carney's hand and heaved it against the wall. He put his left forearm at the end of the desk and then swept everything before him: memo pads, a newspaper, letters, a wire basket, a small bottle of ink. They fell in a shambles on the floor. Carney pulled away from him.

"To hell with consequences!" Malloy roared. "Do you hear me? I said to hell with consequences! I came in here an hour ago to tell you about a man's death! That doesn't matter to you, does it, Carney? I'm sure it doesn't matter to Maladotti, or to any of these other be-robed Mafiosi around here. Well, let me tell you something. It matters to *me*. I didn't much like Mr. James Rail. But by fucking Jesus, he was *human!* He had weaknesses and he feared for his soul: he was afraid, very afraid. But he was *human!* Flesh, blood, bones, sinew, guts, lungs, all of it! That was all he had. He didn't paint or sculpt or write; he didn't own motor works or hotels or concrete plants. He didn't do much of anything, except eat, and maybe fill your goddamned treasury. But I'll tell you something, Carney. He was better than a little heartless worm like you. Stick the consequences up your ass!"

Malloy turned to leave.

"If your little speech is over, Father Malloy, there's one further thing you should know."

"What's that?"

"The man you saw at the beach could not have been Mr. Rail. Cardinal Maladotti had breakfast with Mr. Rail an hour ago."

CHAPTER 20

You were a doctor, Fuentes, you started young, beardless, in that long bright moment that was your youth, with a shiny borrowed suit and an office in the parlor of your father's house. You saved lives then; you pulled life squealing and bloody from the womb. You saved lives, you healed, you gave; and it has ended here, in this shabby parlor, with wicker chairs for company, and old copies of *Bohemia* on all the tables. In one room, a man has a rifle, and you do not care. No, Fuentes, you do not care. You choose mists, smoke rising from old time; bold revelry in New Orleans when you were a special student at Tulane and the blond girls with the pink skins all asked you to show them the rhumba; that, and the house in the sweet garden suburbs, with the sprinklers in the mornings, and the discreet limousines and the American girls strapped on the operating tables upstairs and the recuperation cottages in the rear. All the American girls looked like Virginia Hill that season, with padded shoulders and too much lipstick, playing Miguelito Valdes records in the coffee room. You remember that, Fuentes; and sweet Havana gone bad later, the bodies of castrati in Batista's streets, the *barbudos* fighting in the Sierra Maestra. Then in a day, all of it gone, and the parades through the streets, the *barbudos* everywhere, the countryside revenging itself at last

upon the city, the men with the dense black beards re-
ceiving counsel from any gap-toothed crone begging on
a street corner, while men you went to school with were
lined against walls and shot; and that was it. Superman
was banished from the club with blue lights; the prizefighters fled the arenas for Mexico and Spain and America; the cane-cutters took machetes to the silk pillows
and polished tables of the old houses; God's outrage was
complete. And now you sit here, a groper through other
people's rooms, stripping tobacco from the butts in ash-
trays, quarreling in a foreign language over the price of
eggs, knowing that one of your American pilgrims has a
rifle in his suitcase. You discovered it because you had
one final secret muscle of pride; you were instructed to
touch nothing; you touched everything, because it was
one order you could not abide.

Yet, you do not care.

You prefer cold smoke, mists, reveries. You prefer to
think about the mulatto girl in the green room in Santiago
who had done for you what no one else had ever done
as well; who loved you; who bore your bastard children,
while the high white imperial nose of your wife sniffed
expensive scents in the stores of Havana and put Batista's pictures on the walls in the playroom and laughed at
the talk of fighting in the hills. You, Fuentes, who were
wrong: you who fled to the trinkets and watches of Miami, to the boarded winter homes and secret agents of
Key West, to the forlorn clothes-tattering winds of New
York, enduring those iced canyons in solitude and desperation until you took what remained of all those mur-
dered embryos, those knifed punctuations to weekends
of martinis and laughter, those dry guilty American

vaginas, you took what was left from the lining of the sheepskin coat in the boarding house in East Harlem, and the ticket was purchased, and you set out on your journey, the penultimate leg of your final journey. It was too long. The days have paled. The Lord died for your sins, Fuentes, between two thieves. You will go home and try to die well.

The doorbell rang.

"Who is it?"

"A package. Special delivery."

A delivery boy with a large brown paper package wrapped with thin white twine. The boy is beardless, in a borrowed suit, as you were in the parlor of the old house where your father sat smoking panatelas and reading Calderón. A package for Mr. Harwell. Mr. Harwell? Oh yes. Of course. Mr. Harwell.

The boy is gone, down the three flights of peeling paint and ageless stone. Yes. Mr. Harwell. You lie behind your door, *maricón*. Tiny features, white teeth, hard little body with a rifle, broken down, with a fancy wooden stock, hidden in the suitcase on top of the clothes closet. Listen: I deliver.

"Go away."

"There is a package here for you. And a letter."

No reply. The package is not heavy. So you will not be assembling an armory, *maricón*. It is something else. Perhaps it is ticking. No. Someone sending flowers, perhaps. To apologize for the blue welts across your face? The welts that were not yours yesterday? You were smooth when you went out, *maricón*, out into our shared prison city of exile and light.

The door opened.

"Let's have it."

A hand, darkness beyond, the shutters closed. The hand has a delicate surface, *maricón*. From running against your own hard flesh? You leave evidence about you. Ah. See, Fuentes? The door closes, but there is no tip.

And where are all the hairless boys who delivered boxes, flowers, whips, and penicillin to all the suites in the high buildings along the shore, the buildings that stood gleaming in the sun like giant boxes carved from salt? They must be cabinet ministers now, with beards and good cigars, sitting in boardrooms. It is warm today. I should go out. I should walk in the sun. But I will not. The sun burns away memory. It is nature's scalpel, and you will tremble if you forget completely, Fuentes; your hands will shudder, the hands that worked with confidence and brilliance in the old house and were sold for a winter cabana, trips to New York and Miami, silver vessels stacked in closets, trunks with ivory linings for your wife, an air-conditioned Cadillac, and the luxury of the mulatto girl you loved so well in the green room in Santiago. Your hands will tremble if you cease to remember, Fuentes. If the sun burns away memory, you will be dead.

"I'm checking out."

The hard voice, the tiny pinched face, masked with dark glasses. He had promised four nights; he gives you two. But you will not complain, Fuentes. You write the tally on a slip of paper.

"Two thousand lire, senõr."

"Too much for a crummy dump like this."

"The price was agreed."

Ah, whoever gave you those welts, whoever forced upon you the mask of those dark glasses, I would kiss him if I could.

"Here."

The bills are on the table. They are crisp. New bills from the bank at the airport. You do not touch them.

"What's the matter with my money?" he says to you. "Is it dirt? It's money, isn't it?"

"It is money."

You lift it. You will not thank him. He has his suitcase with the hidden weapon, the large cardboard box, the sunglasses, the blue welts.

"If you expect mail," you say, without conviction, "I will forward it."

He snarls: "Forward it to the Vatican."

And he is gone. The *pensione* is completely empty now. First open the shutters. Yes. Smell the fountain, distant and wet. The boards near the window squeak beneath your feet. Let in the air. Blow the smell of the gringo *maricón* away. Next week, a woman will come to scrub the hardwood floor. For now, you will remove the presence. Change the sheets. Leave the door wide open, and hope that a taxi will bring a new pilgrim. A taxi, yes: there he is now, in his sunglasses, his package, his suitcase. I pity you, poor driver. You will transport him somewhere else, and your reward will be accusations of thievery and bad manners. I see your number. My eyes have never failed. Twenty-one forty-eight. Ah, if there were a lottery today, I would play that number. At twenty-one, you saved lives, you helped create life, you gave; at forty-eight, you became a long-distance runner. Running toward what was left behind, running toward sun, palms, tobacco, harbors, girls eating ice cream cones in starched dresses, and God. Tomorrow, I will go to Mass. I have been a long time away.

CHAPTER 21

Richards leaned back in the cracked leather chair, feeling pleased with himself. The think piece had gone with the morning cables; the 1,500-worder was finished, waiting for the messenger boy. The think piece had some thought in it, but not too much to be dangerous to an editor. The 1,500-worder was 1,500 words. He took the cellophane off a new pack of Schimmelpennincks, crackled the cellophane ostentatiously, and took a long thin cigar from the tin box. If I were still drinking hard liquor, he thought, I would open the file cabinet and take out the bottle. The B-copy is out of the way; I can do the rest standing on my left pinkie. I will even survive those crowds tomorrow. Hell, I could even watch it on TV, if I wanted to sleep late. He took a drag on the thin cigar, and sat up. The chair squeaked. One of these days I will have to get that chair oiled, he thought, moving around the desk. He rinsed the glass coffeepot in the small sink, cleaned it with paper towels, then filled it. He scooped coffee into the perforated wheel and placed it on the glass spindle. He switched on the hot plate, breathing in the rich smell of the Kenya coffee. He leaned on the window frame, smoking the cigar, with his hands jammed in his pockets. A robin fluttered in the oleander trees. That's something, he thought. A robin. Summer is here. The telephone rang.

"*Irish Echo*. Harrigan speaking. Duffy ain't here."

"Hey, Frank. This is Malloy."

"Greetings. I just saw my first robin. About forty-one seconds ago."

"Congratulations," Malloy said. "Listen, are you free?"

"I'm waiting for a messenger. What's up?"

"Something weird."

"Don't tell me your gang couldn't get the tomb open? I'll blow my day tomorrow."

"I'm serious, Frank. Can I come up?"

"Sure. I got a coffeepot on."

"I'll see you in twenty minutes."

Richards poured himself a cup of the steaming coffee. The robin was gone. He took the coffee over to the desk and picked up the telephone. He called the messenger service again, shouting at them in Italian, and hung up. Then he sat down, slipped a sheet of paper into the typewriter, adjusted the roller to single space, and wrote a letter to his daughters. He hoped they were well; he hoped they were applying themselves at school. He was glad the oldest one was still in the ballet class, and he hoped that someday soon he would see them both. Rome was beautiful today. It was the day before Easter, the day when the Catholics held their vigil. The town was very crowded, and tomorrow there would be a mob scene at St. Peter's. But he had already seen his first robin. He told them to keep working hard at school, because it was the only life they would ever have, and they needed a brain to get them through it. He sent them his love, enclosed a money order for ten American dollars, slid the letter in an envelope, and sealed it. He finished the cup of coffee and was filling another when Malloy walked in.

"Jesus," Richards said. "You look like you just wrestled the Devil to a draw."

"Hello, Frank."

"You'd better have some coffee. What the hell is up?"

"The fat man is dead."

Richards handed Malloy a cup of coffee. "Sorry there's no cream or sugar around here. I don't use the stuff. What fat man?"

"Rail. The man I've been showing around town. The very important Catholic layman I told you about. He was washed up on the beach at Fragene this morning. He was nude and he was dead. I gave him the last rites myself."

"Drowned?"

"Yeah. I saw him last night at Rienzi's house. There was some kind of party on a yacht later."

"Sounds like you really celebrated Good Friday," Richards said.

"The guy's dead."

"So he went swimming," Richards said. "He was drunk, and he thought he could swim better than he could. He went out too far, and got himself dead."

"He didn't know how to swim, Frank," Malloy said. "He didn't know how to do anything except eat."

"I don't know what you're trying to say, Bob."

"I mean there's something weird about the whole thing. Rail was Maladotti's charge. Maladotti turned him over to Carney, the Canadian. Then Carney turned him over to me. I know I saw him on the beach this morning. I gave him the last rites and then the cops took the body away. I went to see Maladotti, to tell him his man was dead. Maladotti wasn't in. I talked to Carney. I blew my stack with him a bit. He just didn't give a good goddamn. Then he told me it couldn't have been Rail. He said Rail had a late breakfast with Maladotti, around the time the cops were lugging the remains away."

Richards was quiet for a long time. He didn't look at Malloy. He was sipping his coffee. "You were sober?"

"I had a hangover, Frank. I was up drinking pretty late."

"But you were sober?"

"Yeah, I was sober. It was late. Maybe ten, ten thirty in the morning. I had slept. I was sober."

"Did Franca see him?"

"Franca didn't come home last night."

"Oh." Richards poured another cup of coffee.

"I *know* it was Rail on the beach, Frank."

"Look," Richards said, "it just might be a mix-up. The Carney-Maladotti part, I mean. Carney probably gets his boss's schedule the night before. Maybe the Cardinal never saw the fat guy. But maybe he didn't bother calling his flunkie to tell him. So all you might have is a dead guy."

"Maybe."

That was probably what had happened, Malloy thought. It was Rail, all right. He had drowned. He was naked, he was probably chasing a girl, and he fell off the yacht. That was probably it. And Maladotti never bothered to call Carney.

"Why?" Richards said suddenly.

"Why what?"

"Why do you care? The other day you talked about

the fat guy like he was a godless, slobbering, degenerate Communist. Or a Protestant."

"Frank," Malloy said flatly, "the man's dead."

"I know. The question is why you should care about him."

"Because he died alone. Because when I saw him last night, he was terrified. Because when we went larking around the hills yesterday, I kind of liked him. He wanted me to hear his confession and I refused. If he's dead, he's got the right to a decent burial. Someone in the States must want to know. Someone must want the body back."

"The Fragene cops picked him up?"

"It must have been them."

Richards took out a small blue book with a gold seal on the cover. He thumbed through it, found the page he was looking for, and dialed the telephone. He spoke into it for a few minutes, talking rapidly in colloquial Italian and scribbling on a piece of paper. Then he said, "*Grazie*," and hung up. He stared at the notes, and turned in the chair. The chair squeaked.

"Yeah," he said. "They had a floater out there. He was fat. The body was picked up about forty-five minutes ago. Some people had been directed out there by headquarters. They had his passport and his return plane ticket to the States. They said he was a cousin, a teacher. The body was released to them. The dead guy's name was Parsons."

"Parsons?"

"Parsons."

There was a knock at the door and Richards got up to answer it. A very young messenger boy with a scarlet cap stood in the doorway. Richards took a manila envelope from the desk, told the kid to take it immediately to the telegraph office, and slipped him a fifty-lire piece. The kid nodded and was gone.

"I give the kid two hours," Richards said moodily.

"Listen, Frank. I know you think this is crazy. But I'd like to find out some more about what happened to Rail."

"Why don't you try finding out what happened to Parsons?"

"Frank, I *know* that was Rail's body on the beach."

"What are you going to do about it?"

"He was staying at the Excalibur. Let's walk over there and see what they know about it. You know those people."

"Yeah, they love me over there. They love me so much they start nailing the carpets down when I go in the door so I won't steal them."

"Do me this favor, Frank."

Richards sighed.

"Come on," he said. "This should make my day."

They walked over to the Excalibur. The day was light and sunny and the cafés were overflowing. Outside Doney's, there were extra tables on the sidewalk. Tourists were drinking red drinks in frosted glasses and eating pastry and chattering with great energy. Some of the more expensive whores were walking their dogs. Crowds ringed the newspaper kiosks, looking over the newspapers and dirty books. The animals were in full possession of the zoo. It was a beautiful Saturday in spring, a day perfect, Malloy thought, for making your First Holy Communion. It wasn't until they turned into the damp entrance to the hotel that he remembered Rail's dead eyes and cold sagging flesh.

"At least they can see I hang out with moral types once in a while," Richards said. "With that collar, they have to take you for someone from the Vatican Tourist Board."

"They don't have one."

"I know. But these bums don't."

Richards turned right and walked straight to the desk. The lobby was filled with people. They were buying newspapers and postcards at the small glass counter to the left. The large sitting room was almost empty; it only filled when it rained. A gray young man came out of an office to the left of the desk. He saw it was Richards and his face twitched; he looked as if he had just eaten a bad clam.

"Jerry, do you have a guest here named Rail?" Richards said.

"Why?"

"I want to see him, that's why. What do you think I'm doing—making a census?"

The man behind the desk might have been young; Malloy could not tell; he wore a fine dusty pallor like a mask, and his mouth kept twitching.

"Just a moment, please, Mr. Richards."

He went back through the door to the left. Richards raised his eyebrows and puckered his lips, as if to say, yeah, maybe there is something smelly here. The man with the dusty face came back.

"No one by that name here, Mr. Richards."

"Let me see your guest cards for Thursday and Friday," Richards said.

"Sir, you know we don't permit that."

"Why not?"

"It's a rule of the house, sir."

Richards leaned across the desk. "Let me ask you something, Jerry, old pal," he said. "How do you think it would be if four million readers in New York tomorrow morning were to read a story about what goes on up in room 810? A great big beautiful story, something like 'Girls Romp in Plush Hotel During Sacred Rites'? You know, something along those lines? How do you think that would wash, old buddy? Look real good when the Tourist Board got a copy, wouldn't it? That would look real good for a high-class hotel like this, wouldn't it, Jerry?"

The man's face grew dustier. "We do not presume to monitor the private lives of our guests . . ."

"Get the cards, Jerry."

Jerry came back with a thick clump of white cards, wrapped in a rubber band. Richards started thumbing through them.

"Kelly, O'Brien, Fitzgerald . . . You Irish bastards only stay in the best places, don't you? . . . Hemmings, Montoya, Ashley . . . These people think alphabetical order is something you go through in a police lineup . . . Goodrich, Heenan . . . Yeah, here it is. Rail. James F. Rail . . . 233 West 21st Street, New York City. Occupation: publisher."

"It's a crummy address," Malloy said, and thought: Fire escapes, hydrants, bodegas, a Spanish movie house, dogs. He saw the round, rolling handwriting. The dusty man's eyes looked like spoiled ice water.

"He checked out last night," Richards said.

"Last night?"

"Jerry, old buddy, did Mr. Rail leave a forwarding address?"

"No sir."

"Did he leave with anyone?"

"He hired a car and left alone."

"Thanks, old pal. You're a great fella. My friend here will pray for you."

Richards dropped the bundle of cards on the desk. They went out through the revolving doors.

"You'd make a hell of a cop, Frank," Malloy said.

"Stop talking dirty. It's a sin."

"I didn't know you had four million readers, though."

"It's just under two million. But your friendly innkeeper back there would worry if the circulation was twenty-six, including handball champions. Let's have a beer."

A heavy woman with a wide yellow hat and a flowered green dress was getting up from a table. Her husband, a frail man with horn-rimmed glasses and a Tyrolean hat, stood up at her signal. He was three inches shorter than she was.

"My fren's," Richards said elaborately, sliding the chair out from behind the woman. "Allow me."

"Oh, are you American?"

"I'm a from Napoli," he said. "I'm a good fella. My friend here, he's the nex' pope. Remember her inna you prayer."

"Oh, but we're not Catholics," she said. She had a round soprano voice.

"Aaah, but that's a the bes' thing a these day. It's all because of the Economical Compass. Pope Giovanni is a make alla the people inna worl' the same things under the sheets."

"Yes," she said thinly. "Well, thank you so much for the chat. We must be going. Come on, Harold."

Richards and Malloy sat down in the vacant seats.

"How much you want to bet they're going right to the house where Keats died?" Richards said.

"I don't like the odds," Malloy said. "What about Rail?"

"What about him?"

"If he was having breakfast with Maladotti, why did he check out of the hotel last night?"

Richards stopped waving at the waiter for a moment. He started to say something, stopped, then said: "Maybe he hated the big dump. Maybe he just went to another hotel."

"Maybe," Malloy said.

A young waiter came over. He was not one of the regulars. They asked for two beers and he bowed stiffly. An actor with a heavy beard said hello to Richards, and Richards waved. I should have grown a beard, Malloy thought. The young waiter brought the beers. Malloy poured for both of them. Richards took a long drink, almost draining the glass. Then he put the glass down.

"Wait here a minute," he said. "Guard the chair with your life."

Malloy tipped the empty chair forward, leaving it against the table, and watched Richards walk into the knot of drivers standing in front of the Excalibur. After a while, he took one of them aside, a squat, powerfully built man with heavy eyebrows. Richards and the driver strolled together, back and forth to the corner, the driver talking but never looking up at Richards. Malloy finished his beer and called for another. For a moment he remembered Rail's terrified eyes. Three strikes and you're out.

"We're in luck," Richards said, sitting down.

"What's up?"

"I found the guy who drove your friend Rail in from the airport. It was a straight commercial job. He doesn't know who booked it. He took Rail to the Excalibur. They stopped once on the way in, to eat. Rail tried to buy the girl who served him. There was another guy with him."

"Another guy?"

"A little guy. Young. Maybe twenty, twenty-five. Thin, blond, nasty. He dropped the little guy off first, at some crummy little *pensione* near the Trevi Fountain. Then he took Rail to the Excalibur."

"This was Holy Thursday?"

"Right," Richards said. He called for another beer, snapping his fingers and holding up the empty bottle. "There's more."

"Tell me."

"Last night, early, about seven o'clock, Rail talks to our friend, the duty driver. He wants to know how much to drive to Milan. The driver tells him a hundred bucks. The fat guy agrees. They take a suitcase and put it in the trunk. Rail says he has to go someplace first. The driver takes him out to Rienzi's place. He tells the driver to wait, he'll be back in forty-five minutes. The driver sits in the parking lot and falls asleep. He wakes up this morning with two private cops telling him to beat it. He never saw Rail again."

Richards poured out the beer. The sky was beginning to lose its brightness, but there were no clouds. It would not rain.

"He's got Rail's luggage in the car. If there was anything valuable in it, you can be sure it's gone."

"I've got to go down and find the other guy," Malloy said.

"He's taking us at three thirty," Richards said. "He can't remember the address, but he can show us the place. He wants five bucks. I told him we were good for it, with a couple of plenary indulgences thrown in." He checked his watch. "Have another beer."

The approaches to the Trevi Fountain were sealed off. Automobiles, people, horse-carts, cops. For almost ten minutes, the big limousine did not move. Richards asked the driver to pull over and park. He couldn't do that either.

"Let us out."

"Okay, mister."

"Which building is it?" Richards asked.

"Right down there," he said, not moving, and pointing vaguely with a stubby finger.

"The gray one?"

"No, no," he said. "The red one. Right there."

"All right," Richards said. He gave the driver three thousand lire. The driver folded the bills neatly and put them in a shirt pocket. "There's another three thousand if you take the luggage to my office and give it to the *portiere*," Richards said. "There's nothing worth stealing in it by now."

The driver looked insulted. Italians didn't steal, he said. I'm sorry, Richards said. They shouted at each other, and then Richards patted him gently on the shoulder. He slipped him a thousand-lire deposit on the luggage. Then he and Malloy got out and watched the driver try to ram three nuns, with the car in reverse.

"You, too, can be Sisyphus-for-a-Day," Richards said. "A long-running Italian TV show."

"I don't see any red house."

"He must mean the pink one. Italians think everything is red or blue, except stone and the Church."

They walked down the crowded street. A horse-drawn carriage was jammed between a taxi and an Oldsmobile. There were no sidewalks. They could hear the sound of the fountain grow louder. They stopped in front of a tall building with a faded pink façade. An expensive leather-goods store was on the ground floor, its windows filled with handbags, belts, and shoes, and a card explaining that English, French, and German were spoken there. There were three plastic plaques on the wall beside the shop, each advertising for *pensiones*.

"Shit," Richards said. "There must be one on every floor. We'll have to work a little."

They went into a dank hall, and started climbing stairs with worn steps. Paint was flaking from the walls. It was very damp.

"Real class," Richards said. "I wonder if they handle bar mitzvahs."

"Keep going."

The first floor was entirely occupied by Danes. The woman had no Americans and didn't want any after what those beatniks did to her place last summer. The second floor was filled with a French choir; they were singing in the parlor about the glory of God when the woman opened the door.

"Do you have Americans here?" Richards asked.

"Some. Are you the police?"

"Yes, my friend here is the prison chaplain."

She started to close the door.

"Excuse me, a joke. We're looking for a friend. Thin, small, blond hair."

"Not here," she said. "I only have a professor and his wife."

Richards breathed hard through his nose.

On the third floor, Fuentes answered the door. "Yes," he said in heavily accented English, "I have plenty of room."

"No, no," Malloy said. "We don't want a room."

Fuentes's face started to sag.

"We're looking for a friend," Richards said. "Small, thin, blond hair."

"*¿Mande?*"

"Let me do this," Malloy said. "*¿Hablas Español?*"

"*Sí, sí.*"

"*¿Es Mexicano?*"

"*No,*" Fuentes said. "*Cubano.*"

"May we come in?"

"*Cómo no.*"

Malloy and Richards walked into the empty parlor. A cigar was burning low in an ashtray on a cane table against the far wall. Fuentes seemed happy to be speaking Spanish. Then Malloy asked him again about the thin American.

"He was here," he said in English.

"He's not here now?" Malloy said.

"He checked out a couple of hours ago."

"Do you know where he went?" Richards said. "His name, how he left, anything about him?"

Fuentes turned to Malloy and started talking very rapidly in Spanish. He stopped to offer cigars and apologized for their quality. Neither accepted. He lit one himself. He talked more, and then stopped again to bring in coffee. He apologized for using Spanish in front of Richards, but Richards said that was all right, he understood a little bit, he had been in Mexico many years before. Aaah, Mexico, Fuentes said. That was a beautiful country. Yes. When they were finished talking, Malloy and Richards stood up. Fuentes asked them to stay for dinner. Malloy thanked him, but they had to go. They all shook hands. Fuentes followed them to the door and asked them to come back whenever they wanted to.

"Did you get all of that?" Malloy said, as they went down the stairs.

"Some of it," Richards said. "The guy's name is Harwell. He might be a fag. Our friend didn't like him very much. He was supposed to stay until Monday, but he left today."

They came out on the crowded street. It was getting dark.

"There was something else."

"I know," Richards said. "The guy was a submarine commander under the Czar."

"No," Malloy said, lighting a cigarette as they walked toward the cab stand at the fountain. "He left in cab number 2148. He had a suitcase and a large brown package that arrived about a half hour before he checked out. He had bruises all over his face that he picked up last night somewhere."

"He probably grabbed the wrong guy by the yo-yo."

"Possibly," Malloy said. "There was one other thing."

"What's that?"
"He had a rifle in the suitcase."

CHAPTER 22

This was more like it, Harwell thought. No noise. No horses riding up and down the street. No fumes from cars. No nosy spic owner. I like this place. It's nice and bare. It's pure. It reminds me of the barracks. It's even cleaner than the barracks. The Leader never washed his clothes. Someday he would be hit by a car and they would take him to a hospital and the world would see his underwear. Soggy and smelly. That was his trouble. He was soggy and smelly.

That shower is more like it, too. That water comes out like needles. Not like that other dump. Water all over the floor. You could get athlete's foot there. This is nice. Very nice and shiny and white. It's not hot either. The air conditioner must be German. I won't need so much deodorant. They picked a winner for me this time. It's better I don't know who they are. It's better. They know how to do these things.

Harwell got off the bed and walked over to the small desk in front of the mirror. He took stationery out of the drawer. Then he looked up and saw himself in the mirror.

I'll get that son of a bitch. I almost had him too. Picks me up like he's saving me, then beats the shit out of me. A Limey or something. Working for them. They were tailing me all night. Didn't want me to leave the room. Fuck him. I wasn't going to stay in that room all night. Why should I listen to that bastard Rail anyway? I almost had the Limey prick. Out in the field. Almost broke his leg with that karate kick. When this is over, I'll go and find him. I'll wait for him in the bushes someplace. Then I'll hit him with something. A mace. One of those maces with the spikes sticking out. Right on the back of the skull. Then I'll throw water on him and wake him up. And then I'll kick his face in. Kick and kick and kick. He'll look like hamburger. I'll snap his teeth off at the gums, like we did to Ralph.

He unfolded the sheet of paper, and studied the neat handwriting and the careful map. I have to do this right, he thought. Now that Rail is out of it, I have to pull it off myself. Rail won't be driving. They have some girl. That doesn't sound too good. But it's better than Rail. I knew he would pull out. That disgusting pile of shit. A real pus sack, he was. Smart guy with the mouth. But no balls. All fat guys are like that. No balls. They're like guys with moustaches. Moustache guys never want to fight. They're too busy chasing broads. We used to call moustaches "womb brooms" in the old neighborhood. That's pretty good. But fat guys won't fight. They only want to eat. Even Goering. He didn't want to fight at the end. No balls. If he had balls, he would of been in the bunker too. He wasn't there. A fat guy.

He made copy after copy of the drawing, tracing his future movements with a ballpoint pen, following arrows, traveling streets with Italian names, into the building, into the unlocked room, up the elevator to the roof. Each copy was meticulously accurate. He worked in silence and never looked up again at his face. I must

226 † A Killing for Christ

be able to do this with my eyes closed, he thought. Even with my eyes closed.

After a while, his hand grew tired. He peeked through the blinds and saw that the streets were now dark. To his left, a large gloomy building rose above the others. That must be the railroad station. There was a taxi rank below him, and a newspaper kiosk. They seemed minute and distant from the height. He saw a man get out of a car to buy a newspaper, and he looked suddenly very large.

It will be easy.

He took the brown carton down off the shelf. I have to practice with this. I have to make it look right. He took the soft black garment out of the box and pulled it over his head. It was loose at the shoulders, but the length was perfect. It's the collar I have to get perfect. That has to be really perfect. It can't pop out when I'm showing the pass to the guards.

He caught a glimpse of himself in the mirror and started to glide softly across the carpet. Do I hear an orchestra? Yes, you may, sir. Your name? Charles. How wonderful. *I feel pretty, oh so pretty, I feel pretty and witty and* . . . Oh, sir, I've never done the waltz before. Are you a captain in the guards? I thought so. Your scar makes you so distinguished.

Rail was disgusting. No balls at the end. All mouth at the beginning, and then he whimpers away. He was a big shot in that place on Christopher Street. A trip to Rome, money, performing a service to Christianity. He's probably on his way home now. In some plane, with his tail between his legs. I don't need him. I don't need anybody now. And when this is over, he'll be dealt with. Him and all the others.

He lay down on the bed and let his hand touch the weapon. You're beautiful.

He thought about Barbara Colfield's thighs, milky white in the fields.

It would be easy. A pass, a priest's uniform, the gun underneath, elevators, a car: everything. It would be easy. I can do it with my eyes shut. Except when I pull the trigger.

She'll come looking for me when this is over. She had her chance. Barbara Colfield, with her big tits and her pretty smile. She'll be around. But I'll just look at her and laugh. I'll be as cold as ice. She won't understand about the salamanders and the snakes behind the glass. How could she? She doesn't know where I've been. I'll just be cold to her, and she'll look at my boots, high and shiny, and she'll get down and kiss them and lick them, and I won't even smile.

He lay there for a long while. Then he reached over for the weapon. He ran both hands along the barrel. You're beautiful, he thought. After a while, he let the stock slide gently between his updrawn legs. He gripped the barrel a few inches from the end. Then he put it in his mouth. You're beautiful, he thought.

Beautiful.

Chapter 23

Malloy stopped for gasoline at a small, poorly lit station a half-mile from the Count's house. An old man with wispy hair and a gnarled face peered in at him. Malloy told him to fill the tank, and then opened the door, got out, and took off his raincoat. It was very warm; insects hummed in the dark beyond the station. A torn strip of newspaper rattled against a wall, caught in a tight dense breeze. Malloy thought: This is an evening Rail would have enjoyed. An evening made for small pleasures: food, wine, bread, for lying alone in a dim room. But Rail has become a was; so has Franca; so have I. We are not; we were. I should be at the sea, far from God and intricacy, listening to the far gong-gonging of the buoys. Instead I am trapped again: caught in the detail, shabbiness, and mystery of another man's epilogue. He paid for the gasoline, climbed into the car, and drove slowly down the road, wondering about the neat tiny man with the rifle.

No limousines thumped richly in the driveway; no laughter drifted across the night; no special guards stood as sentries at the entrance. But with the sole addition of barking dogs, the house was as it had been the night before. Malloy stopped in front, went up the steps, and knocked. The huge British butler answered. He wore a white dinner jacket instead of the tuxedo. If anything, he looked wider.

"Well, well," he said. "Look who's 'ere."

"I'd like to see Count Rienzi."

"He's not at 'ome."

"Look, I don't want to argue with you. Where's your boss?"

Malloy fought down a shudder of fear; he hadn't talked like that to anyone in fifteen years. The big man smiled with his mouth, the lips moving vertically to show hard yellow teeth.

"I just don't get it," he said slowly, breathing deeply, the mouth locked in a smile. "You're a bloody priest, ain't you? A bloody R.C. priest. And yet 'ere you are, talking like a fecking 'Umphrey Bogart. I don't make it, chum."

Malloy stepped up and tried to get past him. The blow caught him on the chest; he felt his breath vanish like air from a pricked balloon. His head hummed and he saw bright pinwheels on a black field. He went a long way away, and then he was back, and he was still standing. He was holding the frame of the door, with a sound like a dog whistle blowing somewhere in his ears, and the big blond face and yellow teeth still smiling at him.

"Now," the man said, "now, get out of 'ere, cunt. Fast. The next one might kill you."

A door clicked; he heard feet pattering; the yellow teeth remained. If I could remember how to stand I could get out of this; if I could remember which way to lean; remember some pure anger; if I could remember what it was like to hit a man and dump him in a shambling pile; if I could remember.

"George, what on earth is going on out here?"

Sweet voice, honey voice; and an impression of distant height and elegance and rescue coming down the corridor.

"What on earth is going on here?"

And remembering away off, in some other place, a body lifting silently in the air, arms and legs extended, the beautiful first movement of some fantastic ballet, the moment before he heard the thundering of the explosion.

"What on earth is going on?"

And then he was going down the hall, into other rooms, following her. The sound of the dog whistle stopped and he was sipping whiskey and the impacted wad in his chest stopped its timid protest.

"What is it that you want, Father?" The voice did not seem to be attached to her, as he watched her familiar face come out of the blur, thinking: She doesn't look like a countess; she doesn't look like her photographs either.

"I'd like to talk to your husband."

I'd like to talk to him here, he thought, not in the room with the desk and the books and the dark chapel to the right; I want no reminder of a line of hip, of hair, of black hosts in a red light.

"Ah, yes," she said. "But Googie is in Milan. Can I help you in any way?"

"A man is dead."

Malloy looked around him. There were canvases stacked against all the walls. I must be in her studio. A glass roof climbed two stories above them. They were sitting opposite each other in canvas director's chairs on a paint-spattered floor. One wall was made of the same chocolate-colored cork he had seen the night before in the Count's den. There were posters of W.C. Fields surrounded by psychedelic flowers, of Laurel and

Hardy, of King Kong; and tacked everywhere, between the big posters, there were photographs from newspapers and magazines: pictures of refugees, women and dying children, soldiers, the wounded and the dying. The air was heavy with the smell of turpentine, linseed oil, thinner. Tables were covered with tubes and paint cans; brushes, spray guns, rollers; and in the corner, in a pile of wrecked bicycles, auto fenders, remnants of sinks and plumbing, scraps of kitchenware and coal scuttles, and one lonely spoked wheel, he saw a welder's rig.

"A man is dead, Father?"

"Yes."

"I don't understand. Was he a friend of yours?"

"He almost was."

If I had given him a chance he would have been my friend. My fat glutton friend. I could not tell you much about him, Countess, neither how he lived nor how he died. But I might have saved his soul.

"I don't understand."

"The man's name was Rail, Countess," Malloy said. Spit it out. "He was short and fat. He was at your husband's party last night . . ."

"It was *our* party . . ."

"Your party, then. I saw him here. The next time I saw him he was dead. I'm trying to find out how he died."

She stood up, dressed in long lavender slacks, a lilac shirt, as tall and elegant as the pictures. I understand now what you need, Countess: you need distance. She circled away from him.

"I never heard of any Mr. Rail, Father. How did you say he died?"

"I don't know. He was probably drowned. His body

was found this morning on the beach at Fragene."

She leaned against a table.

"What could Googie possibly know about him?"

"I saw Rail here. Later, there was a party on your husband's yacht. He might have fallen overboard. I just don't know. Nobody that Rail knew in Rome cares much about what happened. I'd like to find out what happened and tell his relatives, if he has any."

She took a good swallow of the Scotch.

"Well, I don't know what to tell you, Father. There was a party on the yacht last night. But Googie wasn't there."

"He wasn't there?"

"He took the two o'clock night train to Milan."

"You're sure."

"Father, my husband and I made one solemn agreement, a long, long time ago. We promised never to question each other and never to doubt. It was the only certain way we could survive each other. I have never questioned him, he has never doubted me." She drained the glass. "But he did call me from Milan this morning after breakfast."

Malloy stood up. "I'm sorry I wasted your time, Countess."

"Oh, please don't feel that way," she said calmly. "It's a relief to be interrupted sometimes. I hope that George didn't hurt you."

"What's his problem?"

"He's really a sort of bodyguard," she said. "Some reformed thug Googie hired a couple of years ago. Our regular butler was killed in an auto crash last month and we haven't found a replacement yet."

"I'm sorry," Malloy said, automatically.

"For the old butler? Oh no. The old butler was a bastard and a thief. He had better manners than George, but no character."

She walked with him into the corridor.

"Do you know anyone named Harwell, Countess?"

"No."

"How about Parsons?"

"I went to the Parsons School of Design in New York one summer a long time ago. I don't know anyone *real* by that name."

"Neither do I."

He saw George peeking from behind the door to the roulette room. He touched his brow in salute. The door clicked shut.

"One other thing, Countess, and excuse my nosing around like this."

"Yes?"

"If your husband wasn't on the boat last night, who was?"

Her face flushed. "Well, for a while, *I* was. But I left after an hour."

"You're sure you didn't see a fat man?"

"No," she said. "The crowd was very wild and noisy, and he might have been there. But I'm sure I would have noticed him. I spent most of my time worrying about the ship capsizing. They were sailing it to Sardinia, all friends of ours. We have some property down there, and we'll join them next week."

"Thanks. Good night, Countess."

"Good night."

He turned the car around and left the house behind.

He went down the road, through the hedges and the silent hills, wondering what it was that he had walked into. A dead man, an opaque wife, a corrupt count, a man with a rifle in a suitcase, a breakfast that had never taken place. Maybe Richards would figure it out. Richards had wired his office for information about Rail and Harwell. There was nothing in the luggage that explained anything. Maybe the little chauffeur would find the driver of cab 2148. Perhaps someone would turn up something: some relative or friend, some connection, some personal history. For now, he thought, I don't care. I'm too tired and something is moving like a traitor in my chest.

When he reached the beach, Franca was waiting for him. She was in bed and the incense was burning.

EASTER SUNDAY

Q. *What is the Fifth Commandment?*
A. *The Fifth Commandment is: Thou shalt not kill.*

—ADVANCED CATECHISM OF CATHOLIC FAITH AND PRACTICE

But the stars that marked our starting fall away.
We must go deeper into greater pain,
For it is not permitted that we stay.

—Dante, THE INFERNO

CHAPTER 24

At dawn, a motor coughed and kicked off and Malloy came out of his sea dream, engulfed in a panic of engines, his eyes still filled with the dream of the small thin man in black, moving in slow vaulting steps through the green fathoms of the ocean bottom. He smelled the remnants of the incense and the deep heavy mud smell of her absent body, knowing from the cold damp beside him that she was gone, really gone this time, taking all of him with her, taking the smell of leaves and morning coffee and sand on the wood floors and night. Gone, taking warmth, wet mouth, laced limbs, hair, impenetrable silence, the ice within, and the roar of the sea. And leaving him in the sea-dark room with the implements of her perverse benedictions and the drying taste of her wafered flesh and the memory of her face gone mad and her sudden, furious, wild, and ungiving lust. Gone. In his own car. The sound told him that. Out past the town and the beach, on to Rome, traveling in dark velocities to some murderous appointment that excluded him forever; leaving him with all duties forgotten, all certainties eroded, all promises betrayed. A frail chipped casing filled with foul gropings and a blasphemer's mutinous heart.

She said: They are going to murder the Pope, ha ha.

She had been waiting for him; in the dark with the

light out and the incense burning in her own private rite; the lust on her smelling like mud when he walked in, his throat crying, asking nothing of her, demanding no facts, no chart of time, no explanations, no intricacy, no history; wanting her, wanting it as it had been on all chill mornings through all wet nights; wanting her there as she had been when he had run from the mangrove swamp, when the dark fog seeped into his brain, in and out, slippery and poisonous as a water moccasin; wanting her when the accusation of Shaw's eyes had been the most terrible judgment of all; wanting her.

Wanting her because he had not expected her there at all. But she was there, in fierce silence, touching him as he pulled the T-shirt over his head, rubbing him again, demanding explosions, working him, and he had gone away into dark channels where no buoy tolled, his heart filled with wet loins and warm mud and the promise of safety, pounding with longing and desire, his arms crushing, his thighs digging, jamming to far reaches, touching walls of caves, seeking escape and safety, wanting her. Falling back away, beaten into softness and pity, he did not care what she had ever done, or what lessons she had learned; he wanted her to stay. And she had lain there on the pillow the color of Lent, filled with him and demanding more, her hands moving again, tongue into and against and around him, working him with old practiced hands, older than he would ever be, older than house and town and ruins, older than history, as old in that moment as the sea. And again, going out of himself, he heard himself telling her all of it, telling her—Franca—that he wanted her back. Franca, that he wanted Franca back, that Franca he wanted back. No reply. No answer. Just taking, with the heavy engines of her hips, taking, gripping, bringing him into the longest of all journeys, taking him down into deepest cunt. And when the fierce wounded rush of self began, she replied to him at last, in a long, low, moaning, rising, terrified laughing scream.

I'm going to kill God, going to help kill God, help kill fucking God, kill God, help kill, God, God. God.

Over and over it came, long and extended and terrifying, her eyes gone, her abdomen arching and raging, deep muscles pressing him, a dark vise, pressing and contracting, and pulling him out again, out beyond the lips of waves, over the shoals beyond the reefs, beyond endurance, until he was himself murdering, ripping, tearing, searching for victims, joining her in the killing of God, insulting the sun, damning the stars, cutting away to exit and freedom, crucifying her, punishing her, scourging her, savage and remorseless at last, beyond pity or terror, an engine of vengeance and lust, beyond God.

And then the void of silence afterward, except for the red smear of her face in the light of a match, when he saw for the first time that her eyes had gone as dead as Rail's gray flesh. And then he had felt the other presence in the dark room: a movement from another region, something that occupied the back of the dead gray eyes, that had driven the warm flesh, that had touched him in the wet gash she had offered him once as solace; knowing something had inhabited her, feeling it in her and the room, feeling its chill and its cold fire, something that had taken her from him, something that smelled of carrion and was beyond the forgiveness of the sea.

Roberto, she said: They are going to murder the Pope, ha ha.

Laughter at last, and words. But he could not believe their message, until the frenzy rose again, and she roamed the small house with the unwelcome guest, tearing shirts and clothing into small bits, pounding walls, laughing all the while, lying down again, rubbing herself, bringing herself to ecstasy and orgasm, again and again, while he stood away, letting the words sink in, and when she was through, the details. Rail was thrown overboard, she said, because he panicked, and I am taking his place. They have a gunman, dressed as a priest, carrying his weapon to a high altitude. The Count had a true devil's prick; he did not fear God. Count and Cardinal, and she would be with them in the act, united. Laughing through it all, laughing because she asked no absolution. Knowing then it was no joke, because of the other presence in the room, because of her mockery; they would kill him from a high altitude and she would rescue their black saint.

It was what he could not give her: he had given her body and night; he could not give her death. And it was that which she lusted for, that which brought her back. You did not conspire against God in solitude, but you risked nothing either. He had slept then, knowing that no one would listen, neither cops nor priests nor God. If they killed the Pope, they insulted God. He was the Vicar of Christ on Earth. And he had slept to dream of Harwell, the man he had never seen, leaping through dark green waters in slow viscous bounds.

And he awoke to her departure.

He lay awake for a long time, imagining Rail's poor death: Franca laughing while they kicked at Rail's fat

fingers, pushing down on his heavy face, while his terrified eyes pleaded for a few seconds more, a minute, an
hour, just a day, and the boots stamped remorselessly,
and they all giggled as if it were some intellectual exercise, and not the Count, Franca, the blond British killer,
the wife, all of them conspiring to destroy a life. For the
first time in three years, Malloy prayed.

When light came, he woke up completely. He shaved,
washed, and dressed. He picked up all the torn garments
on the floor, swept up a broken glass, put all in a paper
bag. He put on a checkered green sports shirt and slacks
and he packed the suitcase. He took the incense pot and
put it in the garbage bag. He removed the colored repro-
duction of the Virgin from its tin frame, and tore it up,
first into long strips, then crosswise, then again. He put
the shreds in a glass ashtray and lit them with a match.
He straightened the bed, and then put the suitcase on
top of it. He closed all the shutters, tightened the water taps, flushed the toilet, picked up the suitcase, and
went out. He locked the door. Then he threw the key
toward the sea, and started walking through the sand.
It was very hot; he was thirsty; but he had moved beyond betrayal, beyond pity, beyond discomfort, beyond
lust, beyond hope. It was a morning before the birth of
Christ, in a desert where locusts played with tarantulas
and the wells had all gone black. He was left only with
the picture of Rail's fingers being stamped against the
side of a bark. That picture, and outrage.

CHAPTER 25

Mary Wilson had not yet gone to bed. She came to the door in a pale blue nightgown, her eyes bleary with whiskey and lost sleep.

"Oh, it's you. Hey, you made some racket last night, you two."

"Mary, can I borrow your car?"

"She took the car, too?"

"I just need it for the day."

"She takes your balls, and then she takes your fuckin' car, too. Some broad, Father. You really picked a winner."

He stood on the sand, looking up at her. She seemed grosser and more drunken than she was the last time he had seen her.

"Come on in out of the fuckin' sun, nit."

Malloy laughed; he couldn't help it; Mary Wilson was all right.

"What's the suitcase for?" she said. "You running away from home?"

"I've got to go into Rome."

"I tole ya the other night. You better get out of Rome. Go into some kind of monastery. Join the Foreign Legion. Anything. Want a belt?"

"No thanks."

"Come on," she said. "What the hell. It's Easter. No Easter, you guys wouldn't have a job."

"I need your car, Mary. It's important."

"I'll tell ya," she said. "I'm supposed to use it this afternoon. Some little creep of a Spanish banjo player is suppose ta take me dancing. He says he can't afford cab fare."

"I'll have a cab come out to pick you up. I'll leave your car at the Excalibur. There are no taxis out here today."

She poured a tumbler of whiskey for herself, and stood up and walked to the sink. She poured another tumbler of cold water. The bed was unmade. There were bottles under the sink, and clothes piled in the corner of the bedroom. She took a long drink of the whiskey and a small swallow of the water.

"Fuck it," she said. "Take the car. That little creep won't show up anyway."

"Thanks, Mary."

"You're not coming back, are you, Father?"

"No, I'm not, Mary. I'll get the car back to you. I promise you that."

"Who's worrying?"

"Thanks for everything, Mary."

"It was good knowing you, Father."

"It was good knowing you."

She gave him the keys and he walked through the sand to the street. He unlocked Mary Wilson's car, put the suitcase in the back, and started to get in. Then he saw the cop watching him from the doorway across the street. It was the young cop who had seen Rail's body at the edge of the sea. Malloy walked across the street.

"Good morning," Malloy said.

"Good morning."

"What happened yesterday?"

"What do you mean?" the young cop said.

"The fat man."

"He drowned."

"I know that. I mean what happened to his body?"

"They came and took it away."

"Who took it away?"

"I think it was, well, Caputo says it was his brother."

"They showed you identification?"

"They didn't show me, they showed the captain. I think it was a passport."

"What kind of passport?"

"American."

"Who showed it to you?"

"I told you, he showed it to the captain."

"Who showed it to the captain?"

"His brother."

"Was he big and blond?"

"Yes. That's him."

"Thank you. God bless you."

"It was nothing."

Malloy drove out onto the highway. He went a few miles and stopped for gas. There was a small restaurant back off the road. He walked to the door. It was locked. He knocked.

"Yes?" A woman's voice.

"Are you open?"

"Half an hour," the woman's voice snapped.

"I'd just like some breakfast. Is it possible? I am on a journey."

He heard a latch slide noisily, and then the door opened. A woman with a worn Sicilian face looked at him.

"Well, I suppose it's all right."

"Thank you."

He sat at a corner table. The eggs were fresh and delicious, the bread still warm from the oven. He ate quickly and got up to pay.

"Well," the woman said, "today's the big day."

"For who?"

"For the Pope. All the foreigners are here, emptying their pockets for him."

"Maybe you're right."

"Maybe?" she said. "Who do you think keeps the gold on St. Peter's roof? It's not the angels, citizen."

"That's for certain."

"Did you ever hear of a priest dying of starvation?" she said, cackling in a high voice.

"Not of the body," Malloy said.

"That's why my husband and I always vote Communist. The Communists never win, but they're clean."

"I guess they are," Malloy said. "I really wouldn't know."

"Goodbye, citizen."

"Thanks for the breakfast. Goodbye."

He drove very quickly to Rome.

CHAPTER 26

Harwell tried adjusting the collar again, but it popped out. I can't lose my temper, he thought. If I do, I might blow the whole thing. Nice and easy. Can't blow my stack. If I do, I'll tear the collar apart, and it's Sunday and Easter too and all the stores will be closed and I won't be able to buy another one and I will blow the whole fucking thing. Steady. Walk around. Run cold water on a washcloth. That's it.

The room was very bright, and a tray lay on the single bed, where Harwell had eaten his boiled egg and unbuttered toast and drank his tea. Beside the tray was his suitcase, and beside the suitcase was the weapon. He covered the weapon with a bath towel, and then stared at himself in the mirror for a long time. He patted the bruised flesh with the cold washcloth. After this is over, he thought, I will get that big blond bastard. I'll break his goddamned neck.

He put the washcloth back on the sink and tamped his face dry. He went back to the mirror. This time the collar stud snapped in perfectly.

Perfect. That's the way it will be all day. Everything perfect. Split-second timing. He sat down and went over the instructions one final time. The instructions Rail gave me, so nice and neatly typed. He didn't write them, that's for sure. Not that messy mountain of pus. Someone did it for him. Someone smart. He looked again at the passport from the Vatican State and the special pass admitting him to the courtyard. Perfect. I really look like a priest. It will be simple.

He looked at his watch. Seventeen more minutes before I go down. Use the back stairs. Walk boldly through the lobby. He looked at the instructions again. Rail said I should destroy them. Fuck him. He thought of the Leader's mocking face. I need proof. I need something to prove it. They will get rid of the weapon. They will drive me to an airport. But what proof do I have? He looked at the suitcase.

Then he practiced again, walking with the weapon under the flowing habit. The right hand was better. But I need to use both hands. Try it again. I'm not afraid. I got balls. I got real balls. Brass balls. That cunt last night. I really showed her. No, the night before it was. All Jews are whores.

At ten minutes after eleven, he went out. He walked down the back stairs and out through the lobby. He tried to look very grave. The lobby was packed with Germans, all practicing their singing. They were good people, Harwell thought. They would appreciate what I'm doing.

He walked into the bright sunlight, took a right, and turned the corner. The car was waiting just as they said it would be waiting. He opened the door with his free hand and slipped in beside Franca. She said nothing. Her legs were a long way out of her skirt. She pushed down on the accelerator and moved the car out into the traffic. Harwell took a deep breath and let it out slowly. It will be easy, he thought. Easy.

CHAPTER 27

Richards was not in his office. Malloy left the suitcase outside the door and walked around the block twice. He bought a paper, but there was nothing in it about anyone named Rail or Parsons. There were a lot of pictures about Easter, and all the weekly magazines had the Pope on the cover. He stopped at a coffee bar and had a cappucino and coffee. When he went back, Richards was there.

"I've got something for you," Richards said, waving a piece of yellow cable paper.

"I've got something for you, too," Malloy said. "They're going to kill the Pope today." He felt Richards staring at him, felt his incredulity. He didn't care. It was true.

"Why don't you say that again?" Richards said. "Nice and slow."

"They're going to kill the Pope. Today. In St. Peter's Square. At the outdoor Mass. Our friend Harwell has the job. He was brought in to do it by Rail. They're getting him in, with false papers, dressed as a priest. Rienzi's in on it. So is Maladotti."

Richards put the cables down softly. He went over and poured two cups of coffee. The room was very bright. Malloy sat down in the chair. It squeaked. He saw Rail's suitcase on a table across the room. His own was inside the door.

"Well?" Malloy said.

"I think you need a rest."

"It's true, Frank. I know it's true. Franca told me."

"I thought she was gone."

"She came back last night. I went out to see Rienzi's wife, and she didn't tell me anything. Franca was there when I got back to Fragene."

"Is she in this, uh, plot?"

"She's driving the car when it's over. It's my car. She took it this morning."

"Why would you believe her? Maybe she's just putting you on."

"I don't know," Malloy heard himself saying. "It was just that last night . . . The hell with it. I believe her. What have you got for me?"

"First, the cab driver who picked up Harwell. He went to the Hotel Metropole, a new icebox near the railroad station, a very big place with visiting YMCA leaders. Second, Rail's suitcase. There's nothing much in it. Clothes, an old Baedeker, a Michelin with restaurants marked off, *Europe on Five Dollars a Day*. And some correspondence with Carney and Maladotti."

"What's in the correspondence?"

"It doesn't mean anything much," Richards said. "Rail was trying to land a catechism. Some big catechism that's coming out next year. I guess it will have all the new liturgy, the changes in penance and fasting and all that stuff in it. No personal correspondence. He keeps referring to a meeting he had with Carney in Paris at some booksellers' convention."

"What else?" Malloy said, leaning forward, the chair squeaking.

"Nothing else in the suitcase. That's it. But the office came up with something else. Read it."

Malloy looked at the cablegram.

PRORICHARDS EXJOURNAL RAIL CONVICTED 1937 VIOLATION POSTAL LAWS YEAR LEWISBURG HARWELL MEMBER NATIONAL SOCIALIST ALLIANCE SIX ARRESTS WASHINGTON YORKVILLE PHILADELPHIA TIP FROM ADL REAL NAME HOROWITZ BAR-MITZVAHED TEMPLE ISRAEL BRONX COULD MAKE GOOD FEATURE JEWISH NAZI LOOKING HARWELL FIVE MONTHS LAST ADDRESS BANK STREET VILLAGE REGARDS SANN

"What does it mean?"

"It means that Rail broke into the publishing business pushing pornography and did a year in the federal can in Lewisburg. It means that Harwell is a member of the National Socialist Alliance, a splinter group of the American Nazis." Richards sipped from the coffee. "It gets better." He picked a half-smoked cigar from the ashtray and lit it. "It means that his real name is Horowitz, at least according to the Anti-Defamation League, and he's Jewish. He was bar-mitzvahed at the Temple of Israel in the Bronx. He's been arrested six times, which means he is one of those degenerates who are always getting punched around by the Jewish War Veterans, after they start with the gas ovens routine. The desk has been looking for him for five months, and his last known address was Bank Street, in the Village."

"Beautiful," Malloy said. He stood up, walking slowly around the room. It was beautiful. Maladotti, mad on sin and God, offers Rail the new catechism if he will provide a gunman to assassinate the Pope. He gets double his money, because Rail finds a Jewish Nazi, of all people, to do the job. Harwell pulls off the killing, is taken somewhere, and killed himself. Then he is found out to be a Jew. Maladotti tells all the cardinals that it was just one more instance of the perfidy of the Jews, that the softening of the line had led to deicide again. The whole Church is turned around. Rail is killed because he goes soft, and would probably be killed anyway. The Count laughs, and makes more money on the stock market, entertaining himself with his latest piece of intellectual outrageousness. It was beautiful. He even had Franca worked in, at the last minute. The girlfriend of a debauched priest would drive the killer to safety, and to death.

"I don't know what all of this means," Richards said. "But I'm sure it doesn't mean killing the Pope."

"Maybe you're right."

"Do you want a drink?" Richards said. "I could use one myself, for a change."

"All right."

Richards opened the second drawer of the file cabinet and took a bottle of Chivas Regal from behind a wall of files. He rinsed out two coffee cups and half-filled them with Scotch.

"You really believe this, don't you, Bob?"

"Yes."

They each sipped the whiskey.

"I can't go much further on this today," Richards said. "I've got to get the hell over there and cover the Mass. They expect the Communists to show up with banners, and sixty people from some Dutch birth control conference."

"I understand, Frank."

Richards peered at him. "Why are you wearing the sports shirt, old buddy?"

"I'm packing it in."

"Just like that?"

"Just like that."

"What the hell for?"

"I don't believe it anymore."

Richards drained the glass. "You want to talk about it?"

"No."

"That's okay with me."

"I knew it would be."

"Can I drop you anywhere?"

"Yeah. The Metropole."

"Come on. Think about it. If you believe the story, why don't you call the cops?"

"They get seventy-five assassination calls every Sunday, Frank. You know it. They just wouldn't believe it."

"What are you going to do?"

"I'm going to stop him myself."

CHAPTER 28

The helicopter beat its way through the air, high over the city, soaring higher, then dropping, then soaring again. It was impervious to the sun, and as it soared and dipped and fell, its occupants busied themselves with film and meter readings, with cameras and lenses, with the mechanics of stopped time. The pilot felt like a Sunday driver, on a day clean with sea breeze, and he soared above the birds, above the red rectangles of roof, the dark-green patches of park, the great brown river; it was a job; they would come down soon over the great square, to film the multitudes, to zoom in upon the Bishop of Rome, the Vicar of Christ on Earth. At that moment he could not shudder, he could make no mistake. His boss, Firenze, was paid too much by the agents of the news agencies and the magazine people behind him. He could not be an amateur. But for now, as they readied themselves, he would soar, playing in the streams of the air, defying the birds, a gull himself, a raven, a hawk. Free. Free to play over the great stinking streets of the city, over the traffic and the affairs of men and the garbage piled in corners. Free to soar over the street where Fuentes stood looking at himself in the mirror, his face ashen, his tie thickly knotted, in a suit he bought in New York, with underwear he bought in Miami, hope and desire moving in him again, as he went for the first time in years to pray. "I will ask your forgiveness, God," he was saying to himself. "I will ask you to forgive all my sins, to forgive what I did to the women on the table with the straps in the back of the house in my old suburb; I will ask you to forgive my cowardice; I will ask you to forgive my spoilation of talent, my sullying of spirit; I will ask you to forgive my flight . . ." Soaring, in verticals, in figure eights, in long slow arcs against the cobalt sky; free, as he soared over the hidden building among the trees with the gods in front and high red chipped stucco walls and a cold slab hidden in a chapel off an office and the long thin woman on the floor of the studio with a tape recording playing the sounds of artillery, of dog fights, of screaming men, the agony and terror of combat, shells exploding, the moaning of refugees, the snapping of small-arms fire, groaning as the sounds rammed the walls of the studio, groaning, "Oh God, George, oh God, oh God, oh George, don't let it stop, oh George, oh God, oh God, oh God . . ." The engine sweet and powerful, carrying him away to the rim of the atmosphere, circling, spinning off wet air, challenging the sun; soaring above the birds, above the streets, above money, above the room in the deluxe hotel where the distinguished man with the gray hair sat up suddenly to look at his watch, ignoring the fifteen-year-old beside him, ignoring her little buds of breast, her pale shamed face, ignoring her, reaching for a cigarette, standing up naked to wrap himself in a silken robe, switching on the television set. "It is almost time," he said to her, and to himself, and to the room, "it is almost time. How droll. How magnificent and how droll. We must order champagne." Soaring: the engines pumping their small controlled whirlwinds, the men in back finished with preparations, smoking cigarettes, and a white speck appearing on the river, and away off, the great blue bowl of the sea, as he soared. High. Free. Pinwheeling over the city, over the hills, swinging out toward the sea, to see the outline of the ruined port at Ostia Antica and away off the squash of houses where Mary Wilson lay alone in the bed, smoking, telling herself about herself, remembering a time when morning was a fable, when she was young and veins did not throb and men always made attempts and she always turned them down. "I wanted to give it away to him," she told herself. "I wanted to give it away. Help the poor bastard. I just wanted to help the poor bastard and give it away and he didn't want nothing at all. He didn't want nothing at all." The pilot had learned to fly the way other people learned to drive, but he liked this silly machine most of all. He liked its control and its power, its beating blades. It freed him of space, and on most days, of time. It freed him, because he saw everything and saw nothing: saw the red roofs, the green swatches of park, the great brown worm of river, and did not see Franca driving the car through the filling streets, with the strange American beside her, the man with the gun; did not see her sliding her skirt back to expose her dark thighs, did not see or hear or feel what she had become, did not know the animal rising in her, the wetness between her legs, the shudder of desire, the feeling she had of the thin blond man's power, and her knowing that he felt it too, knew that under the priest's black robe his penis was throbbing with excitement and desire and the smell of her in the car; wanting to stop; wanting to pull over in some dark alley to have him rush at her, all power and evil, with his great hard hammering God-killing power; a priest of evil and darkness; her priest; her true priest; knowing that she couldn't stop anywhere and must go on and park in the Street of the Two Angels beside the tobacco shop; park and wait until he had climbed to his high altitude and demolished God. The pilot was free of that. "We've got a half hour yet," he said through the intercom, and the man from *Life* nodded his white helmet, and said, "All right, go down close whenever you want to." None of them saw Richards, pushing through the crowds in the square, cursing, wondering what had happened to his friend, and the strange girl he had introduced to him, and where he was going. They did not see Malloy in the room in the cold hotel, the bribed bellboy guarding the door while he stared at the paper with its arrows and neat directions; Malloy, trying to remember how to get to the aeries on the roof; Malloy, remembering the back elevator that would at least bring him close; Malloy, who was remembering Rail's cold flesh; Malloy, trembling, as he walked to the waiting cab. Instead, the pilot was making one final arc around the edge of the city, heading down to the red tile rectangles, down into the city, where the great multicolored black ants were crowding the Via della Conciliazione; where the old Cardinal sat alone in his room, away from his office, with his head filled with serpents and thurifers, carved virgins and bloody pietàs, certain of the future, of the clamor of heavenly hosts rising white in his own mind, contemplating skulls and death, praying: "Oh, God who art the most Holy and Most Powerful, consecrate this act which is raised in Thy eternal and most powerful name. Protect the souls of Thy servants and send to the fires of hell the heathen and the unbelievers. Know O great Lord that on this day shall be born again the spirit of the Church of old, the Church of Thy greatest majesty and power. The Church of heavenly hosts, of warriors and priests. That Church shall return, O my Lord. The sentence of Thy revelation is to be carried out and I, Thy most humble and obedient servant, pray for its success."

"I'm bringing it down," the helicopter pilot said.

"Everything is Go."

Its great rotors beating against the sky, the helicopter descended into Rome.

CHAPTER 29

Harwell stepped out of the car quickly, nodded to Franca, and walked down the street. He knew every move. He could do it with his eyes closed. No one will even notice me. They won't see my face with these glasses. They won't see the rifle. This black thing is perfect. Slots in the sides for your hands. I can hold the weapon all the way. I don't have to worry about it sliding out of my coat.

He turned the corner and walked down a long crowded street. There were cops with shiny Napoleon hats, fat women, old people, tweedy-looking people. All of them going to St. Peter's. Wow, if they only knew what was going to happen. They wouldn't be walking along so nice and easy. It would be like a picnic.

I could have had that broad. Never found out her name. But I could see she was looking at me funny. Breathing kind of funny. She knew I was looking at her legs, but she didn't try to cover them up or anything. Filthy slut. I'll get her later. She's gonna drive me out in the country after. First the hotel, then the country. I'll make her pull over somewhere. In the fields. I'll take her into the woods. I'll lie her down. Little by little, I'll make her take those clothes off. First, the blouse. She'll be lying there with just the brassiere and the skirt. Then I'll make her take off the skirt. She'll be lying there. Then she takes off the slip. No, she didn't have no slip. She'll just be there with her brassiere and panties. Then I'll throw dirt on her. I'll tie her arms down to pegs, and throw dirt on her. Then I'll piss on her. Rub the dirt all over her. Mud and piss. Then I'll cut the brassiere off with a knife. Then I'll take the panties off, little by little, with her starting to scream and no one around for miles. Just her hands tied to the pegs. Her legs waving in the air. I'll take the pants off and then I'll screw her. I'll make her do a somersault, and kneel with her head on the ground and her hair hanging. Then I'll stick it in her ass and she'll scream. Then I'll make cuts in her ass. Tiny ones. Pop, like that. I'll take the knife and—

"*Scusi.*" A man bumped into him and almost knocked Harwell off the sidewalk.

I hope he didn't feel it. The man looked at him and shrugged an apology. You'll go too. You and the blond guy who hit me. All of you. Ahead of him, he saw the walls of the Vatican and his heart started pounding.

A group of Boy Scouts went past him in uniform, singing French songs. A fat moustached man was leading them, gesturing violently with his hands. Harwell stopped and let them go by. As he crossed the street, a motorcycle backfired behind him, and he jumped. What the hell was that? He saw nothing behind him. People were swirling around him now, and his hand tightened on the rifle, sweating, slippery, his heart pounding harder.

He was in an area of small walls, shops, dead-end streets. He tried to remember the map, but it was difficult. The map did not show people. Then ahead of him, a street away, he saw the gate. He swallowed hard. I can go back, he thought. I can go back and forget about it. And then he saw the face of the Leader, sitting in the room back at the barracks, his coarse potato-face leering as he listened to another tale of failure. No, Harwell thought. I have heart. I'm strong. I'll show them. I'm going to change the history of the world. The whole fucking world.

He went to the gate. A tall Swiss Guard in full regalia stared at him impassively. He handed the guard the pass, trying to look nonchalant, watching the crowds turning through the barricades of pillars, stone, brick, and mortar, heading for the square. Under the robe, his hand gripped the weapon. If I was a priest, what would I do? Hello, folks, how are you? How's things? Beautiful weather we're having, isn't it? Terrific day for Easter. Nice clothes you got on there.

The guard nodded.

He was in.

I made it in. I made it in. It was simple. It was so easy they'll never believe me when I tell them.

He walked through courtyards and gardens, through swarms of priests and seminarians; through male choirboys and crew cuts; through lolling monsignors, and officials, and men with dress suits and top hats and great silver medals and different-colored sashes. If they knew what I had in my hand. If they only knew.

He found the building, yellow, tawny, with shuttered windows. The door was open, just as the map said. He went in, closing the door softly behind him. A long hall yawned before him, gray in the half-light. He tried to remember the map, and closed his eyes. I remember now. He walked along, counting doors. At the eleventh door, he stopped. It was open. He saw a small room with a desk covered with papers. It was very dark.

He took the rifle out from under the robe and wiped his sweaty hand on his chest. Then he opened the door at the back of the small room, and was inside another room, this one larger, with portraits of the popes on the walls, no windows, another door on his left. A skull sat on the bare desk. It was silent. Too silent for me, Harwell thought. It's like a goddamned tomb. I wonder who the hell works in this mortuary. He opened the door to his left. Just like the map said. The elevator was waiting. Harwell looked at his watch.

Too early. Too goddamned early. I got eleven minutes left. The pounding in his heart had stopped, but his bowels were now loose. He let the door to the elevator click shut. There's gotta be a john here someplace. He looked around the barren office. The only other door was the one he had come in through. I really have to go now. I have to find a place.

He went into the outer office and opened the door leading to the hall. He opened it softly. He heard nothing. Then he looked out. It was still gray, still empty. He let the door close behind him. He went down the corridor, trying doors. Jesus Christ, I'll shit in my pants, he thought. He tried door after door, but they were all locked. He felt something shifting in his stomach. I'll go back to the office. I can't take any chances. I'll shit in a drawer or something. Holy God, what if the door is locked? What door is it? They all look the same. The eleventh door. I have to go back and start again. He walked the length of the corridor, hearing the distant murmur of the crowd. He counted the doors again. The eleventh door was not locked.

I can't waste any more time, he thought. He forgot his

bowels and opened the door to the elevator. There were only five buttons. There was no light. He pushed the top one and nothing happened. What the hell is this? Then he let the door close. He could no longer see the panel. He shifted the rifle to his left hand. He felt along the wall of the elevator and found the buttons again. He pressed the top one and nothing happened. Jesus, don't tell me they had a power failure or something. No. Not now. He swung around and the butt of the rifle clattered against the gate. The gate! That's it. The goddamned gate! He closed the gate, and heard a motor kick off loudly, and then, very slowly, standing in the dark, with his hand on the rifle, he felt himself rising.

When the elevator stopped, he pulled the gate aside and opened the door.

He was in a long sloping stone room. It reminded him of an empty garage. There were no doors, no furniture, no sign of human beings. Pigeon droppings covered everything. And at the far end, about fifteen feet away, a low lip rose toward the open sky. I'm minutes away from it, Harwell thought. Minutes, inches, and then everything. He left the gate open to the elevator, and set the door ajar. He took off the soutane, folded it neatly, and placed it next to the elevator. Then he opened the breech of the weapon. It was loaded. He snapped it shut, and got down on the floor. He inched forward, using his elbows to push him, the hard droppings reminding him of a scab. The walls went on past the lip, and a roof above him jutted out about two feet. Set into the lip, like the eye of a target, was the drain. I have to keep as flat as I can. Flat as hell. He reached the drain and looked down.

St. Peter's Square was spread out before him, like a great colored lake. There were more people there than Harwell had ever seen before. Thousands, hundreds of thousands. There must be half a million of them, he thought. It's fantastic. It must be what Mussolini saw. A half-million of them. To his left, on the steps leading to the cathedral, an altar had been set out. The target had not yet arrived, but there were priests and monsignors, all in royal purple, sitting on chairs on all sides of the altar. It was a simple shot. A good, clear, direct shot. He looked above him, and felt secure in the shadow of the eaves. Then he sighted the rifle down the drain. It would be easy. It would be so easy. No noise from the gun either. This beautiful German silencer. Hard-jacketed shell too. It will go right through. I can hit him three times if I have to. The first one will take him. It's like Jerry used to say when he would fight with the Jews. That Jerry was a card. I only need three punches for a Jew, Jerry would say. The first one hits his stomach, the second one hits his jaw, the third one hits air. Him I can tell everything when I come back. Jerry is a stand-up guy. Maybe I can make him a minister or something. Yeah. He'd get the nigger problem straightened out, all right. He would get everything straightened out. Those goddamned beatniks for openers. They would go. The colleges are filled with them. We'd get rid of those motherfuckers. That slut driving the car. She'd go too. I wonder where they got her. Not bad-looking, but I could see she was a whore. She let her dress slide up so far I could practically see her snatch. Just like all bitches. A beautiful face and the head like a can of worms. That's how the Leader talked about his first wife. A beautiful face and inside just a can

"Who's there?" he whispered. The singing roared through the skies.

"Harwell! I know you're there! I'm on the other side of this wall! Stop what you're doing!"

A voice. Speaking English. There must be alcoves like this all along here, Harwell thought. He looked to his right, but the stone jutted out over the lip. He could not climb around and shoot the voice.

"Harwell!"

The choirs filled the air, splitting it, breaking it apart.

"Fuck you!" Harwell shouted.

"Harwell, listen. You don't know me, but I know you. I know what you're going to do!"

"Try and stop me!"

"I found the maps in your hotel, Harwell. I know where you're going to meet the girl."

It was a joke. No one knew where he was. No one could have found the hotel. I took a cab there. Just an ordinary cab. There must be a million cabs in Rome. It's a bluff. But how did he know about the slut?

"Don't do it, Harwell!"

His mind raced. Whoever the voice was, it must have come up here the way I did. I'll take my shot, go down in the elevator, wait in the corridor, and shoot him. That's it. That's the way. It'll be easy.

"Are you a cop?"

"I'm a priest."

"Go and fuck yourself, Father."

He sighted down the rifle again. The target was bowed forward. The chorus was softer now, and then it stopped. Now, Harwell thought. Now. Just squeeze it off. Just squeeze it off. Now.

"Harwell, I know you're a Jew!"

He looked away from the sight. He heard a high noise starting somewhere in the distance, and a whirling rhythmic sound coming closer.

"Don't you see what they're doing to you, Horowitz!"

No.

"They're using you, you *schmuck*."

No. It's not Horowitz, I tell you. Christians get circumcised. No.

"You're a Jew, Horowitz, and that's what they want. A Jew to kill the Pope."

No. That's bullshit. I'm a Christian. I'm no filthy Jew. You've got it wrong. His mind started filling with candles, the warm table at a seder, the taste of soup. It's bullshit. I'm a goy. I'm a tough son of a bitch. I ain't no four-eyed bottle-sucker.

"I have a friend from the *Journal* waiting for me, Horowitz," the voice said. "If you don't stop and come down out of there, he's gonna print that you're a Jew all over page one."

"You can't do that!" Harwell screamed. Horowitz was someone else. My name is Harwell. Horowitz was a skinny little kid who used to hang around the school yard. He didn't have any brothers or sisters and the Irish guys used to beat him up all the while. They called him *Jewboy*. That was a different guy altogether. Harwell had blond hair and played basketball with the Irish guys. Horowitz was a little guy. Once in the Catskills, he saw his mother fucking a man in white shorts and tennis shoes. She was a Jew cunt. Harwell was strong.

"You were bar-mitzvahed in the Temple of Israel in the Bronx, Horowitz!" the voice was shouting. "That's going in the paper too, if you don't come down!"

No, that wasn't me. That was some other kid. He made a talk about Ezekiel, and they were proud of him, and he got a beautiful Kodak camera from his Uncle Abe, who drove a taxi in Brooklyn, and his mother cried. That was some other kid.

"Don't let them use you!"

That was someone else, Harwell thought. He started rising off his elbows. He put the gun aside, and started inching away from the edge. It was someone else. He stood up. He backed up, a foot at a time, all the way to the wall. He slid down the wall and huddled for a moment in the corner. That was someone else, a weak skinny kid who tried to fight a man with white tennis shorts in the dark on the grass near the tennis courts. I'm Harwell.

He stood up slowly. I've conquered fear. I'm Harwell. I've seen the dog-faced devil with the silk ladies' bonnet peering from behind the china closet. I've seen rats in the treasure chest. I've seen black giants inserting steel rings in the rectums of Nordic virgins. I've seen them all. I've been brave. What do they know about the woman with the helmet of blue grapes? She had a pet mouse in her mouth and weapons in her cunt and I resisted her in the fields that night when she wanted me to stick flowers up her ass while she played the golden harp. He took a step forward, then another.

They're calling me now. They know. They know. He could hear the choirs roaring in his ears. They know me. They need protection. They're begging me. Listen to them beg. That was another boy, skinny, in a school yard. They need me. They want me to take them through the high white tunnel. They want me. The voices rose in exaltation, and Harwell saw a giant bat coming out of the sun, its wings beating in circles. That's what they want. They want me to fight for them. They want me to grapple with the great black bat of the Devil. Yes. Don't worry. I hear you. I hear your voices. I will protect you. I will save you. And he stepped off the lip to grapple with the sun.

CHAPTER 30

The airport newsstand was connected to the coffee bar. Malloy bought a beer and a copy of the late edition of *Paese Sera*. There were many pictures of the Pope blessing the assembled multitudes, of Frenchmen in Boy Scout uniforms, of women with children in their arms, of Swiss Guards in full regalia. The war was buried on page six. And on page eight, at the end of the continued story of the Easter rites, he saw the item:

> *Mr. Richard Harwell, an American tourist, fell to his death today behind St. Peter's Square while photographing Easter services.*
>
> *Harwell, 24, arrived in Rome on a pilgrimage last week. His body was discovered by an official of the Vatican. He is believed to be a native of New York. Police notified the American Embassy.*

That was all. He had fallen about one hundred and fifty feet, and landed on a roof over the colonnade. Even that wasn't in the story. Malloy finished the beer and walked down the length of the empty terminal to mail the letters. When he came back, the New York flight was delayed another half hour. He hoped it would not be canceled.

He went outside into the night air. The statue of

Leonardo da Vinci looked blue in the hard light. Water played across the fountains. He stood there smoking, and listening to the cab drivers talking.

"Look, if Griffith gives him a chance, Benvenuti will win by two miles . . ."

"Aaaaah, Carmine. You're an idiot. A real idiot."

"Who ever beat him, so far?"

"Who did he ever fight?"

"He knocked out Mazzinghi."

"My mother could knock out Mazzinghi. Besides, Benvenuti's a Fascist."

"So what? Griffith isn't so nice either, I hear."

Malloy suddenly caught a strong smell of the sea, coming from the beach town a few miles to his right. He went inside again. The terminal was empty and vast, its floors as polished as an operating table. He ordered another beer. The girl brought it, took his money, and gave him a receipt. Then he saw the cab stopping outside and the man getting out. It was Richards.

"I thought you might be here."

"I sent you a note, Frank."

"Big deal," Richards said, laughing.

"It was the best I could do."

Richards ordered a beer. "They found Rail's body again," he said.

"Where?"

"In a ravine in the hills," he said. "It just came in on the Italian wires when I left. It was a car crash. There was someone with him."

"Franca."

"Yeah. That's why I came out. I thought you would want to know."

"Thanks, Frank."

"You must feel rotten."

"I don't feel anything."

They heard an accented voice say through the loud-speaker that the New York flight was ready for boarding. They finished the beers and walked toward the departure lounge.

"Are you going to write it, Frank?"

"I might have to. Proving it is something else. They've got everything covered. The cops at Fragene now say they never had a floater, they never heard of Parsons. Rienzi has an alibi. Harwell is dead. Franca is dead. Maladotti is beyond reaching."

"Why did they bring back Rail, Frank? That doesn't figure."

"Well," Richards said, shrugging, "I guess he came into the country using the Rail name. If they didn't have him leaving in that name, there could be trouble. I guess they used the Parsons bit to buy time until they could get rid of him neater."

"Do me a favor, Frank."

"Don't write it?"

"Yeah."

"Jesus, Bob. If I can—"

"Let them be."

"But you can't let them get away with it, Bob."

"Nobody would believe you."

Richards sighed. "I'll see you in the papers," he said, shaking Malloy's hand.

Malloy smiled, and started to walk off. Then he stopped and came back. "You know," he said, "they never really got to know much about Rail at all."

"No?"

"He didn't drive either."

They shook hands again.

"Goodbye, Frank."

"What are you going to do?"

"I don't know. I haven't thought it out that far. I'll let you know. I promise."

"Goodbye, old buddy."

Malloy turned and went through customs and down the long empty inner corridor, past closed souvenir counters, past an empty soda fountain, past a deserted restaurant. He gave his boarding card to a thin girl in a starched blue uniform. Then he walked out across the darkened airfield to go home.